SMASHING PEOPLE

SMASHING PEOPLE

Michael Fishwick

JONATHAN CAPE
LONDON

Published by Jonathan Cape 2001

2 4 6 8 10 9 7 5 3 1

First published in Great Britain in 2001 by
Jonathan Cape
Random House, 20 Vauxhall Bridge Road,
London SW1V 2SA

Random House Australia (Pty) Limited
20 Alfred Street, Milsons Point, Sydney,
New South Wales 2061, Australia

Random House New Zealand Limited
18 Poland Road, Glenfield, Auckland 10, New Zealand

Random House (Pty) Limited
Endulini, 5A Jubilee Road, Parktown 2193, South Africa

The Random House Group Limited Reg. No. 954009
www.randomhouse.co.uk

This is a work of fiction. Any resemblance to actual persons,
living or dead, is entirely coincidental

'Have You Seen Her' Words and Music by Eugene Record and Barbara Acklin
© 1982 Angelshell Music and Six Continents Music Publishing Inc, USA
Warner/Chappell Music Ltd, London W6 8BS
Reproduced by permission of International Music Publications Ltd

'Memphis Soul Stew' Words and Music by Curtis Ousley
© 1981 Killyn Music, Pronto Music and Cotillion Music Inc, USA
Warner/Chappell Music Ltd, London W6 8BS
Reproduced by permission of International Music Publications Ltd

Lines from 'Crow's Song of Himself' by Ted Hughes (from *Crow*,
Faber and Faber, 1970) reproduced by kind permission of Faber and Faber Ltd

A CIP catalogue record for this book
is available from the British Library

ISBN 0-224-06128-3

Papers used by Random House are natural,
recyclable products made from wood grown in sustainable forests.
The manufacturing processes conform to the environmental
regulations of the country of origin

Typeset by SX Composing DTP, Rayleigh, Essex
Printed and bound in Great Britain by
Clays Ltd, St. Ives PLC

To my family, to all those who helped (whether they
knew it or not) and to the small hours,
without whom and which, etc.

Traumatic Personae

WHEN THE CAR left the road it must have been doing well over a hundred.

Left the road. As if it were a tender farewell, or a casual parting, rather than a flight into final darkness. It burst the barrier and spread small fragments of grey Mercedes like a dirty smear over a pretty part of the Sussex countryside. He loved cars, Ferdy, and this was one of his finest: classic, low-slung in beautiful svelte charcoal, like the suits he used to wear. Not that they were low-slung, of course, but they did have a purring self-confidence. He had them made by his own tailor somewhere in the City.

It turned over so many times it was almost tubular when it came to rest, twisted round the trunk of a stout beech at the foot of one of the many steep inclines to be found on the Ditchling Road. I was surprised at this; I'd always assumed that cars like that didn't bend, but this one did. Wheels, mirrors, bonnet, aerial, exhaust, a couple of doors, all were shed in the tumult of descent, as if the car had flung off all accoutrements in ecstatic abandonment. Inside, Ferdy was more pulp than shape.

All in all, a sorry mess, a sorry affair. It was the end for Ferdy, but it was the beginning of something for me.

We were living in Notting Hill then, his daughter and I, and it was good. It's always been one of my favourite bits of London, and the first-floor flat that Grace and I had bought was large and roomy, and we didn't have that much clutter, which made it even roomier. Bare floorboards, kilims covering them, large frenetic oils painted by friends who were just beginning to make their mark, old watercolours of Indian hill-stations passed

1

on by doting uncles (hers, not mine), a rubber-plant that had seen better days but stubbornly refused to die, in spite of or maybe because of the number of old joints that ended up embedded in its soil, a bed, a duvet, a television; what more was there to life? Property prices were surging, which meant we could have jobs for interest's – rather than income's – sake, and still feel pretty smug. The flat was in one of the long, grand streets that lead off Ladbroke Grove – further up, beyond the railway bridge, about where the streets get exciting, especially if you're walking back dead drunk at night, which was often the case with me.

Once, when I was staggering along after some publisher's launch party – a small, literary publisher that gave you large quantities of crisps and hideous wine in a stuffy little room on the walls of which a rather sentimental mural of Kew Gardens had been painted to give one the sense of being in a larger space, where one got very hot, drank prodigiously, and was smashed before nine o'clock – once, as I say, I was staggering thoughtfully along when I brushed someone's shoulder. That's all it was, and I thought no more about it, but on turning the corner for home, I suddenly found a small, agitated man rushing up to me and asking why I had hit him like that. I suppose on reflection he must have been on something, but so was I, and all I could do was stare at him in a fixed sort of way. I think I managed to stammer out a shambles of an apology before he hit me, kicked me full in the chest, which was astonishingly athletic given that he was half my size. The next thing I knew, I was kneeling on the pavement and he had disappeared; which nasty little anecdote, when related to Grace, caused gales of mirth. I must say I thought her reaction misplaced.

'It's not that funny,' I said, frostily. 'He was obviously trained in martial arts.'

'He came up to your shoulder, did he, Wilf?' She fell on the bed and lay there shaking helplessly. She was wearing an ancient T-shirt with 'Knebworth '79' emblazoned across the back, and nothing else, and the sight of her long legs and glorious frame would normally have sent my libido soaring. Instead, I brooded, which she found even funnier, which in turn made me furious, and we ended up having a filthy row – which did not end, as our battles usually did, in several hours of wonderful unbridled sex, but with me lying curled up on the sofa trying to find a position where my spine was not being prodded by an insistent loose spring.

We had known each other since Oxford, where, after the obligatory first-term blues when I had sat in fetid pubs off the High Street staring at a plate of sausage and beans and wondering who I was, I had begun to lead a life which, if it wasn't all parties and free sex, at least gave the impression that it might turn into that. If one could only find the right play to be in, if one could only ingratiate oneself with the happening people, then doors would open. The problem was discerning who was truly happening and who was merely a sideshow. Was it the freckle-faced lesbian separatist, the beautiful boy who spent his holidays learning Northern Soul dance steps in Wigan, the bearded (they were always bearded) director who patently thought himself the Messiah, the anally retentive classicist whose clothes were always immaculate and who didn't need to do anything except *be*, the fur-coated poet with the open-topped Alfa Spider and his coterie of earnest followers, or was it the wildly destructive scions of aristocracy (or at any rate the grander kind of chain store), so little changed since, well, since the dawn of time, I suppose?

Grace was really raven-haired Flora's friend; she possessed a pale, almost translucent, complexion, and an utterly disarming puzzled look to her face, a quizzical flutter between her delicately arching eyebrows, which was quite unworldly. Flora, whose worldliness by contrast was and still is remarkable, and whose eyebrows seemed to curl in unison with her dazzling smile, made a habit of snapping up any male who showed any interest in Grace, to add to her own impressive array of lovelorn scalps. She couldn't help it: whenever Grace was seen in someone's company, somehow, sooner or later, he was to be seen drinking with Grace and Flora, then dancing with Flora,

3

then. . . Usually they became gormless hangers-on, flapping about her, desperately begging for attention.

I fell in love with Grace after she decided to have a party. She and Flora were living in an indescribably unpleasant place up in Headington; not the nice part – Headington Village – but somewhere beyond it. The wallpaper was, like ink dropped on blotting paper, a rash of strange colour separations, and the carpet had a pile so deep things got lost in it. Grace bought all the food and made far too much of it, exhausting herself in the process. I went up there to help out, because – yes, yes – I was at the time more than intrigued by Flora, though – yes, again – my presence didn't seem to send her into paroxysms of spontaneous adoration.

I called round at four o'clock to see how things were. Headington is such a long way out of Oxford that I had to invent some sort of rigmarole about a lightning trip up to London the night before to see the Selecter at Brixton Academy in order to justify this. Grace sat gazing forlornly at the technicolor splodges on the wall.

'Everything all right?' I asked breezily, wondering where Flora was.

'Everything's just fine.'

Even I could tell this was not the whole truth.

'Are you sure about that?'

'Quite sure.' She didn't snap, but if she wanted to sound welcoming she was failing miserably. I looked into the kitchen.

'Looks fantastic. Did you do it all on your own?' I surveyed the massed ranks of homemade pizza and avocado dip approvingly. Standard fare, but in those days any fare was good fare.

'Flora helped.'

And therein, gentle reader, lay the rub. She knew what was coming.

When party-time arrived, Flora was the heart and soul. She took over as one born to command. She knew practically everyone, and everyone came, so the house throbbed with heat and sweat and the languorous sweet odour of dope rolled into

4

perfectly flaring trumpets which glowed suddenly in the semi-darkness. There was only one DJ who counted: a large, eternally grinning boy from Newcastle with a fabulous collection of records – Tamla, Stax, Atlantic, Sue, Chess – you name it, he had it, together with the sort of mature discrimination that marks you out a bit at Oxford. He didn't just play old favourites, he played Hues Corporation and Ohio Players and things a touch out of the ordinary, things you had half heard years before and which struck you with that extra tingle when you heard them again. So he was there, and it was Flora who had booked him up. And as we spilled out on to the raggedy lawn, rank with weeds among towering unkempt rose bushes, everyone danced with the swooning, drugged passion that overpowers you on deep summer nights and grows and grows among the dark, secretive shades of first light. The actors, the ones who had just finished a gruelling run of *Lear*, all black leotards, stark lighting, no props or concessions to the audience, were showing off absurdly; the revolutionaries, who preferred reggae and were pining for the Caribbean Club, chewed their beards and looked scornful; the Northern Soul boys bounded like Cossacks; the punks, mostly maths students from Balliol, lurched and stumbled drunkenly into the bushes, to return reeking of vomit; the mods posed cool and sleek; and the hippies huddled together in a state of happy complacency.

I have a distinct image in my mind – my life is made up of such talismanic recollections – of standing at the top of the stairs wondering whether I was smashed enough to thrust up my nose the snotty five-pound note being used to hoover lines of coke laid out on the lavatory seat in the bathroom, and of looking down to see the first of the revellers picking their way none too carefully through the sprawling mass of bodies to the door. The Chi-Lites were singing 'Have You Seen Her?' and I faintly heard through the immortal, irresistible melancholy of the spoken lines the cries of farewell.

''Night, Flora. Thanks a lot. Oh, and 'night, Grace. Your food was really good, by the way, Flora.'

5

'*One month ago today, I was happy as a lark; but now, I go for walks, to the movies, maybe to the park. . .*'

''Bye, Flora. You're a star.'

'*And have a seat on the same old bench, to watch the children play; you know, tomorrow is their future, but to me, just another day. . .*'

'See you tomorrow, Flora. 'Bye, Grace.'

There she stood, much too sensitive, smiling heroically, waving enthusiastically as a pack of crummy students piled down the road humiliating her. Well, that's the way it seemed to me then, and, in spite of everything, that's the way it seems to me now. You don't really ever fall out of love with someone; and that's when I fell in love with Grace. An odd way to do it, I admit.

'*Tell me have you seen her?*'

You have to know the song. When I was little I used to lie awake at night with the trannie under my pillow waiting for it on Radio Luxembourg, so it has incantatory power for me.

That afternoon I dropped into my favourite café in the Covered Market for the usual bacon sandwich and cup of coffee in the corner with a copy of the *Daily Mail*. I can't say I had thought greatly about Grace because I had been asleep most of the intervening hours, but I was vaguely aware of having made a wonderful discovery, of having found that I actually liked someone rather than merely being desperate to impress them, and I was aware of an entirely new squadron of emotions coursing through my veins. Ones of warmth and kindliness and being good to one another.

The café, where the paint had turned a kind of dirty pale turquoise – at least, I can't imagine anyone deliberately painting it that colour – was full of the animated middle-aged. I was staring abstractedly at the door when it opened and Grace came in.

There are moments, as I say, that stay with you all your life. The dim and dingy world of the café – of my life, too, to be frank – was abruptly penetrated by that glorious grin, by that lopsided face lighting up at me idling in the corner; I felt a surge in my spirits as if I were a diver coming up for air; an upward rush, a flood of heat in the pit of my stomach, a giddy sense of exhilaration. I seem distinctly to recollect the pale, smudged, amorphous presence of her face behind the frosted glass, like something incorporeal, not yet born.

So she was a kind of human sunburst, and the future crystallized instantly before my slightly bloodshot eyes. Walks in the country, appreciative trips to art galleries, great food cooked together, companionship and *Les Enfants du Paradis* late-night at the Penultimate Picture Palace, a mutual vantage-point from which to view the world with approval or disdain, from which to make choices among the chaos of friends, enemies, aspirations and enthusiasms that surrounded us: in short, a *real* relationship. My first grown-up one. There might be great sex, too, but that didn't matter. *That's* how grown-up it was going to be.

She couldn't stop smiling. She smiled at herself smiling. For myself, my jaw ached from smiling. It might be said that the previous night's drugs could have had some lingering effect on our euphoria, but this would have been unkind.

'*Your* party,' I pronounced, with a gallant emphasis on the first word, 'was − magnificent.' I spread my fingers dramatically. Every nerve of me wanted to be nice to her.

'Thank goodness Flora. . .'

'Flora,' I announced in a lordly way. 'Don't you think people talk too much about Flora? She seems to me to be essentially an exploitative person. I know she's your friend,' this as Grace looked at me with startled − and crisply, intensely blue − eyes, 'and I'm very fond of her myself. Well, quite fond.' I modified my feelings judiciously. 'But she likes to use people. She uses you. That is,' thinking I might have overstepped the mark, 'she needs you more than you need her.'

Looking back on this piece of cod psychology I still think it has something in it, but I remember feeling at the time, with surprising complacency, that this was an adroit move on my part.

Grace looked at me for a moment without saying anything.

'Nobody's ever said that before.'

'Well, that's what I think.'

'I don't think she needs me, really.'

'I do. She needs your warmth and kindness and generosity.'

Grace lowered her eyes and a flicker of pain ran across her face. 'That's not true.'

'She's manipulative. She wants people eating out of her hand. She needs to be admired. I mean, I *like* her.' I paused to take a swig of coffee and momentarily despatch the image of Flora's flashing eyes that seemed to rise out of its depths. 'I like her lots. She's good fun, brilliant fun. But she can't bear not to be the centre of attention.'

She hooked a lock of fair, straight hair over her left ear – her ears were slightly too large and were a constant source of self-consciousness – and balanced her chin on her hand, sipping her tea in a hunched fashion.

'I agree. But you're the first person I've heard say that about her.'

I still feel proud. I had stormed to her rescue, and in all my callow protectiveness I was convinced of my righteousness. From then on Grace had me to turn to rather than Flora, and turn she did, and we strode together through Oxford and out into the wide world, soul mates, lovers, sharers of worldly goods and sexual athletes of Olympian stature. I loved her for her quiet intensity, for her gaucheness, for her faded blue Fair Isle jersey and her long, tapering, equally faded jeans, for the way she pulled a tissue out of her sleeve and for her instinct for good in people, for her rounded cheekbones and her smile like the first day of the holidays; for her loyalty to friends who let her down and her surprise at friends who appreciated her. We were pals; I showed off to her; she was too generous and loving to point out my absurdities. And I adored the elegance of her body and the way it swooped and curved from the dear, incisive singularity of her shoulders. It was all too good to last.

It took a small but significant stumble right at the start.

'You know Jimmy, don't you? I can't remember whether he turned up after you'd gone or before. He was very late. He's been

8

in Amsterdam all week, came all the way for my party. Did you see the bike? It's a Harley.'

Why did she have to go and nearly spoil everything? Of course I knew Jimmy – James – Spalding; I'd known him for a long time. When I first came across him in my home village of Monkridge, he was surreptitiously selling farm eggs to local shops at highly competitive rates in order to garner a little extra pocket money, having thieved them from the family henhouses. Both Jimmy and his customers knew that his father's wrath would be terrible should he find out, so they had a mutual interest in keeping it quiet. And I don't think Ranulph ever did find out, but then he was never a great counter of trifles, unlike his son.

I'd seen him arrive, too, the ace face on the smart bike. Why on earth had he, with his finals coming up, been in Amsterdam in term-time? What made him so special? But however well you know someone, if they've got the charisma there's not much you can do about it. You can try copying it, but I gave up trying to copy James Spalding after I went for three twists upside-down on the tree-swing in the woods and nearly broke my neck.

Why didn't she remember whether I'd still been there? I noticed that for the first time she had called it her party, rather than hers and Flora's. Fortunately, the number of women, including Flora, who fawned upon Jimmy had kept him away from her, but they obviously had a real regard for each other, those two, and I couldn't help but like him for that. At least he appreciated her.

So, yes, I knew Jimmy: the wild child from the grand house who had dispensed with his virginity at the age of thirteen in the willing arms of Linda Summersby (seventeen), after whom we other village louts had lusted moistly ever since we knew how to. He never looked back. Neither did Linda Summersby, when she found she was pregnant. She had a hard time explaining that one to her father, the vicar, but she never ratted on the culprit, or so the legend went. It was a feature of Jimmy's exploits that he commanded amazing loyalty from people, even when he had brought them low with careless abandon. He slummed it with us, and we ran, all of us, postmen's daughters and doctors' sons, pack-like together.

I also knew, from experience, that he had built up his tremendous physique by knocking the shit out of poor sods like me, the runts of the village litter. I recall his sitting on my back holding my head by the hair, beating my forehead against the cold floor of the old dairy till the blood ran and I had to tell my ma I had fallen off a gate. I can't remember why he did this; he never seemed to need a reason. Terror for its own sake, I suppose.

It wasn't just his strength, though, or his physical confidence or his uncanny ability to devise games that he always won that gave him his pre-eminence. He had something that was to stay with him all his life: a compelling quality that bound people to him, like the gravitational pull a planet exercises upon its moons. The only person I ever knew to be immune to this, who defied gravity, was my friend Milo, and I loved him for it.

For me, it was different. I could never get away from him; I seemed to be drawn after Jimmy as if in his wake, bobbing along in the afterwrack of a great liner, with all its flotsam floating by: packing-cases and kitchen waste and empty bottles, the detritus of other people's bruised lives, dined upon by rapacious gulls, picked up and caressed by me. There were many who, having endured Jimmy's attentions, would come for solace and explanation.

'He's an elemental force,' I would explain (not in so many words). 'It's not that he doesn't care. It's just that he orders his priorities differently.'

I won't say that men and women flew like moths into the burning flame of his conceit. That's too neat. He didn't even trample on people: he was too clever, too refined, too good at life for that. They simply found, after they had been with him as friends or lovers for a period of time, that there was a complexity in their feelings about him. They would feel battered, drained, listless, nagged by a sense of worthlessness. It wasn't them, it wasn't him, he hadn't stopped loving them or they him. A

10

drabness had entered their lives, that was all, and they felt they were no longer what they were. Something in them was broken. It wouldn't take too much to patch up – most of it could be restored by a little hand-holding – but it would never heal completely: the full glossy plumage of their pride would never quite shine with all its previous complacency.

Naturally he had this effect on me, but I suppose I had been inoculated against the worst of it by early association, as a result of which I was careful to keep my distance. I knew then, I think, and certainly know now, that he awarded me a special place in his affections, but he had, to put it mildly, an odd way of expressing himself, like a loving but difficult parent. As I waltzed round Oxford with Grace I endeavoured to ensure that Jimmy stayed firmly on the other side of the ballroom. And I hugged everything I knew about him to myself.

With the advent of finals Grace and I, like most students, fled to our books in one last attempt to scrape together enough knowledge to con the examiners into begrudging us a workable degree. In our desperation we furthered our burgeoning love by frequent trysts in New College library, where we would surround ourselves with piles of books and work in intimate concentration with the same easy abandon as we might have done after one of our prolonged bouts of lovemaking. Instead of pillows, we made ourselves comfortable among mountains of paper.

One evening in May when I was wondering how much longer I could keep up this relentless assault on my brain, I looked up and saw Jimmy standing there with Flora, looking highly pleased with themselves. Flora was wearing the kind of leather jacket students aren't supposed to be able to afford. Even I would have been dynamite in it.

'Jimmy Spalding, as I live and breathe,' murmured Grace, stretching herself and yawning beside me.

'Hello, dear Grace,' he returned. 'What are you doing here, so far from home?'

I was stung to the quick. Grace wasn't far from home – she was with me, I was with her, home was where we were. Wasn't that obvious?

'You know Wilf?' Grace's tone faltered treacherously.

'We grew up together.'

'Did you? Wilf, you never told me that.'

'Does that make him more interesting?' Flora smiled at me coolly, communicating friendliness rather than mirth. She had no great reason to be fond of me; I was depriving her of Grace's company and she wasn't sure she liked it.

'How's Ferdy?' Jimmy asked. He sat down, hitched one of his long legs over the arm of a chair, revealing a pair of flash cowboy boots bought from down the King's Road, picked up a copy of *Notes and Queries* and began to read with rapt attention.

'He's well. Haven't seen him in a while.' Grace was never forthcoming about her parents. They were not the only thing she was elusive about – there were a number of regions where one's visa was suddenly no longer valid, where shutters came down and mist drifted thickly and you weren't wanted. Some people are like that: they've staked out bits of themselves and are patrolling the perimeter with hounds. At this time Grace and I had been together getting on for a year; I had been to the big house – one of those streets running off the north side of Hyde Park – just once. Her mother had been unfriendly but Ferdy had been the opposite. I found myself wondering, resentment outdone by curiosity, how Jimmy knew him. 'Anyway, I thought you'd left,' she scolded, changing the subject. 'Another eternal student.'

Jimmy was supposed to have departed the year before, but he was making a spectacular killing by touring the Oxford revue comedians who had come to prominence – to everyone's surprise – at the last Edinburgh Festival. Their week at the Oxford Playhouse had just been extended to two. Jimmy wasn't one of those who managed to stay on in the stale elysium of post-graduate life for ever and a day, directing plays and hobnobbing with the less discerning dons and impressing the students no end with their maturity and sang-froid. No one had ever taken Oxford light entertainment seriously before, and now Jimmy's friends had shot to stardom. In the period of time that lay between their sudden notoriety and a TV series he was entrepreneurially making hay.

'How's the antiques biz?' he pursued. There was a deceptive laziness in his speech that almost amounted to a drawl. He was still talking about Ferdy.

Suddenly, to my astonishment, I was enveloped by Flora's hair as she bent over to kiss me – simply, as I knew, to seek attention. Distracted, I didn't catch Grace's reply, only the tone of her voice as it faltered. In a little kaleidoscope of disloyally mixed feelings, I marked the unhappy uncertainty of it, and so did James. His head went back and he fastened soulless eyes on her, like a war-horse hearing the battle trumpet, or, more accurately, scenting exploitable trouble. (It was to be some years before he was able to take advantage of it.) Handsome he may have been, but those were lethal cheekbones. Roman features; the face of a man who would take power and handle it well. Heroic potential by the bucketload.

'Do you want to come to a party?' enjoined Flora, my new special friend.

'I don't think we've got time,' I mumbled feebly. 'Where is it?'

'Simon's. Andy Warhol's going to be there.'

This was entirely possible. Simon Spicer was a newly arrived junior fellow in Anglo-Saxon and Middle English at Christ Church. As one of Britain's brighter young novelists he had brought an air of contemporary literary significance to the place, striding gamely up and down dowdy lecture theatres in his long black gown declaiming earnestly on the vagaries of Anglo-Saxon declension, as the freshly minted English students stared horror-struck from the benches. Fortunately, this apparition had lasted no longer than a few weeks. At the moment when his students revealed that not one had read the texts set for a tutorial he had plunged his head into his hands and murmured: 'Oh, death.'

After which he rather blossomed, shedding sombre gowns for engagingly muddled tweeds, and greeting his students with a cheery wave and radiant grin. He brought his friends to Oxford to feast upon its delights, and his parties became legendary. He did seem to know everybody: Julian Barnes, Richard Ingrams, Tina Brown, yes, but also people like Warren Beatty, Mick Jagger and so forth, strange, exotic birds alighting among the dowdier pigeon-roosts of the British literati.

We shouldn't have gone, really, but you know how it is. Flora and Grace raced for Jimmy's car, a white left-hand-drive Peugeot 505 which he had bought in Brussels and shipped over for tax purposes. For some reason I insisted on cycling, trundling up Banbury Road, getting lost in the process. All the way I was thinking of the work I hadn't done, but north Oxford is a beautiful place on a warm summer evening, the shadows comfortable and embracing, and by the time I found Spicer's house the piquant scents of exuberant vegetation had soothed my jangling nerves.

'Wilfred, how sweet of you to come. Your party have rather preceded you, but I'm sure you'll catch up.' Simon was purring, and his house, the walls of which were a hymn to distemper, was humming with good conversation, the sort you can decant. I was fond of his mischievous demeanour and his real generosity. I remember his white shirt glowed a little in the darkening evening; it was too big for him, accentuating the frail slightness of his form, his mildly feline manner. 'Come and meet some people. You're among friends here.'

I wasn't sure that was true until I clapped eyes on Milo Glover leaning rakishly against the mantelpiece, very much the mannered student, wearing his admired bottle-green velvet suit with a loose-collared cream shirt. His richly red, flowing locks, auburn rather than ginger, combed straight back from his forehead, together with his milky complexion, made him a dead ringer for Thomas Chatterton, a resemblance he exploited mercilessly, quoting great chunks with tremendous vigour at inappropriate moments, safe in the knowledge that no one else knew any better. We had first met on the stage of *Hamlet*, where I was Polonius to Milo's Dark Prince (he looked great but the casting was terrible – he had exactly the wrong temperament); all the unsettling profundity of the play had been knocked out of us by interminable workshops during the Easter holidays, where we had lain side by side in vacant, echoing church halls in Cowley practising breathing, shouting, how to be a vegetable and, ultimately, how to loathe and despise the self-obsessed director of a play about a self-obsessed hero.

'Wilf.' He dropped a hand condescendingly over my shoulder. 'Meet David.' Something in his voice made me inspect his new acquaintance with curiosity. Dressed meticulously in deep grey linen with contrasting pale yellow tie and breast pocket handkerchief, his dandruff-flecked black hair was combed back with determination and panache from a squat, complacent face punctuated by prune-coloured eyes and underhung by a small but distressingly ruthless little chin, with incipient jowls in close support. I learned later that his enemies called him 'the Amphibian'.

'You're on Jimmy's team, are you?' he enquired of me. His manner was aloof, but I sensed he was making a harmless advance of a sort.

'You might say that.'

'David's a terrific swell at the Union.' Milo didn't usually talk like this. 'He's been on the river,' he added laconically.

Perhaps aware of mockery, David smiled broadly.

'Punting, yes. We had a splendid time. Have you tried it recently? You should. One of the girls contrived to fall in, quite deliberately, I'm sure. Rather revealing. We played games in a field, "Blind Man's Buff" and suchlike. When it was my turn they put the blindfold on me and I ran about and couldn't find anyone and when I took it off they had all run away and were doubled-up with laughter. It wasn't really that funny in my opinion,' he ended, with an exaggerated air of rueful reflection meant, I thought, to be both entertaining and disarming. Abruptly, he switched tack. 'Have you been to see *Twelfth Night*? At Magdalen, in the deer park? Rather contrived, I felt, playing it that way.'

'Oh, why?' Milo's tone was cold, and I knew the reason. It occurred to me that David did, too.

'Setting it in prohibition Chicago? Frightful cliché. Jonathan Miller did it years ago.'

'Quite neat making the Duke Capone.'

'You think so? Then I fear your Shakespeare and mine are very different men.' His head waggled slightly as he spoke. 'The Bard would not have approved.'

'Where *did* you find him?' I asked Milo afterwards.

'He was just sort of there. Did you see that smirk?'

'He didn't like your Shakespeare.'

'Oh, well, that was just an idea I threw off.' (Milo was President of the university dramatic society that year.) 'I was surprised anyone picked it up.' I could tell he was rattled. 'He's standing for President of the Union.'

'You surprise me.'

'Are Flora and Grace here?'

'I think so.' Turning, I almost cannoned into a blond figure standing silently to one side. He was dressed entirely in black, his hair was combed very clearly and beautifully, and he hardly moved as others circled about him, talking over and at and through him. Occasionally he was addressed as Andy, sometimes as Mr Warhol; he did not seem to respond to any of it.

Fascinated, I watched, and as I watched I became aware of a ceremonial swirl around him, as if he were one of the lesser gods being venerated by whispering acolytes. A lovely scent filled the air, like old roses, a scent that cleansed the mind at the same moment that it transported it.

I waited for the figure to make some kind of utterance, and as I did so I felt compelled to stay in his presence; it was impossible to tear myself away. I sensed a thick press of murmuring people, drawn as if in search of shelter or blessing.

He neither moved nor spoke, so far as I could tell.

Milo had disappeared, so I went to look for Flora, Jimmy and Grace. The house was packed and it was big, and nowhere could I find them. At last, towards the top of the house, the crowd

16

thinned. I looked from bedroom to bedroom. Clusters of guests were admiring Simon's exquisite ornaments from India and the Far East, most of them brought back by his adventuring grandfather, who had been a fiendish collector.

Opening a small side door, driven simply by shameless inquisitiveness, I found a room in darkness. It was a boxroom, with walls so close together that a couple could lean back on opposite sides and still touch. Indeed, on closer inspection I saw that two people were doing precisely this. Save that one of them had his trousers round his ankles, and the other, kneeling, had the palms of her hands placed decorously on his thighs. His erection glistened in the light from the landing. Two familiar faces turned towards me, blinking suspiciously, unable to identify me with my back to the light.

'Do you think you could close the door, please?'

I complied.

That only left Grace to find. Which took a while, my concentration having becoming a little distrait.

'Your Flora —' I blurted out when I eventually tracked her down.

'Wilf,' she remarked matter-of-factly, to the girl next to her, with an almost imperceptible inclination of her head in my direction.

Her friend, small and dark with short hair and a determined look, smiled briefly. 'Hermione,' she rejoined tersely, her brown eyes glancing cursorily up at me in momentary scrutiny. It transpired they were discussing the merits of the newly appointed Bishop of Oxford.

'He's very good on pastoral care,' Hermione was saying. 'We're a little concerned about whether he still has an active prayer-life, though.'

Grace was gravely sympathetic.

'Where does he stand on women?'

'Not very promising. He's on record as saying there won't be women priests in his lifetime.'

'Anyone with any intelligence can see the Church isn't going to accept women priests,' I offered. 'You can't have a woman administering the sacraments. They're supposed to stand in Christ's place, aren't they? So they have to be men.'

This sort of remark stays with one through the years. When I remember it now I experience a little rush of blood to the cheeks and seem to hear a strange crashing noise, like a gong.

Hermione gave me a look of deep contempt.

'Don't be more of an arsehole than you can help, Wilf,' Grace remarked, witheringly.

I stepped back and threw up my arms in a picture of mock surrender, thereby knocking a glass of champagne out of the hand of the earnest and kindly form of Iris Murdoch and spilling the entire contents over her sumptuously embroidered dress.

The Great Greaves

WITH THE RIGHT degree of irresponsibility it's not hard to make adolescence stretch well into one's thirties. There comes a time, though, when the elastic begins to tighten and some growing-up has to happen. There are those, one meets them occasionally, who avoid this, but they are, curiously, those who have grown old too young; having affected the manners of their elders, and as they imagine them, betters, something has remained unformed inside. Early maturity almost always results in skewed personalities in middle age, like those bimetallic strips used in thermostats, where one metal expands more quickly than the other and forces it to bend in a direction it doesn't want to go.

Another way of side-stepping any consciousness of the ageing process is simply never to change, but you need a tough constitution. My friend Milo has had a good crack at it; even now, he and Tom Phipps are usually out and about doing bars, clubs, coke and the town until the small hours, and neither of them ever looks the worse for it. Tom, who at Oxford was the archetypal denizen of the Union and the kind of creature I used to avoid like the plague but whom I have since come to love, does get rather pasty at five in the morning in Frith Street, but Milo positively blossoms. The more drink, the more fiery he gets; argumentative, yes, but brilliant with it.

What one wants to avoid are the defining moments, when, I suppose, the structures we use in everyday life to understand ourselves and those around us suddenly become terrifyingly inadequate; afterwards we look back and see our lives rewritten,

19

reinterpreted, part of a new understanding that embraces the old, broken one.

Grace once told me that a sect called the Quietists, who were persecuted by the Church, thought that the way to bring good fortune into one's life was to reject any expectations of it, and love God unconditionally. I couldn't do this; I would find it hard to love God without a long Christmas shopping-list of conditions, though I think Grace is drawn by the idea. I don't know how much good it does her. Whether one bullies life or cowers from it, the defining moments will come, and it's how you deal with them that counts, or how you deal with the consequences they unleash.

When Grace found out about her father's death, we were at Monkridge. We hadn't been asked down by Jimmy for ages, not since I'd become part of Kitty's vendetta. And then came the invitation, and very uneasy I was about accepting it, though I didn't really feel I had much choice in the matter.

It was strange to be there again. While I was growing up and Jimmy terrorized the neighbourhood, his father Ranulph was a distant, granitic figure, occasionally seen stalking the Monkridge grounds in splendid isolation. His wife had died in childbirth, and Ranulph had reared four unruly sons with a benign but distant hand. My father being the local doctor, we lived in the village nearby, and most days after school we descended on Monkridge and ran wild among the fabulous gardens, which Ranulph had dedicated himself to restoring. We didn't care for them that much – we were too busy getting to the woods to play 'Forty-forty' and war games – but we were vaguely aware that they were something special. Generations had gardened there with passion and flair, and though the grounds had lapsed during the war Ranulph had set himself to return them to their former glories. Perhaps he found in them some solace for his lost wife. He had loved her very much.

Later, Jimmy would begin hosting his legendary parties there. These were big, blowsy affairs, sumptuous in their way though a little lacking in elegance. He would hire local bands that took his fancy: one moment it was an earnest blues foursome with too much brass and pomposity; another, it was a fleet-footed rockabilly ensemble; the next, some astonishing punks who frightened the daylights out of Jimmy's swisher acquaintances. As he grew in ambition he got them from clubs he frequented in Shrewsbury and then London. The marquees grew larger and larger and the crowds more and more mixed. In those days we used to catch the four forty-five from Euston and were there just in time for dinner: a small band of country-housers, complacently old-fashioned, but by then it was the eighties and *Brideshead* had been and gone, so tweediness and outrageousness went hand in hand. We tumbled from the coaches at Shrewsbury station and though we weren't met by an old retainer with a pony and trap we forgave the oversight.

'Where are we?' I once asked Flora as the train slowed and I awoke.

'Somewhere between Cold Comfort Farm and Blandings Castle, I think.'

Dear Flora. She was just beginning her spectacular career as a literary agent and she tended to overplay the part. But she was right, all the same. I would have thrown in a touch of Mervyn Peake for good measure, for Monkridge, with its low, rambling buildings and outhouses set on rising land, seemed to unfold tower upon tower and roof upon roof as you approached up the main drive. It always gave me a shiver. I once told Jimmy it made me think of Gormenghast, and he looked unhappy at the idea, perhaps because he was in the midst of grandly declaiming on the subject of its Elizabethan architect to an admiring table, perhaps because he wasn't sure whether it was a compliment or not. It was: ever since I was little I had loved to wander the corridors and court-yards, which always seemed larger and more numerous than they really were. When I think of it now I see it both great and small, both as a vast playground for my young imagination and as something more sober and altogether more demure. Then, I used to lose myself in the bowels of the house, much of which had long

21

fallen into disrepair, for Ranulph was far more moved by a damask rose than a damask wallpaper. I would rummage about in the old decaying barns trying doors – usually locked – always half-expecting to see the purple star-embroidered cloak of some fleeing wizard whisking out of sight round a corner. But no matter how many forgotten chests I explored, I never discovered, as I so much wanted to, any hand-painted parchments with strange beasts of unearthly beauty frolicking around an arrestingly cryptic text.

That terrible night when Grace heard about Ferdy I had managed to excuse myself from dinner and escape everyone, in particular a verminous creature who had been trying to impress me with tales of his exploits in some branch of the Special Forces. I don't know why these people unburden themselves to me – perhaps I look the sort of sympathetic creature who would want to know that a prophylactic can hold forty-five pints of water, and other such lore of the fighting man's world. I had made my way through a skylight to a small, flat patch of roof that I liked to think only I knew about. It was quiet, the night was not too cold, and the stars were out. I was just identifying Cassiopeia to myself when I heard a voice calling, faint but with an imitation of urgency to it, a voice that seemed at first to come up from the deep chasm of my own thoughts. The skylight rose, and Jimmy's head shot through.

'Come quickly,' he panted. 'It's Grace. It's Ferdy.'

He seemed to think he had told me all I needed to know. In a moment he was gone and I was blundering at his heels. The way seemed further than it should have done.

Helen, Jimmy's wife, met us.

'It's terrible,' she wept.

'Is he all right?'

She shook her head violently.

It was then that I knew I was not going to find the right words, not even the right feelings. My clothes felt too tight; my head was an unwieldy weight on my shoulders. I was terrified by an aware-ness of a test awaiting me that only I would be able to perceive and only I would know I had failed.

22

Someone I didn't know was holding Grace. She was utterly still. The soldier was machine-gunning the telephone with orders and questions. Such people do know what to do in a crisis. I stood by, and the room and the people revolved about me, and I began to hope I would somehow dematerialize, shaking off my palpable, useless fleshliness like a snake does its skin.

It was not as if I hadn't loved Ferdy. I had, very much, and with good reason. I'd owed him my job. Taking pity on yet another godforsaken student floundering in the miasma of life's golden but on-the-whole-unwanted opportunities, he had shunted me in the direction of Kitty Greaves, that sensational forger of the intellectual horseshoes of our times, whom he had recently appointed as editor of the small, intellectually respectable but commercially dismal arts magazine entitled, with all the éclat of the decade in which it was founded, *Arts Unlimited*. More commonly known, with a hint of derision, perhaps, as the *Arts*, it had started life as a flimsy rag and graduated excitingly over the years to a better quality paper, even, through a succession of editors, attaining the giddy heights of possessing three or four pages of colour reproduction. It had become a respected commentary on the artistic life of the capital, and even the bad editors – and there had been a few – kept up the momentum, for the simple reason that the *Arts* had prestige, and writers and artists through the ages have been drawn to prestige like mice to cheese.

Ferdy, whose business dealings, particularly in artefacts from the Far East, were enveloped in mystery, but who was none the less a generous man, had at some point in the strange trajectory of his career acquired the *Arts*. I don't suppose it cost him a great deal, and I think he genuinely hoped that giving me respectable employment would elevate me in the eyes of Grace's mother. He was a sublime optimist, and wrong.

It wasn't Kitty herself I saw, of course, but one of her serfs, whom she had recently appointed as editor of the *Arts*' book pages, amid a great deal of publicity, having poached him from

23

the *Spectator*. He had moved under the illusion that he would be given his head at the *Arts*, and great was the fluttering among the gossips at his transfer, for upheaval at the *Spectator*, at that point enjoying a tremendous surge in its circulation, was of consuming interest. Unfortunately, Terry Smallish was a kindly, bookish fellow whose musical tastes ran to John Lennon rather than, say, Verdi, and whose distinctly unvoguish, unfogeyish ways soon simply failed to cut ice with Kitty, who could sense the first nervous wing-beats of a newly hatched Big Idea in the cultural jungle at the most prodigious distances.

I was happily unaware of all this as I carefully-casually displayed my invitation to a party at the *Arts'* offices on my temporary sub-editor's desk at the recently launched, soon-to-fold *Marketing People*.

'The job's yours,' Smallish had said when he called me. 'If you're absolutely sure you want it.'

I felt I had arrived. I practised murmuring 'I'm on the *Arts'* book pages' to myself in response to imagined introductions to literary London, though I wasn't exactly sure who literary London was; as I imagined the scene there was a dark silhouette in my mind's eye, with which I would be shaking hands or coolly eyeing over a lunch table in Greek Street.

At the party I was soon out of my depth. Just as I found myself going under for the third time in a conversation about David Hockney's views on the Keith Haring exhibition at the ICA, the waves parted and I found myself confronted by a small atomic explosion in human form.

She approached with the unfettered dignity of an inquisitive shark, hands outstretched to clasp my right one as it swung limply by my side.

'I've heard such a lot about you from Terry. Welcome to *Arts Unlimited*. Tell me, who is your favourite writer?'

'Márquez,' I extemporized. Her face clouded momentarily, then she put her arm through mine and turned to face the room. Out of the corner of my eye, fleetingly, I caught Smallish ironically rolling his.

'That's Berenger Furlong. There's June Hartcher. And that,' she pointed vigorously, 'is Marvin Slowman.'

Furlong and Hartcher were hot, I knew that; one was the son of an MP, the other the daughter of a senior broadcaster. Both had written slim first novels which had been received with rapturous acclaim. Furlong was shit, but Hartcher I rated. Slowman was a new one on me.

'Marvin.' Arm in arm, we followed Kitty's outstretched finger. As I was to learn, she liked to imagine that a playfully excessive demonstrativeness would make do for a sense of humour. Marvin, wearing wraparound shades, was deep in conversation with Angela Carter.

'Marvin's just been published by Chatto. He is our premier rap poet.' Marvin grinned in a pained way and murmured something about Linton Kwesi Johnson. I was acutely aware of the absurdity of standing in such close proximity to Kitty; I was also electrically aware of *her*. I could sense every hair of that beautiful mane, in the dark coils of which the bright lights were glossily refracted. She smiled fixedly up at me and then batted her eyelashes – I had never actually seen this done before – at Marvin.

'This is our new assistant editor,' she intoned. 'Isn't he wonderful? We expect great things.' She turned, looked me up and down abstractedly as if I were a faded poster on the underground or an item of clothing in her wardrobe soon to be discarded, and was gone.

I simpered ingratiatingly at Marvin.

'I love your work.' I couldn't tell whether he had heard me.

'I've just finished *Nights at the Circus*,' I confided in his companion. This was almost true. I had just started it. 'Fantastic.'

As one, they turned towards the drinks table.

Ferdy is going to have a lot to answer for, I thought grimly. I felt a sharp pain under my lower rib, and on inspection found it to be Kitty Greaves' nail.

'I want you in my office at ten o'clock,' she barked flirtatiously.

So began one of life's great partnerships. Every morning at ten the telephone would summon me to Kitty's office, there to be given a task of breathtaking pointlessness, thereafter to be ignored for the rest of the day. As identical treatment was meted out to the other luckless fellow-travellers whom I liked to call colleagues, I was comfortable with this. *Just.*

Kitty was the latest in a long line of revolutionaries at the *Arts*, which like so many dilapidated but august magazines required the attentions of a ruthless, captious, utterly driven megalomaniac at its helm. Though she was not that much older than me, the rest of us simply ran around pumped full of paranoia and a deplorable desire to impress, forever uncertain as to what we were expected to be doing, each of us at the mercy of Kitty's whims. Her brilliant predecessors had used the *Arts* shamelessly as a stepping-stone to the great and glorious upper reaches of Fleet Street, and we all assumed she was in the same line of business, although looking back I think this was unfair. She had revamped the venerable periodical, made it a fortnightly rather than a weekly, and given it a cornucopia of clashing typefaces. She had placed copy lines on the cover and even added artwork to it. She had moved the reviews section from the middle to the back, brought features from the back to the front, and shunted regular slots from the front to the middle. None of which, though eminently sensible, affected the readability, status or circulation of the magazine but all of which considerably enhanced her reputation. The up-and-coming were impressed. The up-and-arrived were nervous. Ferdy was delighted. She had not achieved any particular financial improvement for the *Arts*, but that hardly seemed to matter.

Knowing Ferdy did not hinder my progress, I confess. Often the pair of them met at the Café Pelican in St Martin's Lane for breakfast, and occasionally I was invited, too. Once, very soon after I'd started, as I was walking from Leicester Square past Wyndham's Theatre and the sleeping-bag sleepovers just stirring in the emaciated early morning London sunshine, I found myself wondering quite how sycophantic I was going to be, and the answer was, to my surprise, very. I was young, I was ambitious.

My mortgage was small, and I wanted a bigger one. What did I care for pride?

In the cavernous recesses of the restaurant I found them, Ferdy sleek and patrician, Kitty looking fractionally less wired than usual. I think he was good for her.

'Be seated, young man.' Ferdy's voice possessed a subterranean timbre, and he patronized with such sublime charm that one wanted to laugh and obey at the same time. Even Kitty's eye softened as she looked at me, though the rapidity of her speech scarcely wavered. Ferdy's long, lugubrious face was inclined forward, importing gravitas; this unfortunately gave him a double chin and a hint of fleshliness, of a tendency to excess, that echoed the pink plumpness of his lips. His cunning brown eyes gazed with mournful attentiveness at Kitty as she denounced the London cultural milieu for its bourgeois complacency. She herself hailed from Canada and was convent-educated, while Ferdy came from a long line of Church of Scotland ministers, so rubbishing the English establishment, especially the radical one, was second nature to them.

'All playwrights with a Howard in their name should be hounded out of the theatre and forced to go and live in Surbiton and work in the post office.' She paused for breath. Ferdy's eyes swivelled towards me and he raised his eyebrows interrogatively, slowly unfurling the fingers of his left hand as it lay palm-up on the table. My turn.

Rashly, I opted for opinionated integrity.

'I thought that Barker play at the Royal Court was a work of coruscating genius. And funny.'

'Coruscating shit. You don't know what you're talking about, darling. Boring English male obsession with boring English past. Who cares about the English Civil War? Thatcher's philistinism is a problem *now*. Don't go pretending everything can be solved just because we've been there before. The English always do that. History is their vice.'

She lifted a cup of black coffee before her like a triumphal globe – 'Stately, plump Kitty Greaves', I thought fleetingly – and flashed her radiant smile at Ferdy. It was like switching on the floodlights at the evening game at Stamford Bridge, a smile defensive, offensive and alarming. She sipped the coffee and went on smiling at Ferdy, who tittered quietly while looking sideways at me, cowering mockingly as if to shield himself.

'We've been discussing a new idea of Kitty's,' he said, recovering. 'Why don't you ask Wilf what he thinks?'

'I'm going to have a gardening column.' Kitty was pathologically incapable of asking about anything. The whisper of a possibility had just become a shout of determination. I don't think this had been Ferdy's intention – I could tell by the expression of perplexity that had fallen over his face. His lips pursed, giving him the appearance of a hungry carp. For a moment it looked, strangely, as if he were about to blow her a kiss. Yet as I examine this image I realize it's not the lips but the eyes that are giving me this impression: it's a soupy, dog-like, though still shrewd, look of devotion.

'What a brilliant idea.' I beamed warmly at her. The vagaries of rearing recalcitrant pot-plants at home had given me an overweening desire for the real thing, and I had been hunkering down in bed with colourful volumes by Penelope Hobhouse and trenchant ones by Christopher Lloyd, to Grace's astonishment. So I was greenly, but keenly, green.

'*Isn't* it? Gardens as part of the culture, gardens as art, gardens *in* art, gardens in literature, statuary, lifestyle, everything. Gardening is one of the few creative things the English do.'

'I must defend my countrymen,' said Ferdy, coyly.

'Go right ahead. But, my God, they do it *well*,' she exclaimed.

'I'll write it, if you like,' I threw in.

'*You*? What do you know about horticulture?'

'I'm passionate about it. I live and breathe it. I'm hoovering up every volume on the gardening shelf in our local bookshop. I'm a member of Kew *and* of Chelsea Physic Garden.'

'Hmm. Well, are you a gardener?'

'Not yet.' I was brazen. 'But I will be.'

She seemed to waver.

'Do you know Ranulph Spalding's gardens near Shrewsbury? I could do a piece on them. They're fabulous.'

'Are they in the Yellow Book?'

'No. No one ever sees them. That's why they would be good to do. Quite a coup,' I said, mentally trying to calculate the likelihood of Ranulph opening his precious estate to an intrusive and amateur pen.

'He's not related to James Spalding, is he?'

'Father,' interjected Ferdy, indistinctly, through a last vestige of croissant.

Another pause.

'Well, let's all see if we can think up some names of people to write this lovely new column of mine,' said Kitty, curtly.

Brutal, but effective. I almost cried. Ferdy patted me on the shoulder outside as Kitty hailed a cab. But he didn't say anything.

Jimmy's fame was beginning to spread; and although I had not yet been acquainted with the nature of Kitty's feelings about him, it wasn't to be long before I was. It was the hour of the entrepreneur: the Falklands had been won, Labour had given birth to the SDP, Harry Evans had been fired from *The Times*, Thatcher was trashing the miners and the creator of wealth was the new hero of the business and features pages. Champagne was the popular tipple; rivers of the stuff cascaded down the Square Mile and up Pall Mall, and the frontiers of the state were rolling back like tarpaulins off Wimbledon Centre Court. Play was beginning in earnest, and Jimmy was in close to the net.

He had left the comedians behind and gone into magazines. At first I had hardly noticed; it just seemed a quiet period in his life. The comics had found themselves managers and TV shows and didn't need him any more, and he wanted something of his own. He was a builder at heart, which is not, I suppose, a bad thing.

It started with a funny little item called *Woodland*, a homely, faintly snobbish production that infiltrated the grander reaches of St John's Wood. It was upmarket enough to be seen displayed among other glossies in the local newsagents, this being the condition to which most free periodicals aspire. It was packed full of estate agents' advertisements and mild gossip. Unfortunately, its owner was, well, its owner, but this did not seem to deter James. In a coup of unprecedented ferocity and sheer nerve he put it about that *Woodland* was being run by the leader of a paedophile ring, a story that was howlingly untrue – he was, in fact, in a stable gay partnership of some twenty years' standing – but as is the way with such things he could not face the indignity and revulsion of pursuing his tormentors through the courts, and he fled this entirely fictitious calumny for the more tolerant climes of New York. *Woodland* folded overnight, to be replaced instantaneously by *Grove* (Prop.: J. Spalding), a magazine of uncanny similarity but possessing one additional feature of such cunning that Jimmy was able to pilot his worthless bark among the further populations of Fulham, Chelsea, Battersea and Clapham, where the new wealth of the arrivistes was leading to a mini-boom in the services of plumbers, heating specialists, carpenters and the like. Jimmy's gimmick was to run a page for dissatisfied customers, who were encouraged to write in and complain about shoddy or overpriced jobs; the miscreant's name would be printed and his response to *Grove*'s searching and fearless questioning would be laid out in cold print. A simple device, but devastating. Its entertainment value alone made *Grove* indispensable reading, and it became for a while rather chic, attracting favourable comment in the mainstream press.

Tom Phipps, my corpulent, perspiring, roistering friend, whose penchant for salacious stories had never been impeded by any discernible form of conscience, claimed this was where Jimmy's taste for magazine proprietorship began, and Tom was a seasoned Jimmy-watcher. Jimmy often made appearances in Tom's column in the *Guardian*, where Tom was their bit of rough, and Tom was good, too, on the source of Kitty's virulent loathing for Jimmy.

'She knows just how dodgy he is. She should know. They slept together long enough.'

There was silence for a moment or two. We were sitting in a

French restaurant called the Crepuscule that used to be a favourite of mine, just off Golden Square. I had been at the *Arts* a couple of years by then. Milo was the first to crack.

'That's outrageous, Tom. Bloody outrageous.' I think he carried a small flame for Kitty himself, or at least for the idea of her. He had never in point of fact met her, so far as I knew.

I thought hard.

'I can't imagine any possible time that could have been going on, and I'm sure I would have heard. I mean, what about Helen?'

Tom shrugged infuriatingly.

'I don't see it,' said Milo.

Tom leaned forward to crush out his cigarette, carefully brushing the ash into a neat heap in the corner of the ashtray. Then he settled his bulk back on the small wooden chair, ran a hand through his untidy blond hair, wrapped one arm round his head to scratch his ear and waved to the waitress for more coffee with the other.

'Anyway. Believe what you like. They stopped when he bought up that listings mag she was on; he fired a couple of people and the rest of them walked out in protest. Kitty didn't have much choice but to follow suit. Solidarity and all that. Soured things with Jimmy somewhat.'

'She's moved fast since then. I'd forgotten.'

'She's older than him, isn't she?' put in Milo.

'Older and prettier and much more talented. But unfortunately not nearly so rich. How many magazines does he own now?'

'Twenty-six. He's like a whale chasing plankton.'

'But he started some, didn't he?'

'The bike ones. *Big Wheels*, *Wheelie*, they're called things like that. All in the special interest section in Smith's. Then he resuscitated those two computer mags. You know, he's really admired in that world for what he's done.'

'Oh, I know.'

I did know. Whenever the opportunity arose Kitty ran a paragraph on Jimmy and his business interests. There wasn't that

31

much room for biting gossip in the *Arts* but there was enough. With business being so sexy, she had excuse enough to commission the heavy hitters to write serious pieces about the new young entrepreneurs or the explosion in very focused, very specialized magazines, and they were often briefed – very unprofessionally, and to give her her due this was the only time she did it – to look carefully at James Spalding.

To give me my due, I felt deeply uncomfortable about this. I thought of him as a good friend, and an old friend, too, and there's no one you forgive more easily than someone you have known for a long time, because as they grow slowly but ineluctably into someone you can hardly recognize you excuse their every change for the sake of the person you knew so long ago. So although I had been seeing very little of him because of Kitty's hostilities, when he had recently rung me out of the blue I had answered with alacrity, and as a result I found myself dropping round to his offices early one bright March evening.

Jimmy's first headquarters was in Carnaby Street, and he named his company after it. Unimaginative, perhaps, but if Carnaby had ambitions to be a giant among magazine publishers, its original offices were ideal for one as dedicated to cost control as Jimmy Spalding. Through a small black door in an elegant white façade one wandered up rickety stairs to the top, where all the walls had been removed to leave a large office with sea-grass flooring and two big sofas in primary green and red; Jimmy himself lounged behind a vast but minimalistically concise expression of a desk. The walls were adorned with magazine covers in frames. The whole room screamed, 'My life is my work, and my work is cool.' Which was fine, if you thought that *Knitting Monthly* was cool, but Jimmy was in a white heat of exponential expansion, and business and commerce and making-things-happen were intensely cool – especially if you read the business pages – and there was no one to hear the agonized squawk of the brutalized aesthete. Carnaby was crazy for acquisition and niche marketing, for ratcheting up the potential share value in preparation for the inevitable sell-off, and Jimmy's

32

command–post was a forward position in the onslaught on complacency and shoddy self–indulgence. He was buying small magazines and making them big, shifting their editorial policies, advertising profiles and consumer bases until they became the market leaders in their respective fields. Et cetera.

His feet were on the desk when I entered. He waved his hand and went on talking into the phone cradled by his left cheek. The sky was beginning to darken and both blond hair and brogues were taking on a luminous sheen from the streetlights outside.

I slumped into one of the sofas and busied myself with the company brochure, which chronicled the fantastic ambitions and equally astonishing achievements of Carnaby and its progenitor and guiding light.

'I'm looking to make a major expansion,' Jimmy was explaining languidly into the phone. '*Machine Tools*. They're underfunded and they've completely missed the point about what they're doing. They're very sober, very intense, very dull. I mean, you know, they're really interested in machine tools. But if we take them up to the glossy, feature, quality production level there's a vast readership out there for them. It's big nerd appeal, basically. The problem is the editor. The owner wants to sell but the editor doesn't. Yes. I know, surprises me too. There's some hold he's got over him. They grew up together, I think.' I glared at him, but he was too wrapped up. 'Do you think we need to send someone round to help him make up his mind?'

I found myself wondering what kind of help this paragon might offer: gentle counselling, some acute financial analysis? Suddenly, I found my look returned: nervous, ungenerous, hostile, even.

'I've got to go. Yes, medium pressure, I think. The usual bunch. Let's not take it too far.'

He slapped down the phone.

'Wilf.'

'Serious offices, these.'

'Glad you think so.' The Marlboro Man of old was the

no-holds-barred businessman of today, the pin-stripes ablaze with blistering self-confidence. Of course the pin-stripe is spivvy, that goes without saying, and there is something fabulously brazen about the way the British establishment wears it, as if to declare its fundamental amorality, like the stripes of war. The pin-stripe suit is simultaneously a statement of aggression, formality and absurdity, and it's the last that counts. How possible is it to take someone dressed in such fantastical motley seriously? It's bright, dashing, challenging, vulgar in the extreme, utterly silly and magnificent, appropriate both to the City and the Mob. Threatening and charming at the same time.

Jimmy's made him resplendent. I had not seen him like this before, not quite so much the lion in his den; on his desk, I noticed, was a small sculpture of a cheetah in full flight, claws outstretched, triumphantly claiming the desperate, lunging figure of a gazelle.

'Where shall we go?' he asked, with all the temerity of one who knew the answer.

'The Criterion? Groucho's? Zanzibar?'

He gave me a clever, shrewd look, as if to murmur 'Nearly right'.

'The Ritz, I think,' was what he actually said.

Soon we were sitting with dowagers and duchesses, enjoying champagne and nuts in stately fashion on the dais overlooking the front door.

'I was wondering about your ambitions,' he remarked. 'I'm assuming you have some?'

He was assuming a little too much. Ambition has never been my strong point – indeed, I have never been entirely sure what my strong point *is* – but I was not put out by this.

'World domination,' I replied.

'Bravo,' he responded, pompously, and a trifle sceptically.

'I'd like to be an editor. I'd like to edit the *Arts*,' I went on speculatively, seizing the moment. 'But wouldn't we all? To be honest, James, I'd like to edit anything in sight. Not *Machine Tools*,' I added hastily, raising a finger in the air and hoping that

34

he thought I was simply being frivolous and not that I'd cottoned on to his comments over the phone.

Tom's eyebrows had risen significantly as I told him of my visit to Carnaby, but it was lost on Milo.

'Exquisite,' we heard him remark dreamily.

The large windows of the Crepuscule looked out on to Upper James Street where it meets Beak Street and the busy people of Soho bustle past. Milo was resting his foot on the low sill, observing the passers-by intently.

'Golden Square,' I said. 'Is this where Whittington found his golden pavements?'

'Isn't it "gelding square", from cattle and such?' returned Tom. We looked at Milo meaningfully. He could be very unreconstructed and we liked to pick him up on it when we got a sanctimonious opportunity.

He went on staring regardless.

'Do you think it would be going too far to order some of that *tarte aux pommes normande* you had?' asked Tom earnestly. 'I think I could just squeeze it in. Possibly with a pudding wine of some sort. Milo?'

Tom always hoped to persuade Milo to join in his gastronomic excesses, but you didn't maintain such a bony pallor as Milo's by eating well. Drinking well, yes. With a sigh, Milo turned his attention back to us. Resting his elbows on the red-and-white checked table cloth he looked about him vacantly. The waitress approached.

'Another bottle of the St Émilion, please. That'll see me through the afternoon.' He gazed admiringly at the delicately sculpted shoulder-blades of her departing back.

'How is work?' I asked. Tom and I liked to leave this until last.

'The M.D.'s just left.'

'You only had him a couple of years.'

'Her. Yes, but you know what it's like.'

Milo had ended up, through no particular fault of his own that I could see, in the bowels of a major book-publishing company,

35

one that had tripled in size with the hectic take-over spree that had recently afflicted the industry. It was impossible to open a newspaper without finding a piece on how the dear old traditional values had been scythed by the advent of ruthless corporate men and women with their implacable regard for profit.

'What happened? Bad results?'

'Brilliant results. Best for years. But the sales M.D. didn't like what she was doing with marketing. Neither did the marketing M.D.'

'How many M.D.s do you have?'

'Quite a number. It's a big company, don't forget, so these are big jobs. They all get to be called M.D., anyway. When Pegasus bought us their M.D. told everyone our M.D. was the most talented woman in British publishing, but it seems he's changed his mind.'

Pegasus had been started from scratch five years previously, and their aggression had made them the darlings of the book trade. Milo's company, itself swollen to twice its size after buying up an ailing but nevertheless venerable literary house, had been much the bigger, but its shareholders were thoroughly disenchanted with their miserable dividends, and had decided to sell their shares and retire to Florida. At first it was thought that the grandees of Murgatroyd & Wilson would be slaughtered by the rapacious upstarts with the commercial edge from Pegasus, but as is so often the case the reverse happened. It's a universal law: the fresh-faced energetic newcomers overwhelm the ancient but prestigious relic, then assume the characteristics of their victim. Watch any David Attenborough programme.

'And Grace?' The two of them, the lecher and the glutton, spoke as one.

She was fine. We both were. There was nothing wrong, then, I'm sure of it. It is tempting to rewrite history, of course, but there's really no point. Not when it's difficult enough to write in the first place, and impossible to pin down, even when it's your own history. Especially when it's your own.

'Couldn't be better,' I said.

And that was true, until the news came that her father's car had pirouetted so carelessly into a tree. It was after that the cracks appeared, and we split according to the underlying fault lines.

As she sat on the couch at Monkridge, I took her in my arms. She collapsed against me. Her body felt like a physical weight of pure sorrow, as if all her muscles and bones and flesh were saturated in it, as if it were a subterranean energy possessing her.

Eventually we got her to bed, exhausted by grief but incapable of sleep. She lay in darkness, her face illuminated by the moon, her eyes unseeing but wide open, every part of her seemingly intensely alive to herself but dead to the world.

I stole downstairs in search of whisky. What I found was Jimmy sitting by the curtains of the great windows overlooking the terrace. He was slightly hunched, his legs curled over one arm of the chair, a deep frown on his face.

'How is she?' he asked, without moving.

'Terrible.'

He didn't respond for a while. Then, 'Help yourself.'

I did. The drawing room was quiet, and the noises of the night – the owls in the woods, the occasional lowing of cattle in the fields further up the valley – carried softly into its depths. I remember the pinko-grey torsos of the lovers in one of the paintings, the newspapers folded carelessly into a magazine rack, the deep blood-red of the rounded boll of the port decanter, the tassels on the curtain cords swinging very slightly to and fro so that they brushed delicately against the skirting boards with a noise like distant rain on the surface of a lake, the click of the old clock before it struck two, the light falling on the gilt mirror, refracted over and over again through the cut-glass candlesticks, the cool bright blue of the tape deck's display, and the way in which the wallpaper changed colour from pale lime where the sidelights pressed against it to the dark, indecipherable hues in the corners where little light fell.

It was some time before Jimmy spoke.

'I may as well tell you,' he began. I looked at him. He was

carefully scrutinizing the toe of his shoe. It was a nervous habit he had: he liked to line it up with the edge of the carpet or the side of a table to help his concentration. 'It might take your mind off things.'

He smiled like an apologetic schoolmaster.

'Kitty Greaves resigned yesterday.'

'Oh, good.'

'You're an admirer of hers?' he asked sharply.

As gently as I could, I explained, 'Look, I don't really need this right now, if you don't mind. She *is* my boss.'

'No, it's not what you think. You see, I had something of a hand in it. Not entirely intentionally. I would rather she had stayed, and I told her so. But,' he paused, and waved his hand in mock-despair, 'she didn't want to listen.'

'I don't mean to sound aggressive, but why are you telling me this?'

'I've bought *Arts Unlimited*.'

He let it sink in.

'You've done what? How could you?'

He misunderstood me, wilfully I presume.

'I bought it from someone who needed to sell.'

'Ferdy?'

He inclined his head slightly.

'What are you going to do with it?' It sounds a foolish question, I know, but the magnitude of what he was telling me, the sheer ludicrous inanity of such an unscrupulous operator taking on such a noble enterprise and dumping its guiding spirit in the process beggared belief.

'I would like you to be the editor.'

How to describe what I felt then? The best and the worst, all at once. An adrenalin surge, and profound guilt, and worry about what people would think, and the conviction that I was incapable of doing the job. And fantastic excitement and pride. I was an emotional pressure-cooker.

Jimmy eyed me warily.

'Excuse me,' I said.

I slipped out of the French windows, trotted across the lawn, vaulted the ha–ha, sprinted down to the woods, put back my head and screamed. It was a long, curling scream that rose from the roots of my throat into the inoffensive night. It was ridiculous, irrational, histrionic, hysterical and profoundly therapeutic. Endless pairs of wings rattled round my head. There were scuttlings and hurryings and patterings of paws and a fox barked in the distance. A window opened in the house and a plaintive voice called, 'Is there anything wrong?'

'I'll take that as a yes,' said Jimmy, on my return.

There was one thing that nagged me.

'What's the connection between this crash and you buying the *Arts*?'

He looked back at me sombrely, then his eyebrows puckered uncertainly.

'There isn't one,' he replied. He forced a smile. 'Let's talk about this soon. Not now. But soon.'

I found Grace lying as I had left her, and for a moment I panicked. Then I saw the mounting pile of tissues, dropped mechanically, methodically, as each one soaked up the remorseless flow of tears and was screwed into a tiny ball. She was curled up, as if hugging her grief or protecting herself from it – or both. I sat on the foot of the bed and looked at her. How could I stop those tears? How could I supply the morphine for those feelings? I wanted to take the pain away, to distract her, anything.

So I told her. I prattled on insanely, thinking this good news – let's face it, this extraordinary improvement in my fortunes – would in some way cheer her up. She patted my hand gently, absently. I can't believe I was such a pig. After a while I realized that the tears had not slowed, that the deep tensions in her body had not lessened. And even then I could not quell my churning excitement.

I could write the gardening column myself, now.

The Meaning of Lunch

THE EUPHORIA EVAPORATED the instant I crossed the threshold of Kitty's office. The magnitude of what I was doing struck me like a kick in the chest. I was usurping the throne of the great Greaves, the hottest, most passionate, most committed editor in London, she who walked with ministers for the arts, with royalty, with Katharine Hamnett, with Bob Geldof, with both generations of Amis. She whose editorials made Whitehall quiver, whose reviews closed shows overnight. She whose birthday party on HMS *Belfast* did about as much damage as the mine that broke it in two during the war. She was a gorgeous fire-breathing maniac, a Titan, a Cleopatra, and what was I?

'Before you say anything, read these. I'll be outside.' Kitty's secretary-cum-slave-cum-general-factotum, the much-feared 'Bomber' Sharples (so-called because of her habit of dropping endless jiffy bags stuffed with review copies five floors down the ancient stairwell outside the office to await collection), leered up at me. She thrust seven letters and two newspaper cuttings at me.

'Enjoy.'

I made to sit down, and received a second shock. Kitty had cleared the room entirely. Gone was the old leather-topped desk, gone was the signed poem from Craig Raine, gone was the huge seascape by Patrick Heron, gone the armchairs and sofa, gone the framed original sixties covers from the first editions of the *Arts*, gone the fantastically tasteless sidelights with bases shaped like elephants. The office was utterly, eerily bare, except for an old hatstand.

I squatted gingerly in the corner against the wall and opened the first letter.

Dear Editor (whoever you are),

I would not dream of contributing to your magazine after the disgraceful events of the last few days. You may consider my association with *Arts Unlimited* closed forthwith.

Yours sincerely,
Ludovic Kennedy

The next six letters were, give or take an expletive or two, in much the same vein, from equally august and equally regular contributors. Ex-contributors, as I now supposed they were, with a sub's pedantry.

The first clipping was from the *Standard*'s 'Londoner's Diary'.

We hear there's trouble at mill in Wardour Street, home of the venerable *Arts Unlimited*. With the departure of the inimitable Kitty Greaves, staff are in open revolt over replacement stooge Wilf 'Who he?' Wellingborough. Could his appointment have anything to do with his friendship with James Spalding, the *Arts*' new owner, our Kitty's arch-enemy? Perish the thought.

I won't bother you with the second. It was from the *Guardian*, and slightly more polite.

'Phone for you,' Bomber's voice was looming from her desk outside the office.

'There doesn't appear to be one in here,' I answered testily.

The door opened.

'Oh, she's taken that, too, has she? You'll have to come out here, then.'

It was Simon Spicer. He had usually dealt only with Kitty, so I had rarely had the opportunity of speaking to him since that memorable party in Oxford. Simon had become something of a media-don by now. Novelist, critic, TV-regular, his *Arts* reviews reduced those unfortunate enough to be on the receiving end of them to pulp.

'May I be the first to crawl?' he murmured sweetly. I almost cried.

'Will a column do?' I rejoined.

Thereafter I rang all fifty-six ex-contributors and persuaded twenty-three of them to return to the fold, principally by massively increasing their fees, then sat in the only chair not occupied by Bomber and rested my pulsing temples in my hands.

'In spite of myself, I am impressed.' It was Bomber's voice, not without sympathy in it. I looked up in surprise. Her normally sullen brown eyes were engagingly warm, her shaven head seemed to bristle slightly less aggressively, her Yorkshire vowels were less flat.

'*Is* everyone up in arms?'

'Nothing that a rise in salary all round won't cure.'

'You know, we can't get Kitty back.'

'No.'

'And at least I'm on your side. I'm one of you.'

Her expression cooled slightly and she returned to attack her typewriter.

'Let me give you a bit of advice. Don't try to ingratiate yourself. You've got enough problems without encouraging us to piss all over you. Which we shall undoubtedly do –' here she turned to look at me again, 'given half a chance.'

'Thank you, ma'am,' I muttered, and went in search of furniture.

During those early days my mood oscillated in a slow but horribly certain fashion between a vertiginous sense of vulnerability, as if I were perched on the edge of a high building with great crowds below jeering and hurling abuse and encouraging me to jump – a feeling which never quite left me and at best was an insistent buzz of unhappiness at the back of my mind, at worst a stomach-melting, knee-buckling hysteria – and an exultant surge of adrenalin that stemmed from a recognition that I had absolutely nothing, absolutely sweet fuck all, to lose. I was young enough to screw up and survive, and because nobody expected me to succeed I had everything to gain.

I remember many things about that time, but sleep was not one of them. After the day began at the *Arts* there was no letting up until the early hours of the following morning. There was only a handful of us: myself; the typesetter, Julian, an extravagantly thin character with a wedge of black hair swept back off his forehead who specialized in looks of mysterious thoughtfulness directed for the most part at Bomber; Bomber herself, with whom I entertained a nervously cordial relationship, not because we distrusted each other but because she possessed awesome physical strength and could have beaten me to a paste with ease; the accountant Minna, who was always on antidepressants and as a consequence had a beaming but abstracted, rather owlish demeanour; and Adam Sale, who, unbelievably, did ad sales. That was the permanent staff, and though there were always people around doing tasks of one sort or another, the amount of work even for a fortnightly made me feel as if I were swimming in a swamp of sleep deprivation. I had waking dreams about sleep. I thought of it longingly and imagined it enfolding me in its arms like a nurse or a mother or a lover. I thought of it as a cool southern sea to dive into, as a chilled lager after running the marathon, as a field of corn to roll in; sometimes it was imperious, sometimes it cajoled, sometimes it bent my head to the desk. I flirted with sleep, I dodged it, I ran from it; I did almost everything except simply enjoy some of it.

It wasn't just the work, of course – it was the parties. And the dinners. And the theatre, the opera, the concerts. I could not resist a single one of them. Not a first night, not a launch party, not a gallery opening. I was a cultureholic. And a foodie. And a voguey fogey. And drunk, a lot of the time.

Every morning I stared blankly into my eyes in the bathroom mirror while shaving, and made a little pact with myself.

Scrape.

'I will do it.'

Scrape, scrape.

'I can do it.'

Scrape.

'I will do it.'

Well, I needed to steel myself somehow, even if I did sound like Thomas the Tank Engine. And I wasn't in too bad a condition. Pores a bit frayed, perhaps, skin in need of some renovation, but my general facial structure – that is, lugubrious expression with added podge, a certain endearing frailty around the eyes, hair of a loosely springy nature – was perfectly presentable.

'I can do it. I will do it.'

Careful crunch of razor through bristles and warm lather. Washing of blade sloppily in soapy water. Pat of aftershave, cleansing sting, lung-opening inhalation of alcohol in the scent. On with the gold-rimmed intellectual Bamber-Gasgoigne-crossed-with-John-Lennon glasses and away we go. Hooray, hooray for morning male ablutions. One of life's great rituals.

Grace would be at the living-room table, thoughtfully eating a bowl of cereal, scarcely looking up. She was beginning to work long hours, too, at a firm of solicitors near the Oval that specialized in housing benefit, police brutality and legal aid cases. She loved it, it was her mission; she needed to lose herself in great causes. I profoundly admired that in her; it was her unreachable otherness, countering the all too graspable here-I-am-ness of my own comparatively unbuttoned behaviour.

Quite early on in my editorship Tom Phipps got me invited to a *Private Eye* lunch. I thought that if I could withstand that I could probably withstand anything, and as I was talking to a small woman with thin dark hair cut close to the shape of her head, huge eyes and earrings that appeared to be sardine skeletons in dark-green plastic, a tall, gaunt woman squeezed indecorously past. Turning, she peered closely into my face.

'Do you know quite how despised you are in this city?'

Her skin had the sort of texture that indicated a life well led, her voice a dour mid-Atlantic drawl that seemed penetrating beyond its actual decibelage.

Any number of responses failed to materialize for me.

'Don't be so fucking rude.'

This had not been one of them. I looked at my companion with surprise and not a little affection.

44

'It's not his fault he's got that job. He may be completely useless, but there's no need to talk like that. Just bloody well apologize.'

A chastened sneer slithered over the leathern features of my tormentor, but she had met her match. Not that she said sorry.

At lunch I found myself seated next to my saviour, who held forth demonstratively on the social and cultural importance of South Molton Street to bewildered and disbelieving but nevertheless mesmerized hacks in her vicinity, moving on to the relative significance of *The Face* and *i-D*, before delivering, as a *pièce de résistance* served rather as a master chef does his latest creation in puddings, a huge dollop of gossip about Malcolm McLaren. I had a little lightning-strike of inspiration.

'I'm fantastically grateful to you for helping me out there, earlier,' I began.

'Hideous woman,' she replied, firmly.

'Do you read *Arts Unlimited* much?'

'Never.'

I pressed on.

'What we need,' I said, 'what we really need, is a fashion column. A good one. One with bite. One that's not so much about fashion as about what lies behind it. The economic *raison d'être*. How the cultural references are being manipulated. What it all actually means, rather than what we are intended to think it means. The beast beneath the skin, sort of thing. We could call it "Fashion Victim".'

She gave up sawing tentatively at an overdone piece of steak, sipped some wine carefully, and said, 'You know, that's not a bad idea.'

'Would you like to write it?'

She looked at me incredulously.

'Don't ask me how I know you can.'

'I wasn't going to. I was going to ask you why I should want to.'

Something told me I was on thin ice. I hesitated. 'Well, just think it over, maybe.'

45

'It's Jimmy Spalding's new acquisition, isn't it? I love that man. Do you have a card or something?'

'I haven't quite got them printed yet.' I scribbled hurriedly on a napkin. She looked at it.

'Wilf Wellingborough. What a marvellous name.'

I smiled tentatively. I had always been teased mercilessly about it. But what did ordinary people know? I mentally pushed my *amour propre* lever to the 'pride' position.

'And you know who I am, of course.'

'Of course.' I smiled sweetly back.

'Did I hear Spalding?' A thin man with a long nose, who was attired in a battered blue pin-stripe, broke in from across the table. 'What's he up to now?'

'Well, he bought us.'

'Not wishing to sound like the caterpillar in *Alice*, but – *who* are *you*?' He lengthened the vowels of the words smugly.

'Wilf Wellingborough,' said my neighbour, reading from her napkin. It was no use, I still felt unhappy about it. But then embarrassment is a feeling with which the English are comfortable.

'Ah, yes,' he said, impaling a large chip with his fork. 'Mr Popular. And how is Mr Spalding treating you?'

'Very well, so far, thanks.'

'So far. Good. And his lovely wife?'

I had been expecting some anecdote about Jimmy's business practices.

'Fine. I mean, shouldn't she be?'

He widened his eyes expressively and pulled a face.

'Long-suffering, poor woman.'

'Gordon, that's tosh. What do you know about it?' I was surprised at my neighbour's vehemence.

'Poor is not a word I would use about Helen,' I offered.

'Depends on in what sense you use it.'

'Well, in what sense do you use it?' I saw Tom listening intently from further down the table.

'I mean great warriors of the business world can be very nasty at home, especially if their minds have been unduly influenced by various *substances*.' His voice was so laden with innuendo, there was an unmistakable hiss in the sibilants of the last, heavily emphasized word.

'Bullshit,' came from my right, very loudly.

'Order in the middle there,' came a cheerful voice from the table's end. Tom looked at me and stuck out his lower lip.

To my left, a voice was rumbling querulously, emanating from a grizzled and bewaistcoated, badger-like figure.

'The set of proofs my publisher sent me was riddled with errors, which were nothing to do with me, and then they had the cheek to land me with a bill for three hundred pounds for corrections that were supposed to be mine. Three hundred pounds! They hardly bothered to edit it in the first place. Then they reversed the entire picture section. And the paper they used. *Mon Dieu*! Not fit to wipe your arse on. Because if you did' – he paused for effect – 'you'd get print all over your bum.'

'My friend Milo,' I put in, 'is an editor at Pegasus. You know, the one that took over Murgatroyd & Wilson? He says you need a skin like a rhinoceros to survive in publishing these days.'

'That's true of any business. Take my word for it, publishing companies have always been like this. I should know. It's my thirty-fifth venture between the covers.' He looked at me slightly lasciviously, I thought.

'What's it called?'

His expression became soulful.

'*The Pegasus Anthology of Rude Rhymes and Lubricious Limericks*. With a special section on lavatorial graffiti. Illustrated,' he added helpfully. Before I could stop him, he began to quote some for my benefit, and that of anyone else who could not avoid listening.

As we were leaving the Coach & Horses I caught up with Tom.

'That woman. What's her name? The one I was next to?'

'Sibella? She's at *Cosmopolitan*.'

'Is she on the masthead?'

'She's a contributing editor.'

'Oh. I've just invited her to write a fashion column.'

'You've got the luck of the Wellingboroughs then, if she said yes.'

'I think she might have done. I didn't think the Wellingboroughs had much luck, though.'

'Quite.'

'What, you think I've made a mistake?'

'Actually, you haven't. It's a good idea. You poor lamb,' he concluded, 'you haven't a clue, have you?'

He was right, of course, but not irrevocably so. I had lost some contributors, but not necessarily the best and brightest. Spicer took on the theatre column, and penned elegant dismissals and plaudits while his irascible predecessor bad-mouthed us all around town. Sibella Smallwood dynamited the fashion world and got away with it. I tried to persuade Milo to do a publishing column, but he was too pusillanimous and said that no one would believe the full horror of it all anyway. But there would be others.

'I need something splashy,' I remarked to Grace that evening, as I uncorked an expensive Pinot Grigio I had treated myself to at one of those very suave wine merchants on Holland Park Avenue, the kind where they have real French accents which are always worth a pound or two a bottle. It had been a hot day, full of exhaust fumes and the livid air of unreality that London takes on when the sun really boils and trickles of sweat run down the inside of your arms and everyone smells slightly off, and you worry frequently that you might too. I flopped down beside her in front of the TV. 'It's such a sleepy old place, and Kitty was great, but, I don't know, too noble somehow. We want a bit of swash and buckle. A bit of lip. A bit of attitude. Just a touch. It is the *Arts*, after all. But you know what I mean.'

Holly Johnson was invading the camera lens.

'I can't believe you're watching *Top of the Pops*.'

She was curled up against one end of the sofa, methodically running the tips of her fingers along the strands of her hair to the end, then dropping them. She seemed rapt, concentrated.

'I see we've got a wedding invite.'

48

On the mantelpiece a big, bold, gold-rimmed piece of bright white card stood challengingly. Nothing so confident as a wedding invitation.

'That would be Charlotte and Paul, yes?'

She was tall and rich and in corporate PR; he was short and wily and a barrister. We'd known them at Oxford. I didn't much like either of them – they were more Grace's friends than mine – but I always did enjoy a wedding.

'Correct.'

'Do you want to go?'

'Not really.'

'I know what you mean. Masses of idle chit-chat, too much champagne, wild dancing and a much-needed weekend away.' A slight tinge of sarcasm had crept into my voice.

'You always fall in love with the bride.'

'Only for the day. How can one fail to, when she's dressed like that?'

'Are you going to get me another drink?'

'How many have you had?'

'Oh, for God's sake.'

From the kitchen I called out, 'Went to an *Eye* lunch today.'

No answer. Not impressed.

'Have you heard anything about Helen and Jimmy and Jimmy, kind of . . . well, sort of . . . I don't know. . .' I brought her glass in.

'What you don't seem to realize, Wilf, is that Jimmy is OK. People like him. You're the only exception.'

'That's not fair.'

'Yes, it is fair. Have you eaten?'

'No. Have you?'

'I had lunch.'

'So, what do you want to do?'

'I don't know. I've got some work.'

'Why do you ask if I've eaten if you want to work?'

'Just making conversation. There's no need to snap at me.'

'We could go out.'

49

'Where?'

'192.'

'Been there too many times.'

'Julie's?'

'The same.'

'What about one of those places up by Notting Hill tube? That Greek place, what is it? Costa's.'

'I don't like Greek food. You know I don't.'

'I thought you did. You liked it on Santorini.'

'That was on Santorini.'

'Yes, well, I realize that. The Indian next door, then.'

'I don't feel like an Indian either.'

'Are you being deliberately perverse?'

She looked at me. The first time she had done so that evening. The ghost of a smile played about her lips.

'Are you about to laugh? You are, aren't you? Go on, you're going to laugh.'

The moment passed. She rose and stretched. I felt as if the ghost remained, uneasily, somewhere in the room. The roar of traffic grew suddenly louder, invading the room through the half-open window.

'Are you unhappy, Grace? Is there something wrong?'

'No-o.' Her voice sounded like a couple of musical notes played quickly, one after the other. Airy, dismissive, evasive. I wasn't sure which question she was answering. She gathered some things together and disappeared into the second bedroom, which we used as a study. At the door she turned.

'You do know that's the longest conversation we've had since my father died?'

The door closed.

Well.

What was *that* all about?

I mean, it can't have been true.

I brooded, my head full of grievances. They went off like cannon, rapid but ponderous. Why was it me who always made the effort? Why did I hardly ever see her? She was obsessed by that bunch of south London smartarse sleuths. She didn't respond to me any more, she made me feel like something someone had left out in the rain. That rapturous appreciation of things, the enjoyment of each other's jokes, the more killing the more flagrantly absurd they were, that molten, fused, private world we inhabited, playful and mocking and kind, seemed now to be more concerned with a vexed life of offices and opportunities, of bills and headaches, of finding windows in Filofax diaries and of constant self-sedation. But, I reflected, there was nothing wrong with that. Relationships mature. We still loved each other. We simply had lots and lots and lots of other very pressing things to do. Life changes, life goes on.

Except for Ferdy, of course. Even I could see that Grace was taking it painfully hard, her natural introversion turning to brooding self-absorption and distractedness, coupled with sudden and prolonged moods of morose hostility. And I knew that I wasn't much use to her, though I was a long way from knowing what this blokish hopelessness, as I admitted it to be, was doing to us. It was an unresolved death, that was the trouble. He was, as it turned out, four times over the limit, and driving without a safety-belt. No one could trace where he had been. He had left home just before lunch and not been seen since. He vanished unfollowed into the void, and I suppose the thought arose in some of us that he might have gone there voluntarily; except that Ferdy was a man of self-possession, necessary for bartering ancient artefacts around the world. An arcane business, and one that could turn to unpleasantness very easily, or so Spicer used to say, and he knew a thing or two, being, like his grandfather, a collector himself.

'A smattering of knowledge and a streak of grim ruthlessness, that's all you need,' he told me. 'And exquisite taste, of course,' he added, with his familiar winsome smirk.

I recalled Grace and I visiting her mother shortly after the accident, soon after she had announced her intention to sell their home of twenty-five years. Grace was distraught about this, but her sang-froid was as impressive as ever.

51

'I *think* I can see why you want to go, Mother,' she said, carefully. 'I suppose you feel that with Dad gone. . .'

'I need a change, that's all,' her mother replied, with her customary histrionic air of mystery. 'I have been *me* too long.'

Grace nodded. What reserves of patience she had. The living room was lined with her father's minor treasures from India, Burma, China and Japan. Ferdinand Tomlinson had been many things to many people, and he could call himself author, sometime lecturer, sometime visiting professor, as well as a well-respected authority on oriental art. In a cabinet he kept his remarkable collection of Buddhas from the monasteries of Tibet and Zaskar; his emissaries of sanity, he used to call them.

'So what's it to be, then?' asked Grace. 'Goodbye, much-loved beautiful family house off Hyde Park, hello, crumbling rectory in Gloucestershire?' Interestingly, and despite herself, there was a note of hope in her voice. There could be advantages in her mother's move.

'No. No. You're not going to get rid of me that easily,' her mother replied, coquettishly. She could be a dreadful old bat, really. 'I'd be far too lonely. I want to be surrounded by people. I have my eye on a large flat in Holland Park. Not far from you. Then I can walk in those delightful gardens and shop, just occasionally, in Portobello Road. Don't you think that sounds like fun?'

Grace eyed her speculatively. As I watched the two of them squaring off once more in their lifelong struggle, so little changed by their recent loss, it struck me forcibly that far from ever letting go of Ferdy, Grace was clutching his memory to her, nursing it almost as one would a newborn child, nourishing it from grief and communing with it in her private moments. Was this the shadow that lay ever more blackly between us? And was I jealous of these swaddling clothes of sorrow wrapped about the wound of her father's absence? Knowing my own problem was easy enough: his death reminded me of my own. That was banal, obvious. It was understanding Grace that was the challenge. Her mother seemed no wiser than me. Less so, maybe.

52

'A flat, Mother? Do you think you should? You would be much too solitary living in a flat. It's so alienating, you'd be terribly unhappy.'

Her mother looked peeved. 'I *think* I know what's best for me, Grace.'

'You'd go dotty inside a year.'

'Look here, Grace, I'll damn well decide what I want to do and that's that. After all these years of tolerating your father I think I have a right to live my life as I wish. Or don't you think so?'

She was a woman of passionate furies, Mary Tomlinson. They would come and go like clouds over the moon, bewildering Ferdy and dismaying their children.

'But what's the matter, Mary?' Ferdy would expostulate. 'Just tell us what is wrong. Tell us all. We don't understand. What have we done? Has someone said something to upset you? Are you ill? Do you want to go and lie down? Tell us how we can help.'

And as the children darted nervous looks at one another, Mary Tomlinson would become more and more tight-lipped, and her eyes more accusing, until she would rush from the room, and a door would be heard slamming upstairs. Afterwards, it was as if nothing had happened.

Ferdy, meanwhile, shrugged his shoulders at the children, grimaced and shook his head in a dumb show of incomprehension. The others leapt gladly and with relief on this piece of parental licence, and sniggered complicitously. But Grace – and I had all this from her in a rare moment of reminiscence, for she never talked about her family if she could avoid doing so – was stricken with guilt for not coming to her mother's aid, recognizing in her father's even-tempered reasonableness a truly cunning adversary, one that, though she loved him more than life, she should strenuously oppose for his cruel, patronizing dismissal of her mother's incoherent anger as she was goaded yet further.

I could see such things, but I did nothing about them. Maybe all that happens with the passing of time is this: you locate the background noise of unexpressed and ill-discerned feelings and you turn up the volume, so that you think you were aware of it all the time. And I went on doing nothing. I thought we were still in love in the same old way. I couldn't see what had changed.

For instance, I could see that she wasn't eating well, that she left most of her food at the side of her plate, that she was getting really skinny; that what she did eat was chosen and prepared and consumed with a delicacy bordering on intensity, as if she could feel every calorie, every drop of starch, every milligram of fat, polyunsaturated, monounsaturated or just plain saturated; and that, in short, she behaved as if the evils contained in food could shake her increasingly emaciated body like a tree in the wind. But though I noticed it, in that I saw, I was conscious of what was happening, I was unaware of all the implications. People change. They make different choices. Grace chose to be fussy about her food, and to be obsessive about her work. As far as the latter was concerned, so did I. Even as we diverged, we mirrored each other.

Not that hard work made the *Arts* any easier.

One day I strode in, full of my latest bright ideas, to find Bomber's gimlet eyes fixed triumphantly upon me from the top of the stairs.

'Henry's here.'

'This early?'

'Either he's fresh out of the clinic, or he's been up all night.'

'Presumably you can tell. How does he look?'

'Doesn't make much difference.'

Henry had been a freelance around the *Arts* for so long that no one dared question his right to wander in off the street, park himself in the nearest available chair and let fly with his opinions. His hair was jet black, generally thought to be dyed, his face florid, his eyes slightly protruding, his garb disreputably tweedy – the trainers spoilt any pretensions to decadent gentility – and his ability to hold one spellbound with tales of Old Fleet Street quite outstanding, at least for the first two or three hours.

He was happily ensconced in our latest edition in the only armchair I had been able to palm off on office expenses.

'This Smallwood woman is all right,' he remarked placidly, before getting down to the main business of the day, collecting as many bits of tobacco as he could in his ancient tin and cajoling them into a roll-up. We knew for a fact that most of it came from stubs gathered from litter-bins and café ashtrays, and the sight of this activity never failed to induce nausea. Particularly in the morning.

'Bomber?' I put my head round the door and registered extreme disgust. 'Rollies,' I mouthed. 'Have you heard from Humphrey?' For the TV column I had opted to go right to the top. Humphrey Horsefall was Controller of BBC 2: controversial, left wing, creative. God knew whether he could write, but if I landed him it would generate something of a stir. It would probably compromise him impossibly, too, so I didn't expect him to play. No harm in asking, though.

'His PA rang. Wants to know where you're lunching. I said the Jeu d'Esprit. You can do the ringing.'

'Thanks.'

'And there's this.'

I looked at the handful of rather scrappy pages.

'Oh, shit.'

'Thought you'd like it.'

'Have you read it?'

'That's your job.'

I gave her a scathing look.

'There are some things only the editor can deal with.'

'Sometimes I feel my position very sorely.'

'You bet you do.'

I went back moodily to the office. Henry was chuckling throatily.

'You like my new acquisition, do you?' I enquired, brightening.

'Oh, Smallwood's all right. I told you she's all right. A bit cerebral for my taste. No, I was listening to your conversation with Miss Sharples, there. Don't worry, she told me all before you got here.'

'What *are* you doing here so early?'

'I wander here, I wander there. It *is* after ten o'clock, old thing.' He raised an eyebrow at me theatrically.

'So you know about this Furlong character, then?' The trouble with the London literary world was that it was so small. I'd met Berenger Furlong at my first *Arts* party; after that, though I despised him and him me, we couldn't stop running into each other. Now that I was a force to be reckoned with, I was plagued by his stuff. The pages Bomber had just handed me were only the latest in a very long line. I hated the work, but he had impact. More importantly, he had a champion.

'Only what I've been told. Terrifically rich, I hear, related to all the best families, a novelist to boot –'

'The books are vile.'

'– and a great friend of your proprietor.' He leaned back in the armchair. 'Ah, yes. The proprietor. Someone should write a book about the beast. Beaverbrook, Maxwell, Murdoch, Rothermere. And Spalding. The smaller ones are the worst. So he wants you to stick this in? You'll have to run it, you know.'

'It's supposed to be streetwise literary south London.'

'Thus creating an entirely new genre at a stroke. At least he won't have much competition.'

I started to read.

It's a hot night, and down the Brixton Road the youth are out for a good time, cruising in old Cortinas with missing tail-lights, collecting on street corners, doing deals, looking for money and then some way to spend it. This is south London in the degraded eighties, this meaningless decade of style and greed and intellectual desiccation. You can hear the surly squeaking and clanking of the goods trains not far away on the stale, steaming air; someone else's goods, someone else's money. Sirens are always close at hand; the police are having a good time anyway. In Streatham the whores are out in force; in Tooting there's an acid party in the cemetery. In a small park in Kennington something's going on that will bring the sirens tearing in again, three hours too late. There's too much energy about, and nowhere for it to go. . .

'Oh, God.'

'That bad?' Henry winced sympathetically.

The phone rang.

'Wilf?'

'I speak.'

'It's Milo. The most dreadful thing has happened.'

Bomber appeared at the door carrying a large white sheet of paper. She had written on it in bold felt-tip 'Jeu d'Esprit!', and she proceeded to attach it with Blu-Tack to Henry's forehead.

'What's the problem? I hear you've got the management consultants in.'

'Yes, well, there's nothing new about that. It's not the first time. Anyway, that's not the point.'

'How many times have you had them in?'

'Look, that's really not what I want to talk to you about. I've had a call from Paul Sterne. You know he and Charlotte are getting married?'

'I know. We got the invitation.'

'Why do people do these things? . . . He wants me to be his best man.'

'I didn't know you knew him that well.'

'I don't. None of the others could do it. They're all abroad or something. I think I was fourth choice. What am I going to do?'

'Well, for a start there's the stag party, then there's the speech. . .'

'Yes, I know all that. It's the speech I'm worried about. I need stories about the guy. I mean, as you say, I just don't know him that well.' He sounded petulant.

We made a date for a stories-about-Paul-whom-we-don't-know-that-well-and-frankly-don't-care-that-much-about session and I rang the Jeu d'Esprit. I got nowhere, even when I mentioned Horsefall's name. I fell back on a time-honoured ploy.

'Sorry, I should have mentioned. Mr Horsefall and I are meeting Wayne Sleep. We're thinking of doing a drama–doc about his dancing career. He's a great admirer of your restaurant, you know.'

Worked a treat. I grinned at Henry, who was making a dart out of Bomber's notice.

'What you have to do to get into restaurants nowadays.'

'Lie, you mean?'

'No, not that.' He raised his eyes. 'I mean, Wayne Sleep. Did you have to?'

'He's a lovely man. I've met him. A sweetie, honestly.'

I rang Jimmy to tell him about Horsefall. There was a long silence.

'Well, he's not my favourite.'

'How do you mean, not your favourite?'

'I don't like him,' he snapped.

'I've booked the lunch now.'

'Wilf, you're the editor. You must use your judgement. That's why I put you there.'

'Yes, I see.'

'Has Berenger Furlong sent in his piece?'

'Yes.'

'What's it like?'

Fraction of a second.

'It's good. Needs some work, but it's good.'

'Don't go wild, will you?'

'No, I mean it. It's good.'

Oh, God.

'See what I mean?' beamed Henry.

Hitch or Ditch

I KNEW WHERE SHE kept it. I had always known where it was, and it had never bothered me. I suppose I wondered vaguely what thoughts she harboured there. I had never felt the need for such a thing myself, being content that if a thing was worth remembering I would remember it. Now I wish I had recorded more of my life, because, beyond all those things which seem as bright and vivid as if they were happening this very moment, there are hazy stretches which I don't seem quite able to reach. A lot of my memory is like that. What happened fifteen years ago is still going on in there, still replayable, but getting better as the images are burnished by the desires, and tarnished by the disappointments, of what came after. What you remember is what you are, and sometimes, as you change, whether because you want to or because you have to, you change what you remember. Quite deliberately, even if you're not aware of it. You select different scenes, or they alter imperceptibly. Images don't have tenses, so they are not imprisoned by time. All the stories our parents tell us of our childhood – what we said to Granny at the party, why we were so much better at cricket than football, where we were sick on the car journey home, how we caught twenty crabs off the pier and put them all in a bucket and there were only four left at the end of the day after they had eaten each other – this is the edited slide show of who we are. How we were supposed to be. And why we turned out the way we did.

Maybe I should have kept a diary, too.

Grace kept hers in an old briefcase tucked between the wall and the desk. She didn't write in it that often; at least, I never saw her doing so. But the more I became aware of how little I really knew her, or of how much we were changing, the more I was aware of it. Presumably her diary knew who she was, what was happening in her life. I was probably a touch jealous of it.

In the end it was something Horsefall said. He was a wiry man with the kind of untrimmed beard that appears to edge over the face like a mould, without any readily apparent end or beginning; it just seeped out of his skin and grew straight downwards before being rounded off under the chin. He wore a green corduroy jacket and jeans, brown suede brogues and red socks. His eyes were a bleak blue, his speech almost painstakingly precise.

'Quality programmes,' he said. 'Quality programmes, quality programmes.' He slid a knife into a salmon fishcake and screwed up his eyes amiably at a celebrity on another table.

'That's not the way it's going, though, is it?'

'No, indeed, it is not. But quality will out in the end because no matter how fierce a market there is out there, no matter how many ways and means there are of communicating the product, there's always going to be a need for what works, what's good. People don't want trash. Well, if they do, they want good trash. Quality trash. *Dallas. Dynasty.* They're good. I mean, rubbish to you and me,' he said, eyeing me in a comradely, conspiratorial way, 'but great quality entertainment.'

I swooned a little at being taken for a fellow spirit by one so powerful. This was a man who made television happen. He reached into the hearts and minds of millions and satisfied their televisual needs. He made the programmes what they were. He made the schedule what it was. He was a god.

'You are what you see, you know,' he remarked, reflectively. 'Just like you are what you eat. Just like the people who run Sainsbury's determine – or help to determine, perhaps, because let's not get carried away with this – what you are because your diet is chosen from a series of options – this packet of cereal, that soup – which is determined by them, so people like me – because we determine what you watch – are really making the people, the viewers, the kind of people they are. And it's a big

60

responsibility. I often ask myself, should I have the power to do this? Do I have the right to make these choices? Aren't I just forcing my bundle of neuroses, my set of ingrained preferences, into the minds of millions?'

'Well, they can always switch channels.'

He smiled in a watery kind of way.

'They can. Of course they can.' He suddenly buttered a poppy-seed roll energetically.

'For instance —' he began.

'So what sort of —' I began at the same time. We grinned a little inanely at each other.

'Let me run this one by you.' He held up his forefinger for attention. 'We need,' he said, emphasizing each word as if they were the opening notes of a symphony, 'to reinvent the game show. We need to repackage it. All that "Come on down" stuff is fine as far as it goes. And it goes a long way, I admit. I'm not knocking it. It serves its purpose. But there is an audience for something much more sophisticated. They have grown out of *The Young Ones*, they like Smith and Jones, but they want something with more meat and more bite. What I've got in mind is this. Imagine you've got a couple, and they've been together a long time, and they're thinking about getting married. People are putting it off till much later on in life these days, so there are masses of people like that. What we do is we take a couple like that and we give them an advocate, like a barrister, each. They'd be the fixtures, the stars of the show; the couple would change each week, or maybe midway through each programme. I haven't worked that out, yet. But the advocates are the stars. Mel and Griff, maybe, or Stephen and Hugh. And what they do is they analyse the couple's relationship, using the brief each partner has given them. They defend their partners, if you see what I mean, against criticism from the other party, and they make accusations and ask leading questions in their turn. Like if one partner had dipped into the other's personal correspondence or diaries, or snored in bed, or still saw the old boyfriend or girlfriend, or kept porn magazines in the cupboard, or got drunk

61

every Saturday night, or still played King Crimson records, or ran up gigantic phone bills, or didn't do enough foreplay, or did too much, or didn't like garlic, or wore offensive underwear, or hated ground coffee, or hated Indian food, or didn't make friends with other couples easily, or couldn't play bridge, or spent all their time watching football, or never washed out the bath, or never did the cooking, or let the geraniums dry out, or never paid for any meals, or always forgot birthdays, or never allowed any spontaneity into things, or could never plan a holiday, or had hair growing out of their nostrils. . .'

'Wouldn't it all be a bit embarrassing?'

'Of course it would! Horribly, cringingly, nail-bitingly embarrassing. People would curl up in their chairs at home and they would see themselves and their faults amplified on screen and then they'd turn to one another and say, "But we're not like that, are we?" It would be healing.'

'Or they might have a furious row and walk out.'

'They might do that,' he conceded. 'But it would make fantastic television. Because then what happens is, the audience votes.'

'On what?'

'On whether the contestants should stay together or not.'

'But what if they don't want the audience to decide for them?'

'Well, it wouldn't be binding, you know. But they would know that was the point of the programme, and we could follow up afterwards, and have them back and see what they've done with their lives. It's amazing what people will do to get on television, you know. Anyway, that's the way television is going. People want things that are serious, but don't have to be taken seriously. Things that are watched ironically, like sitting in front of *Captain Scarlet* repeats when you are thirty-five and claiming that they are culturally significant.'

'I do that and I'm only twenty-six.'

'Well, there you are. It's serious entertainment in inverted commas. The trick is that the less sophisticated think you're more serious than you are. Clever people can spot the inverted commas. It's like a secret society. Catching the irony is the only password you need.'

'And of course you're genuinely enjoying it all the time.'

'You've got it.'

'I've got a title for you.'

'What's that, then?'

'*Hitch or Ditch.*'

'*Hitch or Ditch?*'

'*Hitch or Ditch.*'

'That's not particularly ironic.'

'Yes, it is. It's a bit naff and a bit jokey and a bit brutal, but brutal like a Marvel comic. Marvel comics are read by grown-ups in a haze of inverted commas.'

He drew a deep breath.

'It wouldn't work.'

I wasn't all that bothered.

'So what would you say if I asked you to write a column for the *Arts*? We could call it "Inverted Commas".'

I was fast learning that people will fall over themselves to write for a magazine. Even the Controller of BBC 2 could be insecure enough to feel the need to burnish his credentials by writing for us. People will do it for nothing, if it's not their profession. It's the highest accolade there is. When he accepted I wondered if I should have aimed higher.

'You know, I've always wanted to do what you've asked me to do,' Horsefall remarked, as we made our way between the snow-white table cloths and the rich and famous all resplendently reflected in the chrome bar and the seemingly endless wall-mirrors.

A small figure brushed past.

'Hi, Wayne,' said Humphrey.

Glancing round, I thought I could see the waiter giving me a searching look.

Outside, Horsefall shook my hand.

'So you need. . .' he said, with gratifying eagerness.

'A thousand words. . .' I replied, as if prompting a slow child.

63

'. . . twice a month. Got it.' He rubbed his hands, then seemed to remember who he was, and brusquely drew himself upright. 'Well, thanks for lunch. I'll be in touch. I'm going to enjoy this.' He swivelled on his heel and began making his way up Piccadilly. Slowly, I followed him.

Hitch or Ditch. My God.

What would his infernal advocates make of Grace and me?

Personal correspondence or diaries.

It was Horsefall who put the thought into my head, and once there it grew and grew like a bad seed.

I shouldn't have looked at that diary. I don't claim to be remotely justified, apart from the terrible urging of a need to know. There wasn't much to see, anyway. But I shouldn't have looked at it.

I was better at temptation then. I just gave in to it immediately, without recognizing it for what it was. Much simpler. Now, I have a great battle, and argue with myself, and remonstrate, and will myself to be lofty and to take the rockier, narrower, steeper path.

And then I give in just the same. But temptation gets more banal as you grow older, because you have given in to most things and become used to them, and I think these outbreaks of higher moral tone compensate for that, and make the failure more terrifying, more interesting.

The adrenalin rush when I extricated the battered little black leather-bound book from its hiding-place was extraordinary. I took feline care to check everything: its exact position in the briefcase, which way round it was, whether there were any hairs laid across it that might have been placed there to indicate disturbance, what it was lying next to, all that. Then I sat down at the table and read, and puzzled, very calmly.

It wasn't a proper diary, at least not to my mind. Not every day was entered, and sometimes whole months were blank. When she did write, it was often a long piece about one subject. There was a description of Flora that was vitriolic to start with and woozily sentimental at the end. There was a piece about me that

64

was vitriolic all the way through, but only because I had made my feelings about her map-reading rather more clear than I should have done one evening when we got lost in Chiswick. I *thought* she had been quiet over dinner.

Wilf is so bloody overbearing, moronic, selfish, thoughtless, insensitive and cruel. Why do I have to put up with him? What have I done to deserve this? Why could I not have simply asked someone the way? We would have been fine if only he had listened properly. He was just trying to humiliate me.

And so on.

There was a passage about Ferdy's funeral that I was halfway through reading before I realized what I was doing, and I felt like a complete shit and resolved to put the book away. After all, this diary was recording things she didn't always feel: things written in the heat of a passing anger, out of a real but not habitual pain. It wasn't Grace recorded here, but aspects of Grace in extremes of mood.

I was just closing it when my eye alighted on a passage that I didn't at first understand. 'I just can't make up my mind,' it began. I read on, and its implications became clear, but I could not quite digest them. Everyone's suspicious, but it is a frightening thing when one's suspicions, which one had, somewhere at the back of one's mind, hoped and even dared to assume were groundless, turn out to have substance.

The front door slammed. She was home unexpectedly early. The diary leapt into the air, then I caught it and fumbled it back into its hiding-place in panic. This time the adrenalin was such that I could hardly sit down.

'Hiya.' Grace slung a copy of the *Standard* on to the table.

'Woof.' I think that's what I said. It sort of felt that way. My insides were in turmoil. My pulse was going lickety-split. I wouldn't have been surprised if my hair had gone ramrod straight and stood up on end. I felt as if I had just jammed my fingers into an electric socket.

'I'm out with Milo tonight,' I managed to say.

She looked at me laconically. 'Well, you could at least say hello.'

'I just did.'

'Really? It sounded more like "Woof" to me.'

'Sorry. You startled me.'

'Really?' She was cutting now. Could she tell what I had been doing? Was it obvious? She wandered into the kitchen and started ferreting around in the fridge. In a moment, I heard wine gurgling into a glass.

'Want some?' she called. 'It's been a complete pig of a day. We lost that case – you know, the one I was telling you about – and we all felt really bad about it, so we went and had a few drinks at lunchtime, and, I don't know, I think it's all getting to me at the moment, so this afternoon I kept thinking, all I really want to do is get outside a nice cold bottle of white wine in my own place.'

She came out of the kitchen with two big blue and pink glasses and thrust one into my hand, then disappeared into the bedroom to change. I followed her, feeling suddenly turned on by the thought of her naked at this unusually early evening hour. Why, it was practically still daytime. She unbuttoned her shirt in a businesslike way, then snapped off her bra, scarcely aware that I was there. Approaching her, I ran my hands around her broad, too-slim shoulders, then stroked the tip of my finger down her back, weaving gently around her vertebrae. She was very tense, I could feel it. Her shirt dropped to the floor, and the pale spareness of her body seemed released from the dull uniformity of her working clothes. She turned, suddenly, with an urgency I had not seen in her for a long time, like one possessed. For a moment she looked at my throat, as if pausing to consider what she was doing, as if surprised by herself. She looked up at me, and in one swift movement our mouths met. As I held her she trembled. Her tongue worked in and out of my mouth, curling round my tongue and over my teeth. A new sensation coursed through me, this time one that gripped my stomach. She ran her hand down the front of my trousers, undid the zip and slid her hand inside. Picking up my glass I gave her a sip, took one myself, then dribbled some over her breasts. The nipples grew hard. I slipped my fingers into her; she was warmly, slickly wet. Within seconds we were undressed and on the bed. As I knelt she took me in her mouth, and I poured wine down her back so that she was covered in goose pimples. Then we kissed again, and she sat astride me, and she was hot and her thighs were strong and her hair was wettened with perspiration and she went pink with a blush that descended to her chest and she put her head back and came with an agonized shout, her fingers clutching my arms like pincers.

As we lay together afterwards we looked at each other wonderingly. It was to be our last time.

Slowly the evening light cooled in the room, and we became aware of the faint red and orange wash cast by tail–lights passing outside. Bizarre patterns swiftly crossed each other like tides over a shallow shore, and I began to feel that we were, in our room, being cast adrift from the world, that the street and its noise and colour were being abstracted on our ceiling, reduced to their essences of hue and movement.

Then I remembered the diary, and sat up abruptly.

She didn't try to stop me going.

Soho was as fetid and degraded as it always is, especially in the summer after a hot day when the rubbish has rotted inside black bin–liners piled up in disused doorways. I made my way through the crowds in Piccadilly Circus up to Beak Street and the little restaurant – Simon Atkinson's, it was, still there actually – where Milo and I had arranged to meet. It was packed, but Milo had somehow squeezed himself behind a tiny table in the corner and was determinedly wading through a Jilly Cooper.

'I've got to try to get a feel for this stuff,' he said mournfully, his hands tugging fretfully at his great mane of curling red hair, looking more Chattertonian than ever.

'Not quite "Mie love ys dedde, Gone to hys death-bedde"?' I asked, manoeuvring myself delicately into the chair opposite and helping myself to the Sancerre.

'Not as far away as you might think, but a tad more saleable nowadays.' He looked at me good-humouredly. 'I think Jilly might like Thomas C. Hopeless romantics, both of them.'

'So are you enjoying that?'

'My candidate for the Booker.'

'How is the world of publishing?'

'Frantic. Everyone is buying everyone else. Everyone is getting fired and rehired. Advances are going through the roof. It's mayhem.'

'And Pegasus?'

'We just lost the M.D.'

'What, again?'

'He fell out with the Chairman. Apparently there's a big restructuring coming up. P45s in brown envelopes at dawn all over the shop. They do this every two years or so. That way you can't compare results very easily.'

'What do the shareholders think?'

'The shareholders are the Chairman's family and most of them live in Lincolnshire. They're not that interested, I don't think.'

'Have you discovered how to be a thruster, then?'

'Well, I do my best. The trick appears to be getting your name on a successful book.'

'You mean getting the credit for it?'

'It's not that straightforward. For instance, I know people who have got their name on a book simply by telling everyone that they almost acquired it, that they were the underbidder in the auction. There are very successful people in publishing who have done nothing but underbid. You don't have the bother of actually publishing the book, that way. And then there are those who can get their hooks into a book by taking it on after the previous editor has been fired. Or those in a senior position who claim they've bought the book on your behalf. Lightning reactions and a good line in sycophancy are what you need.'

'Sounds to me like you're going off it.'

'Oh, no, I love it. I wouldn't do anything else. I'm just not sure I've quite got the hang of it, that's all. What gets you ahead in your business?'

I thought swiftly.

'Outrageous revelations. Betrayed confidences. Indiscretions captured on tape when the interview has finished. You can ditch a cabinet minister and make your reputation all in one go.'

'But you haven't done that.'

'Not yet.'

'Would you?'

'Truth to tell, until you asked me, I hadn't really thought about it.'

He leaned back and waved for another bottle.

'Who would have thought we would have been talking like this five or six years ago?'

'It's exciting, though, isn't it? The new ruthlessness.'

'The new amorality.'

'Whatever. Tell me about this wedding.'

He plunged his head into his hands with a hollow groan. I poured more wine for him sympathetically. Then he flung his arm out in a gesture of despair and a glass flew from the tray of a passing waiter, shattering upon the next table. Its occupants leapt to their feet, swearing belligerently.

Milo went into another paroxysm of head-clutching, apologized profusely and dropped to his knees to pick up the scattered shards.

'Fuck, fuck, fuck,' came a sudden screech from beneath the table as he cut himself in the darkness. Rising like a rocket, he reached for the nearest object available for bandaging his thumb, knocking the table over as he did so.

'Give me back my bloody roll, you little bleeder,' squawked a besuited, overweight man in the early stages of dishevelment. I am adamant he said this, though neither Milo nor anyone else would believe me afterwards. The dishevelled man rose to his feet. Milo continued to press his thumb into the roll, which turned dark. His face was a lighter shade of porcelain, anyway, and when he sat down with a bump at a third table a woman screamed.

'Oh my God! Look at him! He's bleeding to death! Get an ambulance, someone!'

This stopped the dishevelled man and the occupants of the overturned table in their tracks. You can't mob a dying man in a crowded restaurant, especially when the entire clientele have turned their attention upon you.

A waiter came up, uttered a pious 'Goodness', slipped on a fallen *risotto nero* (some of it spattered blackly over the white table cloth of a fourth table) and went down heavily on what sounded like the broken glass.

'Come on,' I whispered to Milo, seizing our opportunity and his elbow. We approached the counter, conscious of astonished eyes upon us.

'I'll pay. Here's my card. I've got to get him to hospital. What's the damage?'

'Fairly considerable, I'd have thought,' I heard Milo mutter.

'You can't just walk out of here like that,' began the scandalized manager.

Together Milo and I executed a perfect swerve, threatening the neighbouring set of tables.

'I think he's really bad, actually,' I hissed. 'Looks like he's punctured an artery.' I waved the now-glistening roll at him. A sodden piece of it flew into yet another wine glass. The white wine instantly turned red. The manager's eyes widened with horror.

'Out,' he said quietly. 'Just go.'

We did.

An appropriate distance away, Milo leaned back against a wall and raised his eyes to the night sky.

'Jesus,' he said.

'You all right?' I asked. 'Don't worry. I've done similar things. We're just a couple of maladroits.' I had wrapped a hastily snatched napkin round his thumb as we left.

Milo sighed. 'One for the memoirs,' he grinned pallidly. His look turned to consternation as he clutched at his pockets. He was a great one for clutching.

'Where's Jilly? Have I left her behind?'

'I think that's the least you can do. Come on, let's get you home.'

Milo lived in an enormous house in Belsize Park. The house was enormous, but it had long been turned into bedsits. Still, they were ample enough. Whoever had done the job had obviously not returned since, and the walls were caked with grime. Dustballs scuttled like mice down the stairs. In the kitchen area of Milo's room it was as if the oven and all the cooking utensils had been dipped in tar and left to harden. The old grey-green curtains flapped sullenly in the breeze. Up beyond Milo's door, further along the staircase, the walls were dark flakes where fire had raged some time ago. 'One of the water heaters went up in smoke,' Milo had explained. 'They're all about to explode.' Milo's room always looked as if his water heater had already done so. Books and files and records and cassettes littered the floor. Half the bedclothes spilled off the bed. Mugs, some with a crust of mould on them, were to be found in surprising places. Once I discovered an old apple core behind a picture frame; another time I found an old, much-used handkerchief, bristling with withered bogeys, tucked into the plastic tray of what I took to have been a maidenhair fern.

'No wonder it died,' Milo had said. He had made a great play of extricating the handkerchief on the end of a bamboo cane and burning it in the grate, where it refused to combust cleanly and lay glowing malevolently, one half pulsating in the draught that blew down the chimney, the other half indomitably untouched and all the more noisome for it.

By the time we got there Milo's thumb had ceased to trouble him, though I could see that the bloodied napkin was alarming fellow passengers on the tube; I could also see this was delighting Milo, who kept cradling it ostentatiously in his left hand and occasionally giving vent to a low moan.

On the way I picked up a bottle of Jack Daniels from the heavily fortified off-licence on the corner of his street. Pressure was building up behind my eyes and I knew I was going to need some anaesthetic soon.

71

'Now,' I said, when we were ensconced in his two armchairs. 'Let me start again. And this time, no sudden movements. What is there to be said about Paul and Charlotte? In particular, Paul.'

A look of anguish passed over his face.

'Well,' I prompted, 'there was the poem.'

At Oxford, Paul had been writing an epic poem, a sort of satirical contemporary *Beowulf* with lots of crashing Middle English alliteration. Over time, it assumed legendary status. We were all supposed to be in it. If you *weren't* in it you could safely assume that you were socially dead. You were socially dead because if you had been any different you would have been in Paul's poem. Given that Paul was an unprepossessing little lout whose legs were too short and whose ears stuck out and who had a large mole on his forehead, the poem was a brilliant way of exercizing power and influence and getting invited to all the parties and indeed getting laid by beautiful women he didn't deserve. Of course, if I had been in the poem I might have thought differently, but I wasn't and I didn't and I still don't. Milo was. As was Grace. And Jimmy. And Flora. And lots and lots of people. But not me. Not that I begrudged this.

'Yes, there was that. A sort of contemporary *Who's Who*.'

'Hardly.'

Milo smiled. 'Sorry. I forgot. A suitable object for derision, then.'

'Entirely. By the way, how well did you know him?'

'I told you. Only quite well. Not much better than you, I suppose.'

'So why you?'

'I think he thinks I'm relatively safe.'

'He can't know you at all, then.'

'What is the purpose of a best man's speech? In a nutshell?'

'To satirize the groom mercilessly.'

'Which should not be too difficult.'

'There was that time when he tried to climb Magdalen Tower naked on May Day morning and got stuck halfway and had to be brought down by the fire brigade.'

'Who couldn't get through because of the crowds.'

'Which got thicker and thicker as they flocked to take a look.'

'There was that period he went through when he wore a studded dog collar.'

'And that habit he had of driving a nail into his hand to impress women with his mastery of pain.'

'Did that ever work?'

'I'm afraid it did.'

'And that time he screwed his best friend's girlfriend on his best friend's bed.'

'Which wouldn't have been so bad if he hadn't told everyone about it.'

'As a result of which his best friend had a nervous breakdown, took an overdose and was so damaged when they brought him round that he had to leave and now works for the DHSS.'

'Didn't he urinate out of a car window once in Broad Street?'

'No, that was someone else.'

'Was it? I'll tell you one thing, though.' I emptied my glass, refilled it and then went to appraise Milo's musical taste, a favourite pastime for many years. 'He spent a lot of time with the Amphibian. Don't look at me like that. You remember. David Vile or something.'

'David Vale. President of the Union. Didn't like our *Twelfth Night*. Insufferable little prig.'

'We didn't like him, did we?'

'We didn't.'

'What happened to him?'

'Works for the Conservative Research Bureau.'

'So, going back to Paul, and for that matter Charlotte,' I said, as I slipped a record on to Milo's old Pioneer turntable. 'Wasn't she the one who used to go up to men at parties and say "I'm a St Hilda's Virgin and what are you going to do about it?"'

'I think she did. Do you have to put that on? You always play *Astral Weeks*.'

' "Madam George" is a song I love to distraction.'

'I know. I feel the same about "Brown-Eyed Girl".'

'I know. You especially love the bit in the second verse where the organ comes in.'

'So I do. Pass that bottle, old friend.'

'I think we're beginning to generate some good stories.'

'I don't know that they're right for a wedding reception, though.'

'Of course they are.'

That was one of Milo's troubles. He was very sensitive to other people, but this could never be turned in any way to his advantage because he seemed pathologically incapable of understanding them. He lived in his head to the point where he responded to how he imagined others to be feeling rather than how they actually felt. It could be a strength, too, of course; he tended not to be blown off course by every passing anxiety or desire to please. But often, too often, he got it wrong enough to give rise to a litany of embarrassments. There was the evening he and I found ourselves at dinner with a woman who had married a Russian and moved to Moscow, only to return to London within the year. It did not take much wit to discern that something had gone disastrously wrong, but Milo suddenly appeared to wake up from an abstracted trance and thoughtfully began to explain that Moscow was a terrible place for divorce (at which she started and began to stare at Milo with wild consternation, as did I) because all Muscovites had to live in extended families in tiny two-bedroomed apartments and the pressure of such intimate cohabitation became unbearable. Hopeless.

I opened a pair of formica-clad light grey cupboard doors to inspect his wardrobe.

'Now, have you got the appropriate garb?'

'I'll hire it.'

'Well, make sure you get it sorted in plenty of time.' I often found myself mothering him like this. Something caught my eye.

'Cripes, Milo. What's this suit? A bit structured for you, I'd have thought.'

'Regulation Pegasus suit, that. They all wear them. They also like to go round feeling each other's ties and looking at the labels and admiring or sneering and swapping notes on where they bought them. It's quite interesting from a sociological point of view. Ties are the only way they have of expressing their individuality. It's like little boys comparing the size of their willies in the school latrines.'

'Yes, but the suit? Surely you could buy something less boring? Armani, maybe? I mean, I know it's expensive. . .'

'Too unstructured. They'd feel threatened.'

'Oh, come on. Don't they ever loosen up?'

'I did see someone there in an Armani suit once. From systems, I think he was. He was obviously petrified, everyone was looking at him. They didn't even bother to feel his tie. Ghastly, it was. I never saw him wear it again.' He refilled his glass. 'You know, Wilf, I really admire what you're doing at the *Arts*. I know other people who do, too. I mean, not that *many* other people. . .' He broke into a cackle of wheezy laughter, then recovered himself.

'Ha, ha,' I intoned.

'No, I do. Seriously. It was a big challenge and you're coming through it. Do you come through a challenge? Well, whatever you do, you're doing it.'

There are those who would rather believe an insult than a compliment, knowing that the former is normally given with greater sincerity, but I'm not one of them. I like my compliments, and the juicier and even the more unlikely they are the happier I am. Make them big, fat, high-stepping, shameless, glittering, showbiz compliments and as many of them as frequently as possible, that's my view.

'Tell me more,' I said encouragingly.

As I spoke I became aware of an insistent feeling that had been growing surreptitiously for some time, a feeling I had been able to keep at bay, indeed to deny vigorously, facing it down like a whipped cur into some darkened corner of my psyche. But it was coming for me, and nothing would gainsay it in the end; it was palpable, like an enormous balloon full not of air but of a glutinous liquid, hanging perhaps six inches over my head, growing bigger and more threatening all the time, just waiting for a little accidental puncture to drench me in a whole reservoir of misery.

'I just can't make up my mind,' Grace had written, 'between the two.' Just that; a simple, bald little remark which I suppose could have meant anything. She could have been contemplating buying a birthday present. The slippers or the Trouble Funk tape? She could have been thinking of going on holiday. Marrakesh or Florida? She could have been trying out new perfumes in Selfridges or jackets from Jigsaw. She could have been verging on a dissertation about whether Jeremy Beadle's or Noel Edmonds' beard was the more repellent. It could have been anything, and I knew it. But what I assumed, what surely anyone in their right minds would assume, was that she was having an affair. It could have been worse. I took it for granted that I was one of the two, at least. She could not have been dallying amorously with two other lovers, could she? (*Could* she?)

Now, I will admit that the phrase 'dallying amorously' has a very obvious pair of Horsefall's inverted commas around it. Such demureness was very far from what I was imagining, from the images that kept plunging like glowing meteorites into my consciousness all the time I was talking to Milo. I was thinking about sex. I was thinking that the reason sex with Grace had just been so good was that she had been turned on by a new physical relationship, so she was newly sensitized, so to speak. It was nothing to do with me. My stomach was seized with a tight, tearing, jealous thrill; adrenalin again, but this time an unbearably slow burn; the effect of corrosive fear and a wild need to know. Like all such things, the sensation was feeding upon itself. The more I tried to concentrate on Milo, the more I imagined Grace in bed with another man. Not just in bed; in bed and enjoying him. Enjoying the warmth of his skin, the touch of his lips, his cock (much, much bigger than mine, naturally) deep inside her, running her fingers over the small of his back, moaning his name, coaxing him to greater heights of desire, while she herself was aglow with ecstasies which belonged entirely to her and to him, and from which I was utterly and for ever excluded. That was the diamond heart of my jealousy: the excruciating knowledge that someone I loved had learned other experiences, such that new words were required, and that I was not part of that world, and did not understand its language, and never would.

So. Who was he?

'Your go at the turntable, Mr DJ,' said Milo.

Moving mechanically, I succumbed to the decree of the established ritual. Searching through the stacks of old LPs, I found what I was looking for.

'Today's special is Memphis soul stew. We sell so much of this, people wonder what we put in it. We're gonna tell you right now. Gimme about a half a tea-cup of bass. . .'

We called out the King Curtis lines with all the passion of a religious revival meeting. These words were articles of faith. They never let you down.

'Now give me four tablespoons of boilin' Memphis git-tar. This gonna taste all right. . . Place on the burner and bring to a boil. . . Now beat . . . well. . .'

Then it was Milo's turn and as usual he reached for the Four Tops. We had 'Baby I Need Your Loving', 'Without the One You Love' and 'Ask the Lonely' in succession, with 'It's All in the Game' as a sort of encore, then I put on the Undertones' 'Jimmy Jimmy' and T.Rex's 'Ride a White Swan' and Al Green's 'Take Me to the River' because if I hadn't I felt I might have broken down completely, and I needed music that was sensual and driven rather than big-hearted and wide open. So there was Milo putting on 'What Becomes of the Brokenhearted' and me finding weird things like Cockney Rebel (*'Mr Soft . . .'*). We finished the Jack Daniels and I felt my face beginning to crumple and everything started to blur. And then there was a few minutes' silence.

'I take it "Warm and Tender Love" would be out of the question?' I heard Milo say.

I tried to nod vigorously, laugh and say 'I'm sorry' all at the same time without exploding.

'No cause, no cause,' he declared. 'I'd lend you a clean handkerchief, only I'm not sure I know where to find one.' He watched me as I snivelled forlornly, then clambered out of his armchair and came over and put his arm round me. 'I can do cocoa, though,' he said. 'I know where to find that. Then you can tell me about it. Or not.'

'Ever since. . .' I waved with one hand. 'Ever since. . . Well, ever since then, it's just gone. . .' I could hear my voice quavering. I hate it when that happens. 'I mean it's just gone all wrong. I think she's. . .' I waved with the other hand.

Milo patted my shoulder. His long face was so soft and close and reassuring I wanted to stroke it.

'You want to talk?' His right eyebrow rose a little, warm, questioning and thoughtful all at the same time.

I nodded again. Soon I would begin to feel that cold but relieved withdrawal that comes in the aftermath of tears.

'Good,' said Milo, standing up. 'In which case, forget the cocoa. If you've got some spare cash I'll go and get another bottle. I've a feeling this is going to be a long night.'

The Bells of Hell Go
Ting-a-Ling-a-Ling

THE ROPES HOLDING the marquee bowed taut in the wind, their demented threnodies seeming to emanate from the ground beneath our feet. The cold seeped into us, uncaring and relentless. The bleak beauty of the moors lay all around, or it had done before it grew dark. Now we looked up at the stars already appearing overhead, and the wind seemed to rush straight out of the furthest reaches of the abyss.

'Another fucking lovely English wedding,' stuttered Milo. He sucked furiously on the last of his cigarette and flicked it beyond the small arena of light; the wind whipped it immediately into the air and over our heads. I glanced up at the flapping billows of the marquee.

'You may have started a fire, you realize.'

'Don't tempt me.'

'Let's go back. I'm about to expire.'

I returned to the goodbye table.

'I hope there isn't going to be a goodbye table,' Grace had said, on the way up.

'What's that?'

'It's where all the old friends are put. The very old friends. The ones that have been invited for old times' sake whom they don't expect to see again.'

'Why would they be invited in that case?'

'For old times' sake. I told you.'

'Well, then. Why wouldn't they want to see them again?'

'Because they're the old guard. Marriage is a new beginning. It's a way of rounding off the old life, and consigning it to the rubbish heap. You get put on a table somewhere near the gamekeeper, the housekeeper and the old retainer.'

'They're that posh, this lot?'

'They are.'

'Where's the money from?'

'Breweries, farms, you know. There's a hereditary peerage in there somewhere that keeps it all together.'

'Sensible Paul.'

We were sitting in a jam on the M1, just beyond St Albans. This was as much as Grace had said so far, and there was not much more to come. The atmosphere was glutinous. The charm of a Mini lessens in direct proportion to the distance travelled away from the metropolis, and everything felt frail and exposed and ugly, inside and out. The M1 is dead unromantic.

I don't think I really thought that it would end. Us, I mean, not the M1, though the interminable nothingness of that dreary road must have influenced our thoughts. All those people, chugging along, some weaving like crazy to gain a few miles' advantage, some content in the middle lane. It's certainly not a good place to be when your relationship is on the rocks, though 'on the rocks' makes it sound more exciting and rumbustious than it was. We were ending with big, grim silences, more eloquent than any confrontations. Yet I could not bring myself to admit it was over. I'm the sort of person who sees things through to the bitter end, who won't give up until the last rotten dregs have been drained. I don't believe a thing's dead until it doesn't move when kicked.

On and on. Neither of us is putting tapes on, because each one is so loaded with significance it would be like reading statements in court. The Eurythmics are all about Annie Lennox being a strong, vibrant, independent woman. The Womacks are all about smooching. Working Week are about being too jazzy to care. The Housemartins are about being radical, introverted white soul boys. Anita Baker is about being swooningly in love. Joan Armatrading (Grace's possession, not mine) is about being simply unspeakable.

'Who is he?'

I keep imagining saying this. 'So, who is he?' Laconic. Shocking. Her face pales. For that one moment, I'm in charge.

Of course, I don't say it.

Why not?

Because I didn't want to know, that's why not. I hate confrontations. Especially in a confined space in heavy traffic.

On and on. And colder and colder. When we left London it was, as London congenitally is, mild and overcast, as if the world were wrapped in damp blotting paper. Dull, but snug. As we beetled earnestly towards the North Pole we had to switch the heating system on, which was a full-time occupation. The thermostat had gone and scalding air blasted us to extinction until we switched it off, and we waited until we needed it again. It was like travelling in a giant hair-dryer.

We broke the odyssey at Harrogate, after the inevitable filthy row over map-reading. Once upon a time we had blazed with foul-mouthed wrath ('Why don't you bloody well look at the fucking map and tell me where to go?' 'Don't tempt me, arsehole', etc.), but now we steamed monosyllabically ('Is this right?' 'No', etc.) like two outraged kettles.

The doorbell at the guesthouse played 'See the Conquering Hero Comes' with a nasal buzz. Nothing happened. I thought of saying, 'Are you sure you booked this all right?' but a glance at Grace made me think better of it. I turned to look at the huddle of terraced houses lining the deserted cobbled street as it descended precipitously towards the town centre, and shivered. In the distance thunder rolled sullenly and the outriders of the approaching rain cut into our skin like tiny knives. The wind began to rise to a scream and the cold pressed against us tangibly. A 'For Sale' sign squeaked frantically like a vast and demented bat.

'Oh my God,' shrieked Grace suddenly. I swivelled so fast I cricked my neck.

Through the frosted glass panes in the door, silhouetted against the dim pink light, a tiny shadow glided towards us swiftly like some ominous messenger from the inferno. The latch rattled violently as someone or something fumbled at it, and the door swung open hard against its chain. From the darkness came a cracked, eerily androgynous voice.

'Who is it?'

Neither of us could move. A minute or more passed.

'Who's there?' the voice called again, querulously.

'It's a gnome on skates,' I hissed.

Grace gave me a scathing look, and effused benign charm. 'Is this the Roliat Guesthouse?' she enquired sweetly. 'Mrs Roliat, perhaps?'

The chain was released and the door opened. A perfectly ordinary, oldish sort of woman sat perched in a wheelchair beaming up at us.

'Well, that wasn't too bad,' I remarked, as we sped along the scenic route through the Yorkshire Dales the next morning, 'though I could have done without the nylon sheets.' I rubbed my sore neck. 'It's weird, isn't it, the way that static electricity makes all the hair on your body stand on end? Rather sexy, in an unsexy sort of way.'

'Not everyone's as hairy as you are.'

I pursed my lips, inwardly.

'God, you scared me when you yelled.'

'I didn't yell.'

'Yes, you did. Not that I blame you. She was a bit of an apparition.'

'Poor dear. She's just doing it to make ends meet.'

'Be nice if she could save up for some sheets that don't make you feel like a light bulb. I thought I might start to glow. Why was it called the Roliat Guesthouse, anyway?'

'It's Tailor backwards. Her name's Mrs Tailor.'

'Wow.' I switched on the windscreen wipers as a deluge swept down from the fells. 'I think we may have only just escaped with our lives after all.'

'You make it sound like the Bates Motel.'

'The Setab Motel, as it might be.'

Our dialogue lapsed.

We were, of course, late.

I have a theory about this, which very few people think is any good, but which I still believe has something to recommend it. I think we are naturally late, as a species. The human frame is built for tardiness. That is because, as energetic, inquisitive creatures, we want to pack every minute full of activity and interest, and so we are always running late, because we don't want to waste time waiting around for other people to turn up. Waiting is a heinous activity, one notch above genocide in my scale of values. That may be a bit extreme. But humans in their natural habitat are late, and being on time is simply a deeply abnormal form of compensation, a sort of overcorrection of our prelapsarian tendency to breeze in after the party has begun in order to make the more effective entrance. It's connected with guilt and potty-training. Being early is, on the other hand, only ever an accident. I've never known anyone who was early by design.

We were late, but then we were always late for weddings. I still am. I don't know that I have ever seen a bride enter a church, although I did once arrive immediately behind one, and sort of shuffled in after her trying to pretend I wasn't there.

'Bride or groom?' A harassed usher waved us urgently towards a side pew.

'Neither,' said I.

'Both,' said Grace.

He smiled weakly. There was only one place for us to go, anyway. From there a pillar obstructed our view of the happy pair, though the beaming multitude were displayed in all their hideousness. One side were squat and frog-like, eyes bulging and hair sprouting at odd angles from surprising places. Paul's tribe, I assumed. The other side were sleek and well groomed, tall and austere. None of them looked like Charlotte, but then at weddings nobody looks like anyone else. Nowhere does one become so aware of the glorious variety and resplendent ugliness of the human race as at a wedding, where thoughts of our universal destiny played out through the generations spring

83

spontaneously to mind, and one wonders lugubriously whether it has all been worthwhile. A wedding is the epicentre of all that is worst about us: greed, lust, opportunism, snobbery, success, failure, Aunt Aggie's cancer and Uncle Bertram's messy divorce – they hang like a smog drifting sullenly among the guests, all of them dressed in their very, very best, all of them thrown together unnaturally, all of them glowing defensively as if to say, 'We don't know who *you* are but *we're* doing frightfully well.'

I love the part where the vicar asks why they should not be married. 'Just checking,' the service seems to be saying, 'what with the human race being as fallible as it is. You never know. You may have come here today full of idealism and youthful high spirits, but. . .' It's the big 'but' in the sky. 'Let him now speak or else hereafter for ever hold his peace.' Isn't it tempting? It's like being on the edge of a great cliff and wanting to throw oneself off. 'It should have been me!' 'She reads Jeffrey Archer!' 'He's into spanking!' Everyone holds their breath.

'. . . for ever hold his peace.'

Grace sneezed violently, and the entire congregation shuddered.

From deep within me, welling up inexorably, remorselessly, there arose a tickling flutter of sensation, a distant cousin to a sneeze, but horribly different. Like a set of bells I burst out into uncontrollable, explosive giggles. Wave upon wave rolled through me, each one more audible than the last.

I couldn't help it. It was the tension. Grace drove her elbow into my ribs. There was a sibilant rustle as heads turned in our direction. That familiar disembodied feeling overcame me; I felt as if the teacher had just discovered me surreptitiously eating sweets. It lasted all the way through 'Guide me, O Thou Great Redeemer', 'He Who Would Valiant Be' and 'The Lord's My Shepherd', until at last I began to hope that everyone would have forgotten. Judging by Charlotte's look when she and Paul walked sedately back down the aisle, however, I was being too sanguine.

'Wilf,' said Jimmy, striding towards me over the grass as the bitter gale whipped about our ankles. He had a vulpine grin, sly but steely, utterly humourless. 'That was quite a performance of yours. Hello, Grace, dear,' he added, as if to one bereaved. 'Not your fault. Not your fault at all. Everyone's got a cold right now, we've all got them: Helen, Byron.' Byron was their four-year-old.

'Christ, Wilf, was that, strictly speaking, necessary?' Milo's red hair flowed dramatically in the gale against the brooding grey sky. '*Mon Dieu*, it's grim up north,' he added, hugging himself. 'Why November, for Christ's sake? Why couldn't they wait until May? Hello, Jimmy, lovely to see you. Business good?' Without waiting for a reply he grabbed Grace about the waist. 'Keep me warm, darling, keep me warm.' She pushed him away and he made a face. Then she laughed. 'That's better. *Mein Gott*, I need champagne. Always good for circulation. Speaking of which, how's yours?' He eyeballed Jimmy and me at the same time.

'Arteries or *Arts*?' Rather neat, I thought.

'Consider them closely related,' said Jimmy. Why is it that these men of power have to indulge in such pointed banter?

'Behold the blissful duo. Aren't they sweetness itself?' I asked, watching the bride, groom and family being ushered into endless different formations by a sheep-dog of a photographer. His balding pate bounced eerily like a glowing ping-pong ball in the gathering gloom, as he cajoled them into position. Their grins seemed clamped to their faces by the wind, on which was borne his reedy tones.

'No, I want the grandchildren over here now. No, not you, dear. Lovely. Now let's try something over by this wall here. Can you move over to hide the inscription please? That's nice, that's just right. Now can I have all of you. Can you try it with your hats off. More natural. Now hats on. Lovely. Now just the parents. Try and look a bit happier. Remember it's a joyful occasion. You won't be used to this sort of wind, you're not from round here, are you? That's right. . . Now, let's have just the children. Children only. Over here. You go in front, dear. Try kneeling down. Oh, is it? Well, stand up, then. I'm just trying to get a good composition. It won't work so well but there

85

it is. Now let's have all of you together over by this tree. That'll make a lovely composition. Lovely. Now let's do some black and white. Can I have some of you looking over there, the others looking over here. That'll be a good one. Wait a moment while I change the lens. I want to try something a little different now. Where's that box gone? Has anyone seen my lens box?'

'Shouldn't you be over there, Milo?' I asked. 'You *are* the best man.'

'Must I? I suppose I must. Have you seen Flora, by the way? I heard she was going to be here.'

'I thought she was agenting away in New York these days?'

'She is, but that's what I heard.'

'Well, why don't I go and look for her while you attend to your duties?'

Scarcely had I set off, fervently glad of the excuse to circulate, than a shower of freezing sleet drove into us horizontally, and with a chorus of shrieks like that of a host of souls in torment everyone made for their cars.

The next station of the cross was the introductions, possibly the most excruciating of all social rituals.

'That was rather an exhibition you gave in church, wasn't it?' I had no idea whether it was Paul's or Charlotte's father who was addressing me. He was thickly set, his ears stuck out, he had a cleft chin and a broad nose. His handshake was crushing my fingers.

'Wilf Wellingborough. I'm an old friend of Paul's. And Charlotte's. As is Grace, here.' I have a tendency to feign misunderstanding when under pressure.

'Yes, quite an exhibition.' His set grin did not falter. Neither did the extreme pain in my right hand. I winced, and tried to turn it into a smile.

'Well, more Paul, I suppose. Grace is the other way round. More Charlotte. She's looking absolutely radiant, isn't she?' My other ploy, going beyond misunderstanding in the direst of emergencies, is arrant gobbledegook.

'We're very proud,' he said. It had worked. The agony disappeared. I was forgiven. He was obviously Charlotte's father.

'Yes,' I replied, and grinned vastly, which is my tertiary manoeuvre when mutual incomprehension has set in and done its beneficent work.

'You made a real impression there,' commented Grace. I said nothing. I was intent on avoiding Paul and Charlotte.

'I really am very sorry about my hilarity,' I said plaintively.

'Well, perhaps you ought to say so.'

'I would if everyone wasn't making such a fuss about it. Hey, Flora!'

'Hey, Wilf! Grace!'

'How's New York? Just like you pictured it?'

'It's fabulous. No, faaabulous.'

'Faaabulous.'

'Right. Grace, I love that top. Where's it from? Comme des Garcons?'

'Miss Selfridge.'

'Very cool. You look great.'

'So do you. Fifth Avenue can't know what's hit it,' Grace replied, pleased.

'I confess I do spend a little time there.'

'How's litererary life?'

'Litererary life is, well, pretty damn good, really. Pay could be better. Parties are on the whole not bad. I've just done my first NY deal.'

'What's that?' Always scouting for new talent, me.

'First novel. She's a brilliant writer. Sort of dirty realist with a splash of Jackie Collins. Over here I would say that the other way round, of course.'

'Where did you find her?'

'She was writing short stories in this magazine called *Bitch*. She was the best thing in it. She was the *only* thing in it.'

'Would she write for us?'

'If you paid her enough, maybe. And let me tell you, buddy, she's expensive. I mean bucks, lots of them, and make them the higher denominations.'

'So you're now the hottest agent in town?'

87

'I'm getting there. I'm getting there. Anyway, enough about *moi*. What's the gossip? Is Jimmy here? I haven't seen the lovable little bastard for ages.'

'He and his wife are both here.'

'Well, that's good. How *is* Helen? Surviving?'

'We think maybe not all is verdant in the Spalding garden.'

'Oh, really?'

'Wilf thinks that,' said Grace, acidly. 'I don't. You're so boring with that theory of yours.'

'Now then, you two. And what about Charlotte and Paul? Hello, Lucy, I didn't know you were here.' The new arrival was a flouncy friend of practically everybody's.

'Flora, how are *you*? You look *stunning*. How *is* New York? Is it wonderful?'

'New York's great. No, faaabulous. That's how they say it. Sort of Mae West crossed with a sheep.'

'Don't change, Flora. Sorry, I interrupted. What were you saying?'

'I was asking what we all thought about Paul and Charlotte. They've been together how long, Lucy?'

'A few years now. I just think they're so in love, it's really lovely. And did you see Charlotte's mother crying when she walked down the aisle? Blubsville, I thought. And her father's really nice, too. He specializes in great big slobbery kisses.'

'How perfectly foul.'

'No, Wilf, really, he doesn't do it horridly. Isn't it funny how her family are all squat and hairy and his are such smoothies?'

'Yes, I was wondering about that,' said Flora. 'They don't look very nobby, do they, her lot? Knobbly, yes.'

'Well, they're not. I mean, they're farmers really.'

'Lucy, are you being just the teeniest bit snobbish? That's not like you. Anyway, I thought he was Sheriff of Northumberland or something.'

'That's his brother. He's the one with the title.'

'There's Jimmy. Jimmy! He hasn't seen me.' Flora waved vigorously. Lucy stood on tiptoes to peer.

'Do you know him? He's rather dishy.'

'Married, dear. Don't even think about it.'

'Oh, I don't know. You never know your luck.' I thought I would sound a positive note.

'Wilf, how much champagne have you drunk?'

'Not nearly as much as I'm going to, Grace.'

'Who's he talking to?' Flora wanted to know.

'David Vale. A.k.a. "the Amphibian". Shit of the first water.'

'I've heard that name. Doesn't Mrs T. think rather highly of him?'

'The apple of her eye, apparently.'

'How interesting. I think I may have to go over and introduce myself.'

'Don't leave us. It's been so long.' I didn't want to lose her.

'Tell me, how is that magazine of yours? I don't hear much about it in New York.'

'Thanks.'

'You need to pep it up, baby. I read a copy on the train. What you need is a good gossip column. Spice things up. Make a reputation. You do want to make a reputation, don't you? There, he's seen me. Yes, you may well look sheepish, you worm.'

With one bound she was gone, and we were bereft.

'I wish I could wear all that black velvet,' mused Lucy. 'I always think black at a wedding is bad luck, but Flora looks amazing in it, doesn't she?'

'Jimmy clearly doesn't object to it,' remarked Grace. 'Hello, Milo. While we're on the subject of clothes, I like yours. I've always fancied you in green.'

'You're the sweetest, kindest woman. My God, Paul's parents are dire. I've just had a long conversation with them about the importance of the nuclear deterrent.'

'It must have been very one-sided.'

'I couldn't get a word in edgeways, which was just as well. He went on to tell me all about Charlotte's father's financial affairs. He knew every hair on every last sheep on every farm, almost.

Paul's sister's as bad. She's that podgy, ugly one. Lettice, her name is. She wobbles a lot. I don't just mean her embonpoint, I mean her whole face. She has a barely suppressed ecstasy of self-importance. Her eyes glow with it. I think she trashed the whole room while I was listening, with her father beaming approvingly in an affectionate, patrician way. She seems to know the down-side to everyone here. Someone's hair looks too sprayed on. Someone else's dress is too revealing. What's-her-name is too dowdy. This guy's job is on the line but he doesn't know it. This woman's taste in tulips is too common. This man's pictures are fake oils. This couple holidayed in the wrong place in Italy. Charlotte's family have been mean with the wedding. We had at least five minutes on what she had cooked for some dinner and how her *bombe* was so admired, much better, apparently, than that of a friend of hers who is constantly asking for her secret and who is patently not going to get it. She seemed to think she had the last word on everything and yet look at her. She's an outsized frowsty frump with the charisma of a worn chintz sofa. My God, the rapacious, backbiting mean-spiritedness of it all.'

'She got under your skin,' observed Grace.

'Just a little bit.'

'Never mind, Milo. Here, fill your glass.'

'Thanks.'

He was slightly flushed and breathing hard. If one is inclined to get steamed up about the foibles of humanity, weddings are good places to do it. One can, of course, do the decent thing and join in the festivities with the appropriate *joie de vivre*, but Milo had chosen a perverse, thin-skinned anger, which as I watched him I realized had been aided by an enormous quantity of champagne. He was not the only one; we were all trying to drown out the cold, and the shrieks of laughter were beginning to echo the sound of the gale in the guy-ropes.

'Then David Vale came up. He's like Pecksniff horribly interbred with Uriah Heep, don't you think? Suave, oleaginous, lots of bottom, vast bottom, in fact, name-dropping like crazy. Endless references to the Tory hierarchy. Thinks the world of

Jimmy. Sounds to me as if some donating to party coffers has been going on there. He knows the head of Flora's agency and is going to put in a good word for her. He wanted to know how you were, by the way, Wilf. He was telling Lettice about some time you spilled a glass of wine over Iris Murdoch. Is that true?'

'I *had* hoped everyone had forgotten about it.'

'He told the story very affectionately.'

'I bet. So are they all unredeemable here, do you think?'

'Absolutely all unrefuckingdeemable, except for Charlotte, whom I love.'

'Me too. Since when, you?'

'Oh, I don't know. For ever.'

'For ever? You hardly know her, may I remind you.'

'Well, at least the last four hours. You?'

'The same.'

'It's always the way at weddings.'

It was with some trepidation that I piloted Milo to the marquee and the head table. He was getting drunk, he was in an explosive mood, he was exhibiting a distinct tendency towards frivolity (no surprises there, I suppose), and he had a speech to make. As the time drew on for him to make it, his mood simply seemed to get wilder. After I had seen him depositing a half-eaten pear on the hatpin of an evidently befuddled elderly woman on the next table – and after I had discreetly relieved her of it – I took him to one side.

'Milo, what's the matter with you? You're smashed as a fart, aren't you?'

He gazed at me haughtily, then his eyebrows rose in mock surprise.

'Do you know, I do believe I am?'

It was at this point that I took him outside, but it wasn't until a good hour later, when we were both frozen to the bone and his *bonhomie* had soured to an only slightly more sober bad temper, that I let him back in the tent. With a scowl he grabbed a bottle of champagne, put the neck to his lips and downed half of it, then threw me a glance of sour reproof. Fortunately, most of the other

91

guests were too far gone to notice. But my heart sank. The last I saw of him, he was weaving his way among the tables, waving benignly and patting people on the head.

The speeches were terrible.

Then Milo stood up.

'My Lord Sheriff, ladies and gentlemen,' he began, then stopped. He pantomimed peering round him, an idiotic leer on his face. 'I *think* I can see some here tonight. I can't tell you how pleased I am to be Paul's best man. So I won't.'

He grinned broadly, obviously expecting applause. It was not forthcoming.

'Paul tried several others, but they were all suddenly and mysteriously out of the country or attending to emergencies on their uncles' rabbit farms. When he called I had my mouth full of Mars Bar and was unable to reply in the negative quick enough. So the miserable duty falls to me of describing Paul's early life to you, in accordance with the unforgiving demands of the wedding feast. My God, it's cold. I can't believe you actually live up here. Anyway, disreputable is the only word to describe it. Paul's early life, that is. Or so I hear. As I hardly know him I am not in a position to comment. If it wasn't so disreputable, surely there would be some friends left over from his youth who would remember it, but I searched the land high and low, and I couldn't find any. I thought of asking his parents, but after half an hour's conversation I still hadn't managed to interject. His parents, by the way, are those elegant creatures seated appropriately enough on my right, here; I say appropriately because at a rough estimate their politics would make Dr Goebbels look like a fit candidate for the board of Amnesty International. And if you think they're out of the ark you should try their daughter; Lettice by name but not, by jingo, by nature. Her tongue could mince a copy of Debrett's in sixty seconds. Social climber is not in it; social rapist, I would conjecture. But, God rot you all, you want to know about Paul, about as prodigious a sexual athlete as ever slept his way through Oxford sixth-form colleges. "The Priapic Pimple" he was known as, and for those of you without a decent education, and I can see many of you tonight, that means that he was always erect. Can I use the "p" word? Not his pimple, his penis, madam. I presume you know what that is?'

'Oh, dear. Oh, dear, oh, dear, oh, dear,' I heard someone murmur. I felt my cheeks begin to burn. Grace had gone white. Flora wore an uncertain grin. Jimmy was frowning. Behind me, someone whistled slowly through their teeth. Chairs were creaking around us, accentuating the otherwise breathless stillness.

'Paul's attractiveness to women was the stuff of legend. To look at him now, you might wonder with some legitimacy how this could be. We wondered then. Women setting out for lectures in the morning would spy a hooded figure racing past them in the lightening gloom after a night of love with one of their sisters. Like a phantom he was here, there, everywhere. Walking contemplatively through the Parks or down a quiet side street, searching for an apt rhyme or a brilliant *aperçu*, one would find a couple spreadeagled against a tree or a wall and at least one half would prove to be pimpled and priapic. So our theme on this godforsaken day must be, to paraphrase Tom Jones, why, why, why, Charlotte? We can quite well surmise why, why, why, Paul, for with Paul everything was up. At Oxford he, like everyone else, was up the establishment, but since then he has gone on to weasel his way into the very highest echelons of the legal world. Does he take on lost causes on legal aid? Does he, fuck. Well, he does that, as we know, but Paul's briefs, when not being removed by the nimble fingers of his latest conquest, are those of the bigger shipping companies. We are talking seriously fat fees. Paul has come a long way since those Anti-Nazi League marches of yesteryear; all he needed was a leg up with his legover, and that's what he got with Charlotte, offspring of the great and good of Northumberland, and as radiant and beautiful as she is well bred. That's not to say, of course, that she didn't hit Oxford with her knickers around her knees —'

'*What?*' It was the bride. She had gone puce. Milo, magnificent, insane, all notions of taste and personal safety flung to the howling gales, seemed unperturbed. He appeared not only to

93

have taken leave of his script but his senses while wandering giddily off on this appalling peroration.

'And as I look around me now, I see the apogee of English society, the very essence of all that is admirable about our country today. Powdered faces and straining flesh, swollen smugness and monstrous vanities, endless affectations and pretensions, ridiculous mannerisms and shibboleths protecting the mountains of wealth that are defended against all comers by Paul and his ilk, these are what we fought two world wars to preserve —'

'Oh, come *on*.' It was Jimmy.

'Do not ask whether it was for this the clay grew tall, but —'

At this he seemed to falter. I could see he had lost the thread. He swayed gently and looked mildly puzzled. Then a strange, distant gleam appeared in his eyes. It was the desire to outrage for the sheer hell of it.

'Yes. Ah, yes. And whence does all this contagion spring? As all you monarchists will entirely fail to appreciate, while you sit there sensuously fingering your shotguns in your imaginations in preparation for the next grouse holocaust, there is one family at whose portcullis I can fairly lay the blame for all this humbug. The rot begins at the head. Windsor, schmindsor, as I'm sure you'll none of you agree. And that goes especially for the silly old bag on the stamps.'

The room exploded with an artillery of percussive gasps. They could ignore the most outrageous calumnies directed against some of their own number, because most of them could not understand what he was talking about or believe it if they did, but, with some unerring instinct left over, surely, from the time when they were hunter-gatherers together on the pre-glacial uplands they used to roam, they all rose as one to an insult to the Queen, however drunken and footling. Almost every male was on his feet, anxious to be seen to be doing his bit. A chorus of tuts volleyed forth from those still seated. Milo saw the Sheriff — the Queen's officer as I faintly realized; was he going to make an arrest? — advancing towards him with a menacing air, smiled, and sat down with a scarcely credible air of injured innocence.

'You bloody *bastard*,' screeched Charlotte, and with one powerful sweep of her arm she hurled a glass at him. It missed, hit one of the tent pillars decorated lavishly with flowers of the field, and sent broken glass all over the wedding cake. The hubbub ceased instantly. I felt a depressing sense of *déjà vu*. What was it with Milo and broken glass?

In the silence I heard his voice remonstrating plaintively.

'But I had hardly *started*.'

The pandemonium resumed.

'Did you know he was going to say all those things, Wilf?' Grace was looking at me with chill distaste.

'Yes, did you know he was going to do that, Wilf?' Flora and Jimmy, on the other hand, were looking at me with horrified interest. I panicked, hesitated and was lost.

'You did, didn't you? He's ruined the entire bloody wedding,' spat Grace.

She was being unfair . . . at least, I thought she was.

Shaking, I went looking for a fresh bottle, and thereafter Milo.

'Was I Swiftian?' he asked.

Love that man.

If conversation between Grace and me had been slow on the way, it was extinguished utterly on the way back. Partly this was because I felt like death. Milo had wisely accepted my counsel that he should order a taxi – if he could find anyone who would help him do so – beat a sharp retreat to the station, find a warm bench and hole up until the arrival of the morning train.

'Pretend it never happened,' I said.

'But it was such *fun*,' he replied.

'You're mad. I never realized it before, but you are. Mad. Some of the jokes could have been improved, by the way. No offence intended.'

'None taken, dear. It's all becoming a bit opaque, anyway, I'm afraid.'

We were sitting in the kitchen of the main house, far from the rumour of his exploits. It was quiet and warm. Milo had discovered a bottle of cognac.

95

'Misrule!' he toasted. We drank until the taxi came, which in those parts takes quite a while.

As a result, the next morning my head felt as if it had been put in a clamp. Successive waves of nausea swept over me, alternating with humiliation and embarrassment, for I knew that, rightly or wrongly, I was heavily implicated in Milo's strange deeds, and I would never get the chance to explain myself. That's the trouble with these legal people. They never give you a fair trial. Grace didn't even give me a glance, though in fairness I had my eyes closed most of the time.

'Could you just pull into this lay-by?' I murmured somewhere near Richmond. She did so. When we stopped I threw open the door and sprayed the grass verge with vomit, much of which was deposited by the wind on the bonnet of the car, where it slowly congealed as the long day wore on and we made our way back to London.

When Grace brought the Mini to a halt outside our flat she turned and spoke for the first time that day. Her eyes were glacial.

'You and I,' she said, 'need to talk.'

'Just as long as you don't tell me it's not going anywhere.'

'I won't. It's not, as it happens. But you are.'

'Oh, really?' I had lost her for a moment. Maybe this was not what I thought it was.

'Yes. Out of my sodding life.' She got out and slammed the door.

It was what I thought it was.

In Country

I WALLOWED AMONG WAVES of fever. I was a languid albatross, wings ever unfurled, breaking from clouds of unconsciousness suddenly into clear skies and fragile lucidity and back again. As the evenings drew on I could feel my temperature rising, and the sickness made everything too hot or too cold. I was intensely aware of the passing of the light and the loneliness of the bedroom and my own thoughts, lurid and fanciful, flying me out of myself.

My immune system had packed in immediately. I knew it would; it usually does when things go really wrong. It's as if the director of my particular film calls, 'Cut! OK everybody, let's get some rest and try it again in the morning,' and in comes some passing virus, opportunistic as such things are, looks around, likes what it sees and takes over the set. With the result that I am laid low for five days with ample opportunity to reflect upon life's great conundrums.

Convalescence is much underrated as a means of emotional (rather than simply physical) recovery. C. S. Lewis once said that his idea of happiness was to read Italian epics (Tasso and Ariosto, not *The Name of the Rose*, though the latter would do for me), while always convalescent from some small illness, seated in a window overlooking the sea. Convalescence is like a little retreat for the mind; after the tempest passes, while the body is lying weak but relieved to have made it to the other side, one can reflect and think. I remember listening a great deal to Radio 3; they have a habit of repeating performances every now and then, so some beautiful piano music, say, can return to one like a half-familiar, half-remembered but very welcome old friend.

97

Debussy's *Préludes*, their evocative, enigmatic titles announced with relish – 'Brouillards!' 'Bruyères!' – and a whole afternoon of choral music from Llangollen, when sunshine and silken Welsh voices filled the room. It was as if the jangling extremes that had afflicted my senses had quietened to an equally intense but serene receptiveness, like the mirror of a still lake open to the unclouded sky.

It was still too early to understand why it was all over between Grace and me. I knew because Grace had sort of told me – and in her final summing-up she had hardly minced her words – that it was to do with my being emotionally inadequate, but that was so grotesquely hurtful, and, to be honest, my feelings were so raw, that I did what I always do: I set the whole thing aside for a later, happier day, when I could return and place it all in a greater, wider context wherein, with a bit of luck, it could be seen to be either not my fault at all or due to aspects of myself that had long since been corrected. I knew obscurely that I was to blame, but I chose the obscurity. I was sorry, too; sorry I had afforded no help when she needed it, sorry for her sorrow, sorry she was no longer in my life. What could I have said? What should I have said? What the hell had Ferdy been playing at, anyway?

When your girlfriend turfs you out and you feel like death, the one thing you don't do is hang around in the flat you share. What do you do? You go home to your mum and dad, that's what. You may be mature, grown-up, independent and successful (or, let's face it, baby, you may not), but as Robert Frost said, home is somewhere you somehow haven't to deserve, and sometimes that's just what you need. So I staggered off to Euston, that operating-theatre for the damaged soul, that greenhouse for all those looking for a new life, and shivered all the way to Shrewsbury, where Ma picked me up, took me back and put me in my old bedroom; and when I got through the illness I thought, 'Here am I, twenty-seven years old, and I'm still in my old bed with my mother bringing me cups of tea, and I love it.' Because mothers, and fathers for all I know, do like you to recognize who's there when it really counts, if they get the opportunity.

On the fifth day I rose; partly because I was feeling better, partly because Jimmy had been on the phone wanting to know whether I had deserted the *Arts* for good. As had Bomber, who was surprisingly solicitous, and gave me reams of advice and a list of vitamin tablets that seemed to be longer than the alphabet.

'My head's spinning from sitting up,' I quavered faintly at Jimmy on the phone. 'My doctor tells me I need to take a week off.'

'You mean your father does.'

'No, someone else at the surgery,' I lied. 'I am ill, you know; I had a temperature of one hundred and three.' Why did he always make me feel so guilty?

'We need you, that's all. Though even I must admit we need you healthy. When do you think you'll get back here?'

'Get back where? Where are you?'

'London, of course. Where do you think I am?'

I tried to concentrate.

'Monday. I'll try for Monday. I'm sorry, I really don't feel well.'

The voice softened unexpectedly.

'All right. Get some rest. We'll see you next week.'

The following morning a hard frost had encased the world in white and the sun burned in every millionth reflection on every shimmering surface.

'Are we going to have the pleasure of your company for long?' enquired Father, looking at me over the top of the *Telegraph* in the time-honoured paterfamilias way. Breakfast at the breakfast table. The essence of civilization.

'Aren't you supposed to be in the surgery?' I asked in the time-honoured rude offspring way.

'I have the morning off in order to accompany your mother to Shrewsbury,' he replied.

'Sounds like fun.'

'Oh, it will be. We may meet some friends we haven't seen for some time and we may go to Sidoli's to have coffee and cake. Or tea and cake. The possibilities are most invigorating.'

'Don't overdo it, Dad. You're not dead yet.'

'Oh, we won't overdo it.'

'The sarcasm, I meant.'

I helped myself to more coffee.

'Where are you going today, dear?' asked Ma, as if I were still fourteen.

'To be honest I haven't a clue. Last night I told Jimmy I'd be back Monday. So I think I'll just take it easy over the weekend. I might see if Helen's at Monkridge.'

Though I was still a bit wobbly, and Father was suddenly anxious for my well-being, I set out on a brisk walk through the village, the cold air tearing into my lungs and my breath wisping away behind me. I had not bothered to ring, because I needed to get out anyway, and I was in the mood to leave things to chance. The gates lay just beyond the village on the crest of rising ground, and one walked up a slow incline until the ground fell gently away; there on the opposite slope were the unfolding roofs of Monkridge. Today it lay as if cradled in ermine in the great shallow bowl of the surrounding hills. The frost creaked under my feet. By the time I reached the thick, wooden, heavily panelled doors, strangely unassuming in a house so large – but then it was a building that sprawled rather than imposed – my nose felt as if it were about to drop off. Fortunately, it was swiftly attended to by the tongues of two great red setters that bounded out to meet me.

'Donner! Blitzen!' Helen was laughing from the open doors. 'I thought you were ill, Wilf. How lovely to see you. I heard you were here. You've got red setter saliva all over your nose. They obviously like you as much as Milo, and I always thought they liked him because his hair is the same colour. Come in, do come in. Isn't it divine? Look at the colour of that sky. It's a kind of pale blue porcelain, isn't it? Come on, let's get that coat off you. Donner! Blitzen! Get inside, you two!' They were rolling over and over on the frosted grass like russet tornadoes, sending up small clouds of glistening particles.

100

The kitchen at Monkridge was cavernous. Along the walls were ranged great cupboards filled to bursting-point with dinner services and crockery from the exquisite to the plain, the Sunday best to the mundane. Much of it was in use, for though Jimmy's great parties were largely a thing of the past and Ranulph was now frail, the house was important for entertaining Jimmy's friends and business associates and enhancing his circle of influence yet further. The house breathed hospitality. Over the years rooms and wings had fallen into disuse and then been coaxed into life again, and Helen was becoming more and more its mistress, travelling less and less up to London, watching over Ranulph solicitously and preparing the house for weekend guests with the graciousness and proficiency that became her. She was part of the rhythm and fabric of the place.

Overhead hung quantities of dried flowers; saucepans gleamed in rows; ceramic pots stood burbling quietly on not one but two Agas; the odour of freshly made bread and coffee permeated the air; and clusters of kitchen implements like job lots from a torturer's bring-and-buy sale clung to the bars of the hanging racks, making me think of jungle tendrils reaching down from the forest canopy to inspect the quiet forest floor.

I had always sort of loved Helen. She had a wide, sensitive mouth, wider than it needed to be so therefore sensuously ornamental, perhaps the most striking of her features were it not for the large, almost naïve, brooding eyes. Her movements were measured, as if she could hear music and were half-consciously swayed by it. Nothing she did seemed ill-considered, and her clothes, many of which she made herself, were always coolly appropriate, of a piece with the moment. Her laugh was a subdued chuckle – anything more would have been too disruptive – and even then it formed a part of her conversation, an echo of her own thoughts or a fleeting recognition of those of others.

She filled a kettle.

'The gardens are looking beautiful.'

'In the frost? I should imagine they are.'

'Do you want to see them? Shall we go and look?'

I could tell this was what she wanted.

'Why don't we?'

'But you must still be frozen. Why don't we take some coffee out?'

She looked at me half-expectantly. She seemed excited, a little distracted, and I didn't want to disappoint her. I felt a shadow of annoyance that I was made to feel, slightly, the intruder in a house I had known since childhood, but I brushed the feeling aside. I had packed my body so deep in thermals, T-shirts, socks and jerseys that I felt like the Michelin man and warm as toast, so I didn't feel vulnerable to the cold.

I followed Helen bearing a tray with a cafetière of steaming black coffee and two mugs down a passage and through a side door into the open air, where the steam rose volcanically from the pot. Looking up towards the crenellations that ran along the top of the walls I spied a small dark head against some closed curtains which promptly disappeared.

The old courtyard was full of topiary: spirals and globes and cubes and cones, bearing on their shoulders capes of white which seemed to float above the densely packed leaves of the box. Gloomy and stoic, they were huge chiaroscuro enigmas among low, formal hedges and pathways. Beyond them lay the beginnings of Ranulph's long-loved gardens, of walkways where the last great shapes of the autumnal garden stood proudly amid the decay.

Helen placed the tray on a bench by an outer wall, then together we walked, mugs in hand, among the orange dreadlocked kniphofias and the hedgehog-headed teasels, huge outposts of stonecrop and mop-like grasses, old allium seedheads resembling exploding municipal fireworks, and the remains of spiky cardoons, whose leaves in the summer seem to rush like geysers straight out of the ground. Here and there were surprising rashes of colour: attenuated, hungry flames of dogwood, mulberry smoke-bush, glowing rose-hips with their evanescent skins and profuse outpourings of berberis berries. As we went,

Helen cut strange shapes from the borders – a globe thistle, its faded blue like a comfortable afterthought in a seaside boarding-house, a tall yarrow, the yellow essence of summer grown gaunt and aquiline – and as she did so I felt happily irrelevant, serenely post-convalescent, carried along in the wake of her busy harvesting of winter's botanical splendours.

'I should write about this,' I said.

'In that column of yours?'

'Yes. Do you ever read it?'

'I do.'

'Do you like it?'

'You could never tell you didn't have a garden.' Was she mocking? I glowed, anyway.

'Actually, it's the thing I like doing best. I love the magazine and all that, but that's the bit that's all mine. It's where I can most be myself. It's astonishing how the British feel about gardens; it's their vernacular poetry, their common sculpture; it unleashes all their reserve. Gardens are a very British passion, but they make us very un-Britishly passionate.' I prattled on like an excited schoolboy praised by his teacher. She turned to squint at me from beneath a hand shading her eyes from the sun. I was unsure of her expression. 'You're not having me on, are you?'

'Of course I'm not,' she replied, laughing. 'I don't believe you, though. You must love the life. Editors can't be faint-hearted.'

'It's not quite the *Sunday Times*, you know. But I see what you mean,' I added, not wishing to disappoint. Evidently she thought I should be a kind of Wild Bill Hickock of the print media. 'No, I love the *Arts*. It means everything to me. I've woken it up a bit, I think, but there's some way to go. I was thinking of introducing a gossip column. It might make the London Library sit up a bit. What do you think?'

'I don't know.' She bent to tap the ice on the top of a sundial. 'That will help the birds.' She threw the ice to one side. 'I like it the way it is. But you know best.' She looked at me slyly again. 'I hope the proprietor is giving you plenty of independence?'

103

This, I realized, was not the sort of conversation one should have with the proprietor's wife. But I was seized by a desire to explore the opportunity.

'Yes, he just lets me get on with it. I think he likes what I'm doing. I mean, I assume he likes it?' I asked, in an airy, couldn't-care-less fashion. She giggled awkwardly.

'I couldn't possibly say.' A contrary thought seemed to come to her, and she frowned. 'Why shouldn't I, though? I think James likes it the way it is, too. He doesn't like change all that much. You'd be surprised.'

I was, but didn't say so.

'Old-fashioned kind of guy.'

'Old-fashioned? That's not it. He sets a lot of store in possessing *Arts Unlimited*.'

'Quite rightly. It's very prestigious.'

'Yes. Prestigious.' She pronounced the word slowly, testing its consonants with her tongue. 'Correct. And Jimmy is very ambitious.' She did the same with the last word, as if they rhymed. Pre-sti-gious. Am-bi-tious.

'Of course he is,' I said, heartily, not understanding at all what she was driving at. 'Though I don't suppose it adds much to his bottom line. And it's a funny fit with all those computer and bike mags.'

'It's a very odd fit, Wilf. But it does something for him which he badly needs. It's important to him. I think he chose you because he's always had a soft spot for you. But don't think he doesn't watch you like a hawk, either.'

'I can't imagine him doing anything else.'

We were walking back to the house now. The sun had begun to go in and the cold was becoming much more noticeable.

'I can't quite see what it does for him that's so special, though. I mean, *so* special.'

Helen tutted at my ignorance, shivered, pulled her coat tighter about her, picked up the tray and redoubled her pace.

'It impresses people. It says solidity, ballast, old cultural values, things that last, things that mean something. The City is incredibly impressed by all that. It comes from dealing in intangibles all day, futures and what have you, or all-too-tangibles like oil and tin and the price of fertilizer in Saudi Arabia.'

'So he wants to float the company?'

She stopped dead and mimicked astonishment. 'Brilliant.'

'There's no need to be like that. How would I know?'

She laid a patient hand on my arm.

'Wilf, if you had that gossip column you might have picked up the rumours that have been going round for the last week.'

'Ah, well, I've been ill, you see.'

She ran her hand down to mine and applied a gentle pressure. 'So you have. Sorry. It's been preying on my mind a bit, that's all. It will be some years away; the company is not really large enough yet, but it will be. Sometimes even I am surprised by James. Surprised by how much he wants from life. Surprised by what he is capable of doing to get it. He's not a man of much scruple, Wilf.'

'But you love him.'

She didn't answer, and opened the door to the house. As she did so, a whirlwind about knee height engaged with her legs.

'You're supposed to be in bed.' Setting the tray aside, she plucked the child up into her arms in one great swooping movement. He hid his head in her neck for a few moments, then shifted slightly. I could see an eye gleaming askew at me from the vicinity of his mother's left ear. As I moved towards him the eye, indeed the entire face, was buried swiftly from sight, in a small charade of shyness.

'He's not well,' apologized Helen. 'Been running a temperature for two days. I think he's over it now, though.'

Behind her, a small hand reached out surreptitiously to draw patterns on a moisture-clad pane of glass. Helen could feel what he was doing and laughed. The boy sat upright, looked her full in the face and kissed her nose with a passion.

'Can I have a sweet? Please?' he wheedled, brazenly.

'No, you may not,' replied his mother. 'You couldn't keep

105

anything down yesterday and now you want a sweet. You can have a sweet after lunch, if you eat it. Come on, let's get you upstairs to bed. And I want you to stay there.'

I watched her retreating form, small and strong, carrying the boy Byron lodged against her right side. His head leaned against her shoulder, and his left hand absently patted her back.

There was serenity in this house: the serenity of the past, of my own past, indeed, and that of Ranulph and Jimmy and his brothers, now scattered to New York and Paris, to banking and advertising, and one to raise organic carrots near Aberystwyth. While I waited for Helen to return I wandered the familiar corridors, the carpeted and the stone-flagged, and I noticed for the first time the subtle encroachment of Helen's presence. It was there in the clip frames crowded with photographs of recent holidays in the kitchen, in the more formal pictures, framed in heavy silver, which clustered like a dynasty on display in the dining room. There was their wedding and their family, individually, in pairs, in groups, caught in moments of great significance – Byron's christening, his first steps – or relaxing in deck-chairs in sunny Norfolk gardens, lolling like seals on a rock, half-conscious of the camera; grandparents sitting stiffly on a bench surrounded by dogs; Helen's mother in an alarming yellow hat and her sister as a bridesmaid.

There were other details, too: old rugs had disappeared, and carpets had been replaced by sea-grass. Furniture had been reupholstered; faded chintzes had been disposed of in favour of shy pinks and pale greens; and even the untrained eye could not fail to observe the new colour schemes, carefully planned to match each room's mood. The dining room was now clad in a dramatic golden wallpaper with swag curtains in deepest cobalt blue. The kitchen itself had had its regiment of cupboards given a smart beige livery, though it was still struggling gamely to retain its old scruffiness.

I wondered whether Jimmy and his father liked these changes, if they noticed them.

★   ★   ★

106

It had come as a shock when Helen and Jimmy became an item. At the time, I didn't think she'd be his type: not flash or waspish like Flora, not glamorous like his women usually were. I had thought her demure and quiet; at Oxford she had kept herself to herself a lot of the time, and would be seen scurrying along like a furtive tree-animal, keeping close to the wall with an eye out for cats. The rugger-buggers adored her because she made them feel protective, but she didn't say a lot and the girls that they usually consorted with, who wore Jaeger jackets and Hermès scarves from Harvey Nicks like their mums, didn't take to her at all. We once played Monopoly together after getting bored of a party and going back to her rooms, and it was all perfectly innocent, so she took to me after that and thought me funny in an inoffensive way. She used to give me big winks over the desk-dividers in the Upper Reading Room of the Bodleian Library, which were so constructed that you could not look up from your work without gazing straight into someone else's eyes, thereby lending an exciting intensity to the otherwise undifferentiated hours of study.

Flora's phone call announcing the news had been even more raucous than usual.

'Have you *heard*? Darling Jimmy has a new lover and you'll never guess who it is.'

'No, I imagine I won't.'

'Oh.' She sounded disappointed. 'Aren't you even going to try?'

'Flora –'

'All right. Helen.'

'Helen Macreadie?'

'The same. Can you believe it?'

'Well, she *is* lovely, but not quite James, if you know what I mean.'

'I do know what you mean. Rather wispy-looking, wouldn't you say?'

'Do I detect the slightest note of jealousy in your voice?'

'Darling, I'll say this to you because I love you and you're my best and closest friend –'

'For today.'

'– for today, but you know what Jimmy's like; he takes a little piece of all our hearts when he goes. Jimmy's Lost Lovers are a sort of club. We meet every Thursday over a box of tissues and pour out our unrequited longing. I'm thinking of writing a play about it.'

'Could I remind you that you dropped him like a large turd when that actor who was in *Gandhi* came along? What was his name?'

'You are so vulgar. I don't know how I can talk to you.'

'But you did.'

'You don't understand the rag-and-bone shop of the heart, Wilf, you really don't. I didn't mean to leave for ever. I just wanted him to know what it felt like.'

'Whatever. I can understand your feelings about Helen –'

'Big of you.'

'– but I really like her. It'll be nice to see her again. She was in that *King Lear* at the Playhouse. The one where they all wore black leotards.'

'Everyone always wore black leotards. They're disgusting. I hate student theatre.'

'Come on, Flora. She was a wonderful Cordelia.'

'Vacuous part. Give me Goneril and Regan any day. Spirited women with a proper sense of self-esteem. Not some salad-crunching, carrot-nibbling anorexic waif.'

'I don't recall Shakespeare mentioning Cordelia's eating disorders. And if you mean Helen, you're being brutal. You don't know that about her and if you do you're being callous and dastardly.'

'I do know that about her and I apologize. I'm sorry.'

'It's always the ones that mainline lettuce that are the strong ones. And she'll have to be Herculean to keep J. S.'

'Granitic and flinty, more like. She won't keep him.'

But she did. And Flora's words came back to me as I stood in the kitchen at Monkridge washing the coffee things and listening to the quietness of the house, and they returned again when, that evening, out of nowhere, my mother said:

'Of course, you know the rumours about those two, don't you?'

'I've heard. But I can't believe they're true.'

'*Where* have you heard them?' She was piqued; she liked to be first with the news.

Their day in Shrewsbury had not been a success. They had not found anything they wanted, there were roadworks everywhere, Sidoli's had run out of the lemon tarts my father regarded as his only sin, Ma kept slipping on the frosty pavements and their friends had not turned up, having been unable to start their car.

'It's getting to be a rough place.'

'It always was a bit, wasn't it?'

'Worse, now. A car was literally rolled over outside Safeway the other day and they tried to set fire to it. It was one of those three-wheel invalid cars – apparently it's easy to do.'

'The owner must have been cross.'

'He was. He was still inside it. And there's always some shop window boarded up because it's been vandalized.'

'It's all those pubs. There are too many drunks.'

'Someone was stabbed in that lane that runs down the back of the Lion just last week,' my father observed with lugubrious satisfaction.

'Well, I know that the country's going to the dogs because of Thatcherism and the failure of the so-called trickle-down effect, Dad, before you say it –'

'I wasn't going to. But it is.'

'– but most violence is still domestic, isn't it? People who know each other. That's how they get in the door. That's why people lower their guard. It's the intimacy of violence, the violence in intimacy. The anger that festers when we love each other.'

Which brought us to the rumours, and I couldn't say I had heard them at a *Private Eye* lunch because they disapproved of the magazine, and anyway I didn't know how true they were.

'People are talking about Jimmy,' I went on. 'He's a thrusting entrepreneur in a culture that idolizes thrusting entrepreneurs,

109

and the more cut-throat and ruthless they are the better. There are armies of people in London with their ears and noses and indeed every other sensitive organ employed full stretch to gather in hints of other's misfortunes, like a kind of black harvest.'

'Can't think why you live there.'

'So do you think it's true?'

'I don't know. And I wouldn't say even if I did.'

'The doctor is mum, Mum.'

'Well. . .' She hesitated, looking guardedly at Dad. 'We've heard there's unhappiness there. And that he's not above making himself felt in a rather forceful manner. And I'm only telling you this because you're friends and I think you should know. And now. . .' She stood up. 'I'm going to bed.'

The next day I rang Helen.

'I'm coming round.'

'That will be nice.' She sounded as if she meant it.

'This afternoon. And then we're going to go down the back bar of the Prince Rupert and have a drink. I'm going to call Jethro and see if he'll come too.'

It was one of those adolescent jokes that sticks; when Stephen Price was in his teens he had, with the confidence of early male maturity, grown a great deal of facial hair soon after he left school, which as I recollect was remarkably early. The beard was a tribute to his hero Ian Anderson of Jethro Tull; we had never been able to persuade Stephen to take *Thick As A Brick* off the turntable. It was more favoured even than the Sabs' *Master of Reality*, Wishbone Ash's *Argus* or Yes's *Close to the Edge*. (It should be noted here that Jethro was the world's most awesome air guitarist; upper lip flaring, upper front teeth pressed hard against his lower lip, he would mime the opening notes to 'Smoke on the Water' with explosive accuracy – 'dvvv–dvvv–dvvv, dvvv–dvvv–DVVV–dvvv'. Someone once mischievously allowed him some time with an electric guitar and the poor bastard had absolutely no idea what to do with it.) *T As A B* was a 'concept' album with about four tunes on it (or am I being generous here?) but Stephen – Jethro – loved it to banality.

Sometime in 1975 he had dragged us off to see Tull at the Liverpool Empire, where Anderson stood on one leg playing his flute, sporting an immense and lurid codpiece. 'We're going to do an underwater breathing apparatus kind of a song,' Anderson announced balefully. All the lights were suddenly extinguished. '"Aqualung"!' yelled Stephen, gleefully, thereby ruining the whole effect. Over the microphone in the darkness we could hear a whispered growl, 'Smart-alec cunt.'

Jethro ever after, he was a huge, swaggering man who had hung around Jimmy for a bit and who usually wore leather trousers and a black T-shirt emblazoned with the name of the touring 'progressive' band of the moment. In time it had come to have 'Motorhead' written on it and he had mixed with the biker heads at the Admiral Benbow, but after that phase he had softened and was now almost civilized. He was a great comrade from many pre-drinking-age pub crawls, and he had a peculiarly effeminate charm, which I think was related to being so fat and given to mild sensual self-gratification in the form of drinking-chocolate, velvet coats and (of course) leather trousers. I'm sure he harboured dark fantasies about black magic rituals, and he had probably tried to sell his soul to the devil, though whether he had any success in that department I don't know.

The bar at the back of the Rupert was a favourite haunt when we were doing our bored-teenager-in-the-school-holidays bit. It was usually full of public schoolboys from the place up the hill, who all seemed to know the barman personally and were very edgy towards Jimmy, because he was at Eton and therefore several notches up the public school hierarchy. But I was local and middle-class and had a sort of tatty authenticity about me, so I could be an interesting, rather than threatening, acquaintance.

I didn't want to spend the whole evening in the Rupert – just a few drinks and then find somewhere that wasn't a Berni Inn at which to celebrate my release from the clutches of whatever maleficent microbe had so violently laid me low.

I went to Monkridge in Dad's car to pick up Helen. I waited in one of the smaller drawing rooms while she kissed Byron

111

goodnight. I had the car keys in my hand, ready to leave, when she said, 'But you know, Wilf, we haven't really talked about *you*.'

And that was true. I was so surprised I sat down. I had honestly forgotten about Grace and me. Not entirely, of course; I was fully conscious of what had happened. But I wasn't obsessing about it; it was as if the illness had purged me, had gouged out my feelings like a glacier pulverizing a valley out of a mountain. My temperature had scorched them out of me, and had cauterized the surrounding skin. In other words, I felt better about it. Fragile and temporary it might be, but it was so.

'Maybe it was ready to end,' said Helen, matter-of-factly, after we talked it through. 'Maybe it was a failure on nobody's part.'

'I think there was a failure. I wanted to help but I couldn't. I could not feel her feelings. I couldn't imagine how to. It was a failure of my imagination.'

'You don't have to feel the same to help someone.' She hesitated. 'I'm very fond of Grace.'

'She loves you, too.'

'Don't be facetious, I mean it. You know I do.'

'I know.'

'She has a gloomy, absorbed streak in her, though.'

'Self-absorbed?'

'I didn't say that, but I suppose that's what I mean.'

'So?' I was defensive. Old habits die hard.

'So I think she liked you for certain qualities, and vice versa.'

'I don't follow.'

'Well, you have a certain amiability about you, Wilf.'

'You mean I'm feckless.'

'I didn't say that. You do put words in my mouth.'

'But you did mean that.'

'No, I didn't.'

'So what did I want from her?'

'Oh, I imagine a sort of centredness, a sort of gravity.'

'You mean she's morose?'

'Don't be absurd.'

112

'People have said that about her.'

'Well, I'm not one of them.'

We gazed at each other, half hostile, half amused.

I felt the stirring of some piquant, obscure emotion. Getting to my feet, I paced the room to shake it off, and found myself picking books off the shelves at random. Old volumes of Hardy. Slightly younger Penguin paperbacks of Jane Austen with scribbled pencil notes inside; more evidence of Helen's occupancy. Hughes's and Heaney's *The Rattle-Bag*.

Suddenly something very strange.

A slender volume of poetry. Ted Hughes's *Crow*. With hideous, very real, exploded, grey-black-flecked holes through it, ashen and plain as death: three craters in the shape of a trefoil through which I could see the light when I held it up in my hand.

'What the hell is this?'

Helen smiled faintly.

'Ah, yes. Target practice.'

At first I didn't understand. The thing was grotesque.

'These are bullet-holes?'

She nodded.

'Real bullets?'

She looked distracted, irritated even, as if I were being wilfully obtuse.

'Do they look like pretend ones?'

I held the book like something small and frail and precious and outrageously destroyed.

'Jimmy doesn't like Ted Hughes much.'

I prised it open. Flakes sprayed off the pages like ash. I suppose they *were* ash.

'When God went off in despair, Crow stropped his beak and started in on the two thieves.'

My favourite lines were still intact.

'Do you like Ted Hughes?' she asked.

'Sometimes. Not really. Sometimes. Yes.'

There was a kind of engaged stillness between us.

I tried to fit the pages back together.

113

'Well, well,' I said, cradling the violated volume. Gingerly, I returned it to the shelf. 'Does he often do this?'

'Not that often. Depends how bad he thinks the poetry is.'

'Is he a good judge?'

'You know him as well as I do. Almost.'

'I don't think he's that easy to know, however long you've been around him. And I don't know much about his taste. I'm not sure I understand what his taste *is*.'

'He does own a magazine dedicated to the arts, remember.' I was being reproved or mocked, or possibly both.

'Lawdy, so he does. And I'm the editor, as I recall.'

'One would think he knows quite a bit about them, then.'

'One would.'

I felt unnecessarily and infuriatingly provoked, bullied even. Jimmy was a rogue elephant, perhaps, but she wanted me to know that he was *her* rogue elephant.

'Come on,' she said, smiling sweetly. 'Jethro awaits.'

His comfortable bulk rested darkly in a corner of the bar.

'Hail,' he remarked, affably, hand raised. I fetched some drinks.

'You're looking very trim, Jethro,' I ventured as I sat down. I peered at his sideburns. 'Is that a little silver I detect among those curls? Very distinguished. I mean, really,' and I did mean it. There was a svelte healthiness about him, an aura of sudden maturity. Quite sexy. He had lost a lot of weight.

'I work out,' he said, all smugness and self-deprecation.

'What, at that place across from the Bear Steps?'

'Yea, verily.' These ex-heavy-metal freaks love to sound Arthurian.

'So how's Shrewsy Town?'

'Oh, you know. Crap, as usual. And the Smoke?'

'Brilliant. But I long for home.'

'Liar.'

'Yes.'

'What's Jimmy doing?'

'Running the world.'

114

'No change there, then. You work for him now, don't you?'

'Well, it's not like in a garage, you know.'

'Wilf, I'm not a prat, remember?'

'You're a lovely human being, that's what you are. Have a crisp.'

I loved this easy corny old rubbish born of knowing one another too long. And we were both showing off to Helen, which I liked too. She wasn't that impressed – how could she be? – but she was out for an evening, bunking off with a couple of lads, and she was laughing. Jethro had an unceasing supply of local gossip, which gets pretty racy in the country, as they think about sex a lot of the time, surrounded as they are by burgeoning and fructifying and bestial copulation and parturition, and when they're not thinking about it they're engaged upon it like eighteenth-century libertines. In town we're all very prim and well behaved and easily shocked. In the country they're just at it all the time.

As we talked I found myself watching Helen. She was looking younger; her hair was done in a girlish pony-tail, she was wearing freshly minted biker's leathers and she was picking with slow, purposeful relish at a packet of hickory-smoked peanuts. She still sat ramrod straight, still gave the impression of being slightly displaced from the rest of the world, but she was less demure; the strained expression about her eyes and mouth was less pronounced. Occasionally she glanced at me and smiled, then looked back at Jethro, rambling on with one of his steamy chronicles of rural rumpy-pumpy. It must have been the effect of his conversation, but I suddenly found I could not take my eyes off her – in particular the graceful line of her neck before it sank into the animal embrace of the black leather. I think she noticed; every now and then her eyebrows would dip fractionally and admonishingly after our eyes had met.

'But he's a bastard, he is,' Jethro was saying of some farmer out towards the Wrekin. 'He's got about three women on the go, and he's running two farms but he won't let his eldest son get his hands on any of it. The farms, I mean. I've heard he's quite generous about the women. Bashes his wife every Saturday night after he comes home, too.'

'Sounds familiar,' I said.

Jethro looked at me sharply.

Perhaps my mind was clouded by thoughts of Helen. I glanced at her. She was staring at me suspiciously with raised eyebrows.

'What do you mean, Wilf?' Jethro asked. His voice was soft and casual.

Suddenly I was aware of tumbling into some hideous trap I had set for myself.

The colour went from Helen's face and her lips set in a tightly compressed line. 'You little bastards,' she murmured to herself.

Swiftly, with an air of awful finality, she rose, pulling her bag strap over her shoulder, and walked rapidly out without looking back.

'She's got to start talking about it some time, you know,' observed Jethro dispassionately, but with mild disapproval, as if he were discussing a friend's drinking problem.

'You're fucking fatuous, you know, sometimes, Jethro.'

'Excuse me, you introduced the subject, Wilf.'

'Yes, but I didn't know what I was doing.'

'That's because you couldn't keep your fucking eyes off her, you treacherous little worm.'

I was going to reply, but I thought about Helen instead.

'I'm going to find her.'

Jethro snorted.

''Course you are.'

Outside, the remains of the morning's snow had congealed into dirty heaps sparkling fitfully in the lamplight. I couldn't see Helen, and I began walking up the street towards where we had left the car. It was deathly quiet, save for the faint reverberations of a night-club in the distance. Out of the shadow of the wall that ran round the looming blackness of a church stepped two silhouettes.

'Have you got the time?'

It was said in a flat monotone, as if there was nothing in the world he wanted to know less. In the distance, at the end of the road, was a small figure, shrinking all too rapidly.

'Hang on.'

I stepped towards the light, and was conscious that he was in my way. I would have to move round him. His friend, who had a No. 1 crop just like he did, was watching from the pavement.

'Excuse me.'

'I said, have you got the time?'

His friend stepped off the pavement.

'Well, I would if I could see. You're in my light.'

'Speaking of which, have you got one?'

'One what?'

'A fucking light. What do you think I am, stupid?'

'I'm sorry, I'm looking for someone.' I could see the figure in the distance turn its head towards us.

'Can you lend us a fiver?'

'I haven't really —'

'He looks like he might have a fiver, doesn't he?'

'Shall we have a look?'

'Would you like to show us, or shall we have a look all by ourselves?'

There was a subdued chant to their voices, as if they were singing quietly to some inaudible rhythm.

'Look, time, twenty-past nine. Cigarettes, I don't smoke.'

'Funny voice you've got. Where you from?'

I felt the wall at my back. His face was peering into mine, moving slowly from side to side, snake-like, like Jason in *Friday the 13th* when he's hung the guy on a knifeblade through his middle. Inquisitive; innocently interested in extreme violence.

Something scratched my chin. I looked down. A broken bottle. Suddenly his elbow twitched backwards.

I ran.

I didn't get far. I sprawled over an outstretched foot and my head cracked against tarmac.

I heard screaming. A weight landed on my back and a boot crashed into my head. The world exploded into incandescence.

Suddenly the weight lifted. I sat up as if in a dream and saw one figure stumbling into darkness while Jethro had the other by the throat and was beginning to swing his head against the lamppost.

One. Two. Three. The body went limp. His friend had vanished.

Jethro dropped his prize and began kicking it methodically. The head, the eyes, the mouth, the ribs. He jumped on the head and then the stomach.

'For fuck's sake,' I slobbered. My lips were swollen and split and pouring blood.

The screaming went on.

'Come on,' shouted Jethro.

I staggered up. There was Helen, her eyes fixed on Jethro, her face and mouth distended in one long scream after another. As he approached her she reached out her arm. At first I thought it was an embrace; then I realized she was warding him off. The next moment, she ran. I ran after her. Jethro ran too, but he just wanted to be away from that scene. We ran until we reached the English Bridge and stood there panting, looking over the side into the oil-slick-black Severn coiling sensuously beneath us.

Everything was quiet, save for the sobs of the small body collapsed against the balustrade some distance away. I began wiping my face with my handkerchief. My skull hurt like crazy. I was taking in air like a vacuum cleaner, great long shuddering cold draughts of it.

'Fuck,' said Jethro, quietly, with every exhalation of his own breath. 'Fuck, fuck, fuck.'

When the adrenalin had stopped pumping and my body had ceased to quake and my pulse had stopped sounding like a drum roll against my swollen temples, I muttered, 'Jethro?'

'Yea?'

Arthurian to the last.

'Thanks.'

'Any time.'

'Jethro?'

'Yea?'

'Did you kill him, do you think?'

'Nay.'

He spat into the river, a great big flob of phlegm. It hit the surface with a satisfying slap.

'Least, I don't think I did.'

'Not for want of trying.'

He didn't reply.

The sobs to my left kept on coming.

I Heart New York

ONE EVENING I slunk into the Crepuscule to find Milo and Tom Phipps already well established, halfway down their second bottle of Sauvignon. I had been thinking of Helen often, the events of that evening being emblazoned upon my imagination, but I couldn't ring when Jimmy was there, and when he wasn't she left the answering machine on or was out, and I felt she was shutting herself in on her life, tenaciously hanging on to him in his wilder moods, when who knows what damage he did to her psychologically or physically. I had been growing obsessive and angry, and longed to go up there and carry her away, forgetting that there was no particular reason why she should want to come with me.

Milo, on the other hand, was as ever free of doubt and worry, and strangely oblivious to his outlandish behaviour at Charlotte's and Paul's wedding when it came up in conversation, as Tom and I liked it to.

'I actually had rather a nice card from Paul and Charlotte on their honeymoon,' he reminded us proudly, not for the first time, 'thanking me for wrecking their wedding, and saying there was now a contract on my head. Rather witty.' I had not tried to disillusion him. It was possible they had forgiven him. People do like to think happily of such occasions when they can, though it must have taken a formidable tonnage of the milk of human kindness to think so in this case.

I had finally given in. Tom's gossip column had been running fitfully for some time, and pretty anodyne it was too. I wanted a little more spice, and I said so.

'Wilf's right, you know, Tom,' put in Milo. 'Can't you do a

bit better? Or is it that all those other diaries you contribute to get the best stories?'

'They certainly pay better,' retorted Tom robustly. 'I always feel my jewels are worth the price, a price I don't appear to be able to conjure from your august but nevertheless dowdy periodical, proud though I am to be a contributor.'

He did have a line in pomposity, but as this went hand in hand with an endearingly open mild fraudulence, which in turn overlaid a stoatish shrewdness, no one ever seemed to mind.

'Tom, let us not pretend to one another that you have anything but the ethics of an alley cat.'

He pursed his lips in protest.

'A vulnerable and much-loved alley cat, but an alley cat nonetheless,' I went on. 'And although I don't want to have an editorial conversation in front of Milo here —'

'It's never stopped you in the past,' he interjected.

'— I do think the *Arts* deserves better than the impoverished load of junk you've been serving up so far. Where's the fire? Where's the sparkle? Where are the little items gleaned at the stage door? Where is that fresh-from-the-dressing-room feeling? Those hot publishing scoops?'

Here Tom looked accusingly at Milo, who shrugged and pulled a face.

'The tittle-tattle from the first-night party? The raised eyebrows at the gallery opening? Even the odd spit and sizzle from the House? You do it for everyone else.'

'That, surely, is the problem,' said Milo, applying himself to the menu.

'I hear what you're saying,' said Tom, looking browbeaten.

'What about Paris? Berlin? New York?' I was remorseless.

'Talking of which, how's Flora?' Milo interceded.

'I hear she's making quite a name for herself,' I answered, betraying my own purpose for one of my favourite subjects.

'So do I,' added Tom, who hardly knew her, grateful of the deflection.

'Tell you what, Wilf,' said Milo. 'Why don't you go over to

121

New York to see her? You could do a piece about what it's like being the new kid on the literary block – you know she's setting up on her own?'

I gazed at him admiringly.

'Brilliant,' I said. 'I shall do it.'

'Might wake up that crummy little mag of yours, anyway.'

'If you had ideas for books like you had that idea just then, you might be more than a mere publishing skivvy.'

'Seconds out,' called Tom, now entirely in the clear. 'What are you going to eat?'

Milo's idea grew and grew. I conceived a storyline: not simply one piece about what Flora was up to, but several at two-monthly intervals, like a slowly evolving soap, centring on one character, but with many more intertwined. A kind of documentary biography, but recorded by a camera on a slow release, like nature films that speed up a tree's growth or the billowing of a cloud; each episode composed to mark a dramatic shift in Flora's career, which wasn't all that difficult since the woman appeared to be storming New York with awesome celerity.

She had taken an apartment in Greenwich Village. In the evening the local bars and restaurants filled with happening people, and Flora was very definitely one of them. She happened, as it were, with electrifying effectiveness. When I got out there for my first endeavours at slow-release reportage, to which she had at first infuriatingly affected indifference – she was picking up some bad habits, and that eighties can't-see-you-I'm-too-busy-to-notice-you power kick was one of them – her nights seemed unending. The standard pattern appeared to be drinks followed by a party followed by dinner followed by a club, and as soon as I arrived she would charge the lot to my expense account, knowing that I had managed to sell the idea in the States to the emerging and rampaging *Spy* magazine, whose coffers appeared bottomless (as compared to the *Arts*, where we had plenty of bottom but no coffers).

I planned four week-long visits, each at two-monthly intervals, which was all I thought I could get away with, and, in eighties parlance, went for it, bobbing along in the slipstream of Flora's small black dress and padded shoulders. Lunch might be at Michael's, if breakfast had not been, with a gravel-voiced publisher of legendary coke-intake from a boutique publishing house, and the two of them would indulge in a molten flirtation of such intensity that it left me feeling breathless and mute.

'We shipped seventy-five thousand of Clara's new one before publication. Have you read it? Here it is. She's signed it. Specially for you. She said, "What shall I put?" I said, "Oh, to the sexiest agent in New York City, including Trixie Bagnall." '

'Is that what she's put?'

'Well, I *am* her publisher, so she owes me a favour. Of course that's what she put.'

'I'll read it tonight.'

'Do that. I'll call you tomorrow and ask you what you think. It's hot. You'll love it. Sort of upscale Judith Krantz.'

'I know. I know her work.'

As she spoke she wound some of her thick mass of black hair behind her head in a fast, stretching motion which revealed the tectonic splendour of her neck, then shot a scorching smile at our companion.

'Who or what is Trixie Bagnall?' I asked, utterly at sea.

The hair was released, the smile transmuted to fiery disdain. She was being tropical.

'Top agent, darling. Do keep up. Big on suntan, silver bangles and pounces like a cat. Bit of a cliché, but effective.'

'So you're from London?' asked the publisher, kindly. His name was Vernon. I wasn't sure it was possible to be cool and also be called Vernon, but you can get away with a lot in New York. 'Do you know Jimmy Spalding? He's a friend of mine.'

'He's my proprietor.'

'You make him sound like your landlord, Wilf,' said Flora.

'Well, I suppose he is.'

'He's also one of your oldest friends. And mine.'

'Yes, he is. In a way. Sometimes easy to lose sight of, that. Tell me,' I went on, anxious to change the subject, 'how often do you see Flora at a party in any one week?'

'Not nearly often enough,' he replied, and turned a full-beam tungsten-filament headlight of a smile upon her. 'So you know Clara's work? How well? Very well?'

'You could say that.'

'She's not thinking of moving, is she? She hasn't spoken to me about that.'

'Vernon,' said Flora, and here the pair engaged in eye-contact that approached nuclear fission, 'you know I can't discuss things of that sort with you.'

'Why didn't you drop the formalities and have sex on the table?' I asked in the cab afterwards. 'The entire restaurant was beside itself in anticipation. The disappointment was palpable.'

'Are you jealous, darling?'

'Of course I am. So is this Clara woman moving? Moving where? And why should we care? Hardly headline news, I would have thought.'

'Moving agents, pie-face.' To my relief, she was turning back into her more recognizable self.

'I see. And is she?'

'Oh yes. But what Vernon doesn't know is that she is going to be moving publishers, too. Unless —'

'Unless what?'

'Unless he pays about ten times what he's paying her now.'

'And will he?'

'He will.'

'And will he go out of business in so doing?'

'He might.'

'But will he?'

'It's likely.'

'Would his patent desire to sleep with you have anything to do with this?'

She giggled in a girlish way I didn't like. 'Oh, Wilf. You're so coarse. Of course it has.'

124

They lunch fast in New York, so we were back in her office on East 60th Street and Park Avenue by two-thirty, time for forty-five minutes of hanging on her lips, sipping like an attentive humming-bird, before being unceremoniously ejected in favour of the business of the day. I made the most of it.

'So tell me, Flora,' I began, as I slouched on the warm leather and hauled out the tape-recorder. 'What makes a good agent?'

'*Well.*' I could tell instantly this was going to be Grand Guignol. 'You may well ask.' Flora tilted her chair back behind the desk and turned to face out of the window on to the small backyard, filled with palms and *fatsia Japonica*. She gathered her hair and let it fall over the backrest, hooked one long, viciously heeled leg over another and put her hands behind her head. 'Let's see. There are a number of definable approaches to the agent's art, some more effective than others. One can count them rapidly off as follows. There's the boisterously amusing: waggish and laddish and hail-fellow-well-met. There's the thumpingly bullying: condescending, stupid and unstoppable. There's the unfathomably mysterious: sphinx-like, long on *hauteur*. There's the deceptively matey. There's the bustlingly matronly. There's the querulously whiney. There's the instantaneously dismissive, with the drop-dead sneer or the shriek of laughter. We all do that from time to time. There's the extravagantly demanding, naming sums which beggar belief. There's the showbiz swagger. There's the new kid in town. There's the tremulously literary; guaranteed to get editors reaching for their money-boxes, especially the more bone-headed and gullible ones. There's the coolly purring, with its tutting and "Oh, dear me, we'll have to do better than that"-ing. There's the earnestly well meaning. There's the fantastically pompous, though publishers often see through that. Do you want more?'

'What are you?'

'That,' she said, swinging back into position, 'would be telling.'

'That's why I'm asking. I mean' — I saw that she was not disposed towards frivolity — 'let's concentrate on you.'

The phone buzzed.

Instantly her demeanour changed.

'Hello, Harold,' she crooned, in tones lifted straight from the ice-box. 'Oh, have you? Uh-huh. No, do tell me.'

There was a prolonged and high-pitched babble from the earpiece. At one point Flora held it at arm's length, looked at me, raised her eyebrows and yawned theatrically. My heart bled for the poor creature on the other end.

'Well, you can if you want. What would you like to do?'

More babble.

'I'll tell you what *I'm* going to do, Harold. I want three-five for this book.' A prolonged moan came from the phone. 'I know where I can get at least that. I don't think your company has really committed itself to Priscilla's work in the way it should, and that's not a criticism of you, Harold, but it's the truth. The cover was terrible. Those ads just didn't happen. Well, I didn't notice them and I don't know anyone who did. This author deserves better, Harold, and you just need to go away and take another look at your plans for her. Then come back to me.'

The babble rose a semitone in pitch.

'Look, Harold,' snapped Flora suddenly – by this time I was aghast with fear and trembling – 'I think we're going to take a walk. You either pay the price or I get it elsewhere. It's as simple as that.'

What sounded like a subdued shriek emanated from the phone.

'I'm going to be on a plane this time tomorrow. If I don't hear what I want from you before then I'm sending this out to six interested publishers.' Her voice had assumed a testy note. 'It's nothing personal, Harold, but Priscilla has a big future and I need a publisher who can deliver that future. Yes, of course I've discussed it with her. Are you daring to suggest that as her agent – ?' She was ominously threatening now. 'OK. Tomorrow lunchtime, that's right. All right, Harold. I look forward to it.'

She replaced the receiver.

126

'So that would be the electric cattle-prod approach, would it?' I asked.

She gave me a distant look.

'If I may paraphrase Wellington, I don't know what you did to Harold, but you scared the hell out of me,' I went on. 'Do you think there's anything left on the end of that phone? A smouldering, bloody heap of flesh, perhaps?'

She brightened.

'You liked it? Was I devastating?'

'Devastating.' I nodded. 'Devastating you can do.'

She looked thoughtful.

'Perhaps I should have gone a little higher,' I heard her murmur.

'Thirty-five thousand sounds like a lot to me.'

She stared blankly.

'Isn't that what you meant? Three-five?'

'Add a nought, Wilf. I wouldn't pick up the phone for the figure you've got in mind.'

She threw a set of keys at me.

'Here. Let yourself in. I'll be back at six-thirty. And make the vodka substantial.'

I tottered into the sunshine.

Her apartment was mostly bed and television; a huge white divan and a vast screen in one corner, with a washing-machine in the kitchen and a small glass-topped round table in what served as the dining space, whereon Flora would hold hot literary suppers with small but evidently nutritious fare usually featuring fava beans.

I, of course, slept on the floor, which I didn't mind because I loved New York and I sort of loved Flora (different from the way I sort of loved Helen, but I'll come to that), and I very definitely loved the way my articles were causing a sensation at home, where the idea of a British literary agent smiting the city of power shoulders, power breakfasts and power hair was intoxicating.

So I came back to New York and Flora three times more that

year, and I suppose I would be distorting the truth if I denied the fact that some time after my first visit, indeed on the second visit, second night thereof, may its memory never fade, we slipped into bed together and stayed there, and if any men reading this want to know what it's like finally climbing between the sheets with a tall, perfectly formed, drop-dead gorgeous, silken-skinned woman whom you have desired from afar for many years, it was strangely not the fiasco so beloved of our comic masters. It was, in fact, just as good as you can possibly imagine it. Probably better.

For three nights we made love into the small hours and awoke hollow-eyed at dawn for more. Then I noticed something.

'Tell me. . .' I murmured to Flora, as my tongue caressed her left ear lobe.

'Don't talk,' she said. I obliged happily, and ran the tip of my tongue into her ear instead. Her body stiffened with pleasure, and she drove her nails into my ribs by way of return. She was nothing if not a powerful lover.

The thought would not leave me, however, and as I lay watching the television afterwards I returned to it.

'Why do you never switch it off?'

'Mmmm?' She stretched languorously and turned on her side. The sight of her shoulder-blades made me want to start all over again. Immediately.

'The television. It's always on. Always. At night you only turn the sound off. Why is that?'

There was no response. The shoulder-blades proved too much, and I curled myself round her.

I could not rid myself of the knowledge, thereafter, that I would never be the subject of Flora's absolutely undivided attention. Not if even the television could be a competitor. Nor did I ever lose sight of the fact that Flora's apparent and enthusiastic interest in me, Wilf Wellingborough, might have had something to do with the increasing glamour that was attaching itself to her because of my pieces for *Arts Unlimited* and *Spy*. But all in all we were pretty damn pleased with ourselves.

And naturally, as an outward manifestation of our twinned and ever-improving destinies, we were pretty pleased to be lovers. And, what the hell, we liked each other.

Then, one night as I was kneeling by the bed, my head between Flora's thighs and my tongue rapidly bringing her to a sensational climax ('Eat me,' she would command, and I would happily oblige, nibbling her with my lips, cradling and lapping her clitoris with my tongue), I heard the television announcer crowing:

'And now the moment you've been waiting for, it's new, it's compulsive, it's the show that's sweeping the nation coast-to-coast. '*Hitch . . . oooorrrrr Ditch!*'

My tongue ceased in mid-tremble. I particularly noticed the inflection on the 'or', like a little tune. In later years it became famous, that inflection, and everyone said it was intended to echo 'Here Comes the Bride'.

'Don't stop,' moaned Flora, faintly.

There it was on the screen. Horsefall's show. Primetime NBC. Big, crass, embarrassing, mawkish, insane. Wildly successful. My title. *Hitch or Ditch.*

'Fuck me. Fuck me,' I stuttered, standing up.

A foot was pushed between my thighs to hook me back on to the bed.

'What do you think I'm trying to do?'

I struggled up again.

'No, stop, look, listen.'

'Why are you talking like the Green Cross Code?'

'It's Humphrey Horsefall's show. He told me all about it. And it's my title. It was my idea.'

'You know Humphrey Horsefall? This is his? It's dynamite. Everyone's talking about it.' Flora studied the screen thoughtfully. 'I wonder what the book rights situation is?'

'Know him? Of course I do. He writes a column for us. I'm going to kill him.'

He seemed genuinely concerned when I rang the next day.

'I'm sorry, Wilf, you know I was never sure it was going

129

to come off, it was touch and go the whole way through, and then when it did happen, I had to leave the Beeb as you know –'

'I didn't know it was to do this. And what about my title?'

He sounded puzzled.

'You can't copyright a title, you know, Wilf. Anyway, now that we *are* talking about this,' he coughed hesitantly, 'I'm spending a lot of time in the States at the moment and I think I'll probably have to forgo the column for a while. If you want a replacement, probably only temporary, there's a wonderful young man writing pieces for *Time Out*. . .'

'Never mind that. What about my title? I mean, you do know it's mine, don't you? You do remember?'

'. . . frightfully good stuff he's writing, very acerbic. *Any*way, good to talk, coming to your side of the Pond tomorrow, got a hundred and ten things to do, my last contribution's in the post, really must be going. . .' He wittered and faded, the phone clicked, and there was silence.

'Just a thank-you would have been nice,' as I said to Flora.

But the petty gripes of others concerned her little, save inasmuch as they could be transformed alchemically into gossip. Gossip ran in her veins and sparkled in her eyes; it turned her on more than sex. When I was with her the air was alive with it, distracting as a swarm of flies. And as we lay awake at night in the hot New York summer, the talk inevitably dwindled to our own knotty, immovable points of discontent. Flora always returned to Jimmy, and I to Grace. Sometimes I felt it was like one of those slapstick scenes where one party has a piece of sticking plaster stuck to them, and no matter what they do they can't get rid of it; it turns up on an elbow, or a cuff, or the shoulder, or the back of a leg. It's a nuisance, but he just can't shift it. So it was with the grubby remnants of our obsessions; though it was never clear to me how far Flora had taken her interest in Jimmy, and she always changed the subject when I crept stealthily up on it hoping to surprise her, with mine it was always there, nagging away even when I thought it long forgotten.

130

This irked Flora.

'It wasn't your fault her father was killed. And I just don't think it's true you were emotionally inadequate, or even immature – though, on the whole. . . OK, I won't pursue it. No, all that's just cant. You simply can't face the truth, which is that she went off you because she went off you. It happens.'

'Because I was immature. Because of my lack of emotional imagination.'

'Try sensitivity.'

'Well, there you are.'

'Were you a brute?'

'No.'

'Well, then, there *you* are.'

'Will it happen to us?'

'Don't be crass. Of course it will. Did anyone ever find out about that accident? I bet Jimmy had a hand in it.'

'Don't be absurd. He may be everything you think he is, he might even be a bit of a gangster, but I don't think he'd kill someone. Not someone he knew.'

'Do you think he forced Ferdy to sell the *Arts*? Did he have something on him? Something that Ferdy couldn't bear anyone knowing about?'

'He liked Ferdy. Stop speculating.'

'I think it's weird, that's all. It was an accident, wasn't it?'

'Flora, either you want a conspiracy or you don't. Do make up your mind.'

Her mind had already moved on.

'Of course the big, hot story,' she announced suddenly, 'is your old friend.'

I immediately envisaged a thousand acquaintances with teeth bared overtaking me jeeringly in the fast lane of life's motorway, or highway as I suppose I should have said, given where we were.

'Kitty,' she said, taking my look of nervous anticipation for one of imbecilic expectation. 'Kitty Greaves.'

'Oh, ah.'

131

'Condé Nast have asked her to come over and do a start-up. Sort of *New Yorker* crossed with *Vogue*, apparently.'

'That sounds fantastic.'

'It does, doesn't it? I mean, literally so. Completely impossible, one might add.'

'One might. If not utterly absurd.'

'If not sensationally stupid. But that's what they want to do. They want to capitalize on the emerging artistic and intellectual credibility of fashion, and the increasing fashionability of intellectual endeavour.'

'I thought intellectual endeavour had always been reasonably fashionable. I mean, why do it, otherwise?'

'Listen, this isn't my copy, this is the advertising spec I'm quoting from.'

'Will it work?'

'Who knows? Yes, probably, for the first four issues, but after that not really as well as they hoped it would. It's a hybrid. Hybrids never work.'

'So why do it?'

'Because it might work.'

Nations are run on such thinking.

'It might work. And Kitty will make it work.' I reflected on the qualities of my old boss. Passionate, fiery, committed, emotional, energetic to the point of frenzy, fingers alarmingly attached to every button that dared to raise its little head above the vast control panel of media life, combative to a point that would have made Ridley Scott's Alien retire from the ring with an etiolated 'Aw, shucks', she had every chance of screwing up or winning through, both gloriously. 'At any rate it won't be boring.'

'So I'm throwing a party for her.'

'At-a-girl.'

Flora was amazing like that. I suppose it's a New York thing; not a New Yorker thing, because New Yorkers are laid back, cynical and generally easy-going in the way that anyone born into the most extraordinary city on the planet would be. Like people born into capital cities always are: they know they are heirs to a lifetime of intense stimulation, so why hurry? They can always pass the time being rude to people instead. But New York attracts the world on the make, people with blistering, unhappy energy, energy that is never satisfied, that gnaws into itself when it's not making a difference sixty times a minute. They just can't sit on their tails. They want to make money, they want to design clothes, they want to paint pictures, they want to sell anything they can sell, they want to acquire companies, they want to put on shows and manage bands and orchestras, they want to deal in property and jewels and futures and derivatives and toys and lawnmowers and cars and vans and ships and politics and human rights and arms and sex and more property and railways and every single kind of commodity you can think of from swimming-pools to buttons to the rotten fat pimps' rings in Diamond Jewelry Way to bagels and mineral rights and restaurants and cheeses and olives and a really rather considerable amount of crime. If there's anything in the world out of which money can be made, someone in New York will have found a way to do it, with a twenty-four-hours-to-live mayfly intensity. But they probably won't actually be *from* New York. They'll be people like Flora and Kitty. And their parties will be to die for.

Flora liked her parties big, beautiful, outrageous and preferably headline-making. The sort that strip paint from the walls.

The one for Kitty was packed. A bijou yard on the corner of East 60th and Park is madly expensive, but it is still only a bijou yard, and Flora had invited New York's finest – and a few hundred extras, for luck – on a day when I found myself standing under the dripping massed air-conditioning units on 42nd and Seventh hoping for a freezing drop down the back of my neck to ease the effect of the stultifying heat, dallying outside hotel rooms for the cool rush of canned air, and shying away when overheating car engines drew up close. On the way to the party I careered up Fifth Avenue past the Presbyterian Church at breakneck speed in a cab whose driver's name appeared to be written in hieroglyphics. Out of the corner of my eye I saw

133

someone in a wheelchair topple in front of the thundering cavalcade of yellow cabs and be struck whirling like a top by a speeding chrome bumper. We didn't stop. The streets and pavements boiled and bubbled with endless roadworks, tall orange-and-white chequered chimneys belched smoke, pipes ran here and there from silver canisters to manhole covers.

'Who's going to be there?' I had asked Flora.

'The usual.'

'Everyone?'

'Exactly.'

As I got out of the cab the driver noticed my accent and gave me a ferocious glare.

'You from out of town?' he rasped suspiciously.

High summer meant a rash of small black dresses occupied by cool girls and light Versace suits occupied by perspiring boys. I found myself next to Richard Branson, the editor of the *New York Times* and a prominent movie producer who, Flora had warned me, had been in Ted Kennedy's party at Chappaquiddick. I rapidly realized that none of them knew each other particularly well, but all of them were significant enough to feel that they should be paid respect, and the result was a stunning banality in the level of conversation. We were just considering the Warhol retrospective at the Museum of Modern Art with all the alacrity and *joie de vivre* of a 747 running out of fuel and going down over Buenos Aires when I caught sight of a thin, weaselly set of features I knew, and made my excuses.

'Simon!' I almost yelled, catching him by the arm like the importunate beggar I was.

'Wilfred,' he murmured, with a subtle, knowing glance at my erstwhile companions. 'Having a good time?'

'Outstanding, on the whole. But how are *you*? I haven't seen you for ever.'

Oddly this was true. Simon Spicer's column hadn't lasted long; he had departed the shores of the *Arts* for grander things, and since then I had only seen the back of his head here and there as he became more and more sought after and more and more

134

apparently elusive at the same time, thus stoking up his reputation exponentially. Academia hates any of their number who succeed in the grisly world of trade and commerce (understandably, I've always felt; the pure stream of intellectual pursuit sullied by the depredations of Mammon, etc.), but he managed to have *le monde* slavering over his every word, whenever it could be got out of him.

The crowd swayed with one of its episodic spasms and I trod heavily on Jack Nicholson's foot. He was very nice about it.

'My God, she's got pulling power,' I said to Simon, referring to Flora.

'Hasn't she?' he returned, looking over my shoulder. This was the sort of party where looking over people's shoulders was not impolite but mandatory, proof of prestige. I did it; my interlocutor did it; if one watched carefully one could see everyone at it, their mouths galloping away in accordance with one evidently sparkling region of their mind, while their eyes ruthlessly raked their fellow guests in accordance with another. It made one wonder at the awesome power of the human brain that we could all perform two such very different activities at the same time. Someone ought to do scientific research into it.

Simon's glance, however, had an intensity that made me follow it. Just behind me was the belle of the ball, Kitty Greaves, firing on all cylinders, gyrating and glittering like a disco-ball with very slightly more class. I realized he had not been referring to Flora. And pulling power was certainly what Kitty had that night; she was radiant with hot-ness, in-ness and happening-ness. New York was her playpen.

When she saw Simon, however, the effect was extraordinary. Her eyes rolled self-deprecatingly, the edge of her mouth turned under in uncharacteristic self-mockery, and she propelled herself swooningly into his arms. Quite stomach-turningly soppy.

'Wellingborough,' she murmured, catching sight of me as she clasped Simon hungrily. There was no room for me to run. Her eyelashes batted at me with their accustomed shamelessness. Suddenly she sprang back to life.

135

'Darling, that magazine is a feeble shadow of its former self.'

'I'm not surprised,' said Simon. 'He's never there to edit it.'

I was wounded.

Kitty whispered something smouldering into Simon's ear, gazed at him scorchingly, and was swallowed up by the adoring crowd.

I looked Simon up and down. He was dressed in a beautifully flowing Italian suit of deep grey and wore no tie, but apart from that he looked no more nor less attractive than he always had done, which is to say an intriguing blend of the anaemic and the vampiric. He gave me a knowing smile of consummate complacency and then he, too, was gone.

She was a powerful lover, Flora, but she was a flighty one, too. And as the novelty of my pieces wore off, so, I felt, did her interest in me. She began to pick holes in my standards of hygiene, to complain about the clothes I left lying around, to ask pointedly whether I was intending to finish the half-eaten roll I had left on top of the washing-machine. Little things like that.

Soon after I returned from my fourth sojourn with her, I received a call from Jimmy, asking whether I was going to apply myself to improving the circulation figures of *Arts Unlimited* or spend my time socializing in New York. He didn't mind which it was going to be, he said, just so long as I made up my mind and told him. Soon. Within twenty-four hours.

'Well, they're not slumping. On the other hand, they're not soaring,' said Henry, with infinite sagacity. I had called a crisis meeting at the *Arts* immediately, in search of practical remedies, but as I looked about me at my illustrious colleagues I had begun to wonder why I had bothered. They were slumped on repro eighteenth-century kitchen chairs I had purchased from Phillips' auction rooms for next to nothing for the sake of our finances, and my collection of Conran uplighters failed to rescue the office from a feeling of desultory dilapidation.

'Thank you, Henry,' I replied, rubbing my forehead carefully

136

to try to stop my frontal lobe acting up. 'No need to minute that, Bomber.'

'You want minutes?'

'Never mind. The point is that we have a circulation of ten thousand and Mr Spalding wants us to double it.'

'Impossible. Crazy,' opined Adam, loyally. Ad sales weren't all they might have been.

'Nice to do, though,' said Minna, who occasionally thought like the accountant she was, wistfully.

'Why this sudden interest in circulation, anyway?' I mused aloud.

'I think it's understandable, isn't it?' put in Sibella, cuttingly. She might have saved me at the *Private Eye* lunch, but I wasn't sure this entitled her to take liberties. 'Obviously you've been too busy focusing on quality to worry about quantity, but it matters to Jimmy, I think. Anyway, we *still* haven't replaced Humphrey Horsefall.' Sibella had become rather a fixture at the *Arts* recently, and was forever popping into the office to deliver her copy and sit around and chat noisily. I loved having her there, though I couldn't help wondering why she wasn't contributing-editing away at her own gaff.

Before I could open my mouth she said, 'What about Paul Sterne?'

My jaw must have dropped a yard.

'Why on earth would we want him? How do you know about him anyway?'

'Milo Glover. I met him at Joan Collins's launch party. He was telling me about him.'

'Well, apart from his rather successful attempt to ruin his wedding, I don't see what Milo would have to tell you about Paul Sterne.'

'He's commissioned him to write a book.'

'He's commissioned him to write a *what*?'

'A book. You know, rectangular thing with pages.'

'But why? What book?'

'It's already written, isn't it?' put in Bomber. 'Everyone's

137

talking about it. It's a sort of epic poem about life at Oxford and after. It's supposed to be a rhyming *Dance to the Music of Time*. You know him, do you, Wilf? You're probably in it, then.'

I reapplied pressure to my frontal lobes.

'You're out of touch, Wilf,' said Sibella.

'He *has* been away a lot,' said Minna.

'Maybe he should get Flora to come over here,' said Bomber. 'So we can see more of him.'

'Maybe he should,' said Sibella.

'Could you stop talking about me as if I weren't here?' I asked. I didn't like the look Sibella threw in my direction.

As it turned out, Flora flew in of her own accord.

'I'm here to see a potential client,' she breathed down the phone, in an ecstasy of acquisitiveness. 'You'll never guess who. And I want to see *Madam Butterfly*,' she added as an afterthought.

'Whom,' I corrected. 'I can, actually.'

'Who, then?' she asked, unprovoked.

'Paul Sterne.'

'Oh.' She sounded faintly disappointed. 'You *are* on the ball.' I allowed myself a wry smile. 'He's the new Pope, you know.'

'Isn't that blasphemous?'

'Alexander Pope, imbecile.'

'Have you read it?'

'Of course not. How could I?'

'You could ask Milo.'

'He won't let me near it. Poor lamb, he obviously thinks it's his ticket to the stars.'

'I'm sure it's terrible rubbish.'

'Me too.'

'I mean, no one in the States will want to know.'

'I'm sure you're right.'

Even I was not that naïve.

'Flora, are you trying to pretend to me that Paul has written a dull book so that you can have first dibs before anyone else does?'

'To be honest, Wilf, this concerns me significantly less than

138

whether you can obtain tickets to *Madam Butterfly*. What about it?'

'The one at the Coliseum?'

'How many *Madam Butterfly*s are playing in London?' She was sarcastic.

'Three, actually. The English National Opera at the Coliseum, the Robin Hood version at Stratford East and the gay low-life one upstairs at the Royal Court.'

'Touché, baby. We'll take the Coliseum.'

There's something a trifle galling about throwing your heart and soul into a worthy, well-regarded and sometimes amusing arts periodical only to find after a while that it remains simply worthy, well-regarded and sometimes amusing. You might ask: what else did I expect? And, not one to duck self-criticism, I might add: who was I to complain, anyway? Yet something intrinsic to the human condition means editors do like circulation figures to move upward. It's a natural law, like $E = mc^2$. Especially when they have just been prodded hard by the boss.

As Bomber said, 'I don't understand it. Our contributors are of the very highest calibre.'

And as Henry added, 'What you need is the spark of controversy, old son,' before leaning back with a supercilious gleam in his eye and that thin waspish smile on his lips.

'Betray some secrets,' said Flora, as we leaned against the polished wooden rail that runs round the great opening cut like a giant eye between the ground and first floors of the Coliseum, through which we could watch the crowds below. They seemed to mingle with the swaying rhythm of anemones in a sea-pool left behind by the tide. We were spotting minor celebrities – 'Isn't that one there by the pillar always on *Blankety Blank*? Not that I watch it, of course.' 'No, she's that Channel 4 newsreader.' 'I like who he's talking to.' 'She was at school with me.' 'She's very beautiful, isn't she?' 'She's good at that; it's what she does best.' And so on. Very restful after a moody, sweaty day, helped by the crisp, cold glass of wine I pressed to my forehead from time to time. A little cleansing opera; what a treat for a steamed-up Englishman after a steamy English summer's day.

So I only half heard her. A small gathering beneath us had caught my attention.

'Look, it's Kitty. What's she doing here? Has that magazine flopped already? And isn't that Jimmy? That's an unfortunate coincidence.'

The dark-haired tornado, Kitty Greaves, dressed entirely in white, was directing a look of undiluted scorn at my beloved proprietor. Then, leaning slightly forward as he walked by with some blonde on his arm, she deftly flung the contents of her glass in his face. A lot of it splashed on the girl. The nervous smile that had been playing about his lips as he caught sight of her – a look I had never seen in his face before and certainly haven't seen since – turned to one of drenched bemusement. His smile didn't disappear, it just became more fatuous.

'How utterly delicious,' I muttered.

Kitty turned her back in a posture that was pure flamenco, and stalked into the crowd. Even the back of her head looked withering.

'Wilf, let's get another drink,' Flora urged. I was surprised by her indifference.

'Did you see that?'

'Yes, of course I did. But I really want another drink. Come on, Wilf. Now.' She was plucking forcibly at my arm.

'But look. Look at Jimmy. It's priceless. I bet nothing like that has ever happened to him before. I mean, what theatre. This has got to be written up. I'll put it in Tom's diary. No, I can't do that, can I?' The heat must have been getting to me. I looked back and saw with the dull comprehension that attends such moments that the blonde so assiduously running her handkerchief over the lapels of his double-breasted suit, kissing the champagne from his sodden features, giggling into his face and causing him to grin broadly, was someone I knew.

I felt Flora's arm through mine.

'I told you to come away.'

I was pretty stuffed up and misty-eyed after that. I don't think I said much. The performance may have been good, or it may not. All I was aware of was that Grace and Jimmy were sitting side by side somewhere in the auditorium, having happily enjoyed mutual dampness.

Afterwards, we ate Japanese. The restaurant was just off Wardour Street, and as we sliced briskly through the sludgy Soho night air, side-stepping the drunks, the revellers, the hailers of taxis and the tramps roaring from doorways, I found it in myself to utter: 'So how long has that been going on?'

'I don't know.' There was a petulant note in her voice.

'Wilf, I'm getting a little unhappy about this,' she said as we sat down to sushi. 'I mean, who cares? They've always had a thing for each other. And you and I may not be — but you know, we are —'

And we looked at each other, and we both knew we weren't, nor were ever going to be, real lovers. Lovers, yes; really in love, no. I minded about Grace and Jimmy. Whatever they had going, I minded about it. My heart was pounding, I couldn't concentrate, my palms were sweaty, and horrible emotions were gnawing at my gut. I hadn't known I'd mind, so there was the additional shock of finding that I did. The minding, and the shock.

That night, when we went back to Flora's hotel room, paradoxically, we seemed to make love for the first time. Somehow we had been jolted into a new awareness of each other. In the darkness our skin slid together, unbearably soft and snake-like. When we found each other, it was with a fullness and an ecstasy we had not known before. There was sadness, and sympathy, and kindness, and thoughtfulness. It was the beginning of the end, but, looking back on it, perhaps it wasn't such a bad beginning, in its way.

What Friends Are For

'You're fired, Wilf.'

The words lived with me day after day as week after week lengthened into month after month and the *Arts'* decrepit circulation figures remained ineluctably stable. I heard them in my dreams, and when I awoke; I heard them as I stared into my ever-more-sunken eyes while shaving; as I pulled on my socks and scrunched lugubriously through cornflakes; as I boarded the tube at Stockwell, where I had bought a tiny flat after Grace and I split the proceeds from the one in Notting Hill; as I squared my shoulders once more to another day at the offices of the venerable organ. They nagged me at parties in the West End and at dinners in Hampstead. The more the world sought my opinion on everything from Salman Rushdie to salmon fishcakes, the more I seemed to hear Jimmy's lips whispering the dread words in my ear, like some subconscious devil.

'You're fired, Wilf.'

Or, as he might have said, according to the fashionable managerial hypocrisy of the time, 'I'm letting you go, Wilf.' As if he were doing me a favour, while simultaneously releasing me into the abyss.

So I beavered and hustled. I fired Bomber in a fit of pique after she lost a book review by Germaine Greer (whom I had been cultivating assiduously), then had to go to her on bended knees (literally: I tracked her down to a pub in Finchley where the floor was so filthy it took three washes to get the stains out of my jeans) to win her back again; I brought in a parade of new columnists, some of whom even I had not heard of, and set the magazine spinning through a bewildering array of typefaces. For a disastrous trial period I changed it from a limp fortnightly to a larger, stiffer-spined monthly, like *The Face* only without pictures. It stopped selling immediately, so I changed it back.

And if I felt Jimmy's wingéd chariot, or at least his new Roller, purring threateningly at my back, I found that I hated him, not for his power over me, but for whatever was going on between him and Grace. When I was with Flora, on one of her increasing number of predatory trips scouting for fresh, innocent, exploitable talent, I couldn't talk about anything else. Not surprisingly, her attention drifted.

'Do you think Helen knows? He treats her terribly badly, you know.'

It was another early evening in the Crepuscule.

'You *have* mentioned it once or twice recently. Here's Milo, thank God. Milo! Over here! Come and save me!'

'I didn't know Milo was coming.'

'I invited him.'

'Evidently,' I said, peevishly. I peered at my old friend with suspicion.

'Milo, is that a suit? Moreover, is it a new one? Of a fashionable variety, and unashamedly unstructured?'

'Milo's special now, aren't you, Milo? Milo is hot,' cooed Flora, stroking him appreciatively as he sat down.

'Flora has just sold Paul's book in the States. Very effectively.' They exchanged molten looks, the kind people give one another when they are starring in the same success story. Come to think of it, I'd been there with her once myself.

'How much?'

'You're so crude, Wilf. Six.'

'Six hundred dollars? Or six hundred thousand?'

'Figures. Six figures.'

'For a long poem about undergraduate life in a British university? Give me a break.'

Milo was huffy.

'It's going to be a sensation, Wilf. Everyone's raving about it.'

'Oh, I know. I've got the proofs in my briefcase. But, Flora, how did you get the Americans to buy it?'

'I said it was a cross between J. D. Salinger and Hilaire Belloc.'

'And is it?'

'Yes. Some of it. Quite a lot of it, in fact. He has a unique voice.'

'Oh, yes?'

'Yes. He is a pearl beyond price.'

'I thought you said six figures.'

'Wilf, are you going to be obstreperous all evening?'

'I might be.'

'At least we've got him off Jimmy and Grace,' reflected Milo, waving the waitress over for another bottle of Sauvignon. He eyed her appreciatively, plucking a breadstick out of a glass.

'Do you think if I asked her nicely she might chew provocatively on this?' he murmured.

'If you asked her nicely, I'm sure she would.'

'You two are a disgrace,' said Flora.

But as the months went by it didn't get any better. I knew Jimmy was dissatisfied, and I grew restive and irritable because of it. Partly this was because I knew it through hints and rumours and whispers, that unsettling swarm of ironic asides and half-understood slynesses which only coalesce into a meaningful picture afterwards, their sense leaping out at you when you're in the bath or posting a letter or popping the top off a milk-bottle. 'How are you getting on there?' 'He's a hard taskmaster, isn't he?' 'Did I hear you were thinking of leaving?' 'It's very upmarket for that stable, isn't it?' 'Does he interfere a great deal? I bet he's itching to get his fingers into your editorial meetings.' 'How's the circulation? Are you giving Jimmy what he wants?'

When I talked to Jimmy he was cool and distant. 'It's up to you, Wilf, you're the man in charge. I trust you to know how to keep the show on the road.' Why on earth should I? When he gave me the job I thought he could see the makings of a great editor in me. He was successful; he knew what he was doing; my talents must have been manifest. Somewhere between then and now they had obviously ceased to be so, and if he didn't know what they were, I was none the wiser.

Bomber was surly and mutinous after my treatment of her, but Sibella was supportive to the point of omnipresence. She was a cornucopia of ideas: she discovered in Henry a unique and hitherto untapped genius for wordplay, and immediately set him to run a quiz page, full of impossible conundrums, clerihew competitions and a crossword of such fiendishness that it became a legend, the very essence of cussed awkwardness followed by sublime illumination. She persuaded Horsefall to continue writing for us as our man in New York, penning waspish pieces about the marathon social scene of which he was rapidly becoming a connoisseur, being welcome as the producer of the syndicated hit show *Hitch or Ditch*. Paul Sterne was appointed books editor the week before his own book was published, a fortnight before it went to No. 1 on the *Sunday Times* bestseller list. Soon after this Milo was asked to take over the television column, shortly before he was made Editor-in-Chief of Pegasus Books and started to be written up as the smartest thing in publishing, gaining a reputation for leading the new set of media *jeunesse dorée*, 'a restlessly innovative and entrepreneurial gang on the outer fringes of which lie the Nigel Dempster wannabe Tom Phipps and dark horse Wilf Wellingborough, under whose faltering if charming hand lies the tiller of the senescent *Arts Unlimited*', as the *Observer* so kindly put it.

'Tom,' I said to him. The Crepuscule was almost deserted, and we had been there some time. We were at our usual table, and, outside, the lights of Beak Street glowed thinly. People hurried past in the early autumn chill. 'Something has to be done. Otherwise you and I will languish in obscurity for ever more.' I stirred my coffee moodily.

'Well, Wilf,' he said. His fat fingers clasped together over his voluminous stomach as he lolled expansively back in his chair and blew a large smoke ring, which curled in and out of itself as it rolled towards the ceiling. 'I have a story which you may like to run, though I suspect you may not have the bottle for it. Plenty wouldn't. It's about David Vale.'

'Oh, good.'

'Wait. He appears to have been showing a great deal of interest in a young man in his employ. Buys him presents, takes him off to the opera, even took him on holiday.'

'Nothing wrong with that,' I replied, wearily. 'I mean, you might be homophobic, Tom, but I'm not. More to the point, neither are our readers.'

'That's not the point. What *is* the point is that the young man in question doesn't return his interest.'

'I didn't know the Amphibian was gay.'

'Why did you think he was called the Amphibian? By sea and land. AC/DC. Billy Bothways.'

'I thought it was because he looks like a frog.'

Tom considered this. 'Well, there is that,' he conceded.

'But you think he's gay?'

'Oh, he is. For the purposes of this story he is, at any rate. And the crux of it is —' He fixed me with a triumphant glare.

'Yes?'

'Because the boy would not return his advances he ran him down so effectively that he managed to get him sacked.'

'The utter shit.'

'Indeed. Good story, isn't it?'

'So why haven't you run it?'

'Too risky. Not many people know the story, and those that do are too scared.'

'Are you sure of it, yourself?' It did sound a shade unlikely.

'Sure I'm sure.'

'It certainly doesn't sound like the Research Bureau to me.'

'Oh, come. As Peter Cook so memorably put it, buggery is the prerogative of the Tory Party.'

'No, I mean that place is as leaky as a sieve.'

'Well. You've been whingeing at me about not giving you anything hot and now I'm giving you something essentially pretty scalding and you turn your nose up at it. Make up your mind, Wilf.' He waved a hand in an unsteady gesture of generosity. 'It's yours if you want it. For my usual fee.'

I was nettled. And what had Flora said? 'Betray some secrets.' I made the decision.

'At the very least,' I remarked meditatively, 'it will make your column more interesting than it normally is.'

It did. Tom's diary had hitherto confined itself to decorous remarks about the tantrums of minor opera singers, with the result that it was merely one notch up from 'Jennifer's Diary'. Now, the words fairly burned a hole in the page.

Sibella was unhappy.

'Ker-ripes, Wilf,' she ejaculated, looking over my shoulder as we prepared for press. Henry, who had already taken a look, was amusing himself by wearing an old Second World War helmet some wag predictably had given to Bomber as a birthday present and which we always insisted on hanging over her chair. He was marching backwards and forwards across my office, every so often presenting arms and accompanying himself with a sound-track of muffled bomb blasts spluttered from the corner of his mouth.

'Hard news,' I said. 'Blue touchpaper about to be lit, Sibella.' At this, Henry's oral battlefield increased in volume and he began to mime fighting his way through enemy territory. We ignored him as best we could.

'It's pretty strong, isn't it? Can you stand it up?'

'That's down to Tom.'

'Does our blessed proprietor know?'

'I think he wants me to run this show,' I opined, testily. 'At least, so he tells me.'

Sibella liked to wear loud colours – bright, primary ones – to compensate for her diminutive form. Her open face, frank and brave as it was, had a startling ability to collapse into a ferocious scowl when she disapproved of something or someone, so that she'd look like a baleful Pekinese.

She was scowling now. What's more, she was wearing a bright blue suit which made her look like a small electric storm.

'I think you should run it past him.'

'I don't think we've got time.'

'Well, have it your way, but I still think you should. It looks risky to me.'

'Sibella, do you think that, as editor, I might be allowed to make an editorial decision?'

Perhaps if she had not irritated me I would have listened to what she was saying. But we had seen so much of her recently that she was making me uneasy. There should have been no real cause for concern: the *Arts* was traditionally a democratic and welcoming organ, and it was quite usual for contributors to drop in and pontificate. But Sibella, because she did so much more than that, was beginning to feel like a fixture. Jimmy's management technique, as I had heard so many times, consisted of placing previously happy people into situations where they could do nothing but loathe each other and be traumatized and unhappy, and it did occur to me, very, very faintly, that he was doing the same to us.

I had not meant to be offensive, but it was too late. She turned on her heel and swept out.

It was make or break. I let the piece go in.

On the day the issue appeared, to blink in the sunlight optimistically for a brief second before being thrust firmly behind such competitors as *Military News* or *Railway Modeller* in newsagents up and down the land, I popped into our local store to see if they had their fortnightly copy on their grimy shelves, and was instead greeted by a tabloid headline that thundered: 'Thatcher's Pet in Gay Office-Boy Claim!' For several seconds I was unable to move. At first I was nonplussed; then it dawned on me that it was a leak, from the printers perhaps, or maybe they had simply been in time to see an early copy. We had never been that stringent about supplying the shops with the *Arts*: I think we were surprised and pleased if it made it into a newsagent at all. Then I was thrilled by the thought that the story was big, really big, bigger than I'd ever thought it was. Then I was horrified for the same reason. Then I was jealous because our thunder was well and truly stolen. Then I read the story, found we had been given liberal credit and was thrilled again, despite the fact that the paper affected never to have heard of the *Arts* while being careful to blame us entirely for the story. The others were in a similar vein: 'Thatcher Protégé in Gay Smear', ran *The Times*. 'Gay Allegations Shake Research Bureau', rumbled the *Telegraph*. 'Did Spurned Advances Get Him the Boot?', burbled the *Mirror*. My head sang as I sat among the crowds on the tube. It sang all the way down Wardour Street, up the stairs and just up until the moment when I began to open the door, which was wrenched from my grasp by a flushed Bomber.

'Thank Christ you're here,' she said, breathlessly. 'Why aren't you answering your phone?'

'I'm not in my office yet,' I replied, reasonably, I thought.

'Your home phone, Wilf. The press are going crazy.'

'I suppose they would be. It may be that I haven't paid the telephone bill. In fact,' I said, remembering the pile of unopened envelopes, all of which looked as if they were after my money, 'that's quite a likely explanation.'

'They're after you big-time, baby. Oh, and Mr Spalding rang. And David Vale's solicitors. And the *Guardian* want to do a profile on you. And *Newsnight* want you and Tom. As do,' she glanced down at a sheet of paper, '*Channel 4 News*, *Any Questions*, the *Today* programme and *Wogan*.'

'*Wogan*? So this is *really* serious? Wellingborough goes commercial. What about *Desert Island Discs*?'

The *Arts* went commercial, too; we went back to press four times that day. The phone was relentless. It seemed as if the entire might of the Tory Party was being hurled against us. Tom was untraceable, and I fended off everything with confident bluster while committing the whole office to the simple duty of locating Phipps. He had just been seen at Patisserie Valerie, he had been seen on his way to *Time Out*, he had lunched at the Groucho, he had been meeting someone at the Savoy; it was a fascinating insight into Tom's world, but it was not much use to us, and it

149

was becoming increasingly obvious that we needed him desperately. My temper began to fray.

'Where the flaming fuck have you been?' I snarled into the receiver when at last Tom came through.

'Hither and yon.'

'Hither and *yon*? Have you *seen* the papers today?'

'Of course I have.' There was a defiant note in his voice I did not like.

'Well? Shouldn't you be here helping me out?'

'Oh, "should". Such a short word with such complex meanings.'

'Seems pretty clear to me. Anyway, never mind semantics. I've been dealing with the media all day and I need better answers than the ones I'm giving.'

'Have you heard from the solicitors?'

'Yes, this morning. Haven't heard from them since, mind you. Maybe they've decided not to bother.'

'Maybe. Maybe they're talking to someone else.'

'Like whom?'

'I should think there's only one candidate. But I must dash. I have a train to catch to Newmarket in half an hour.'

'You're spending a day at the races when your story is bringing the skies down about our heads?'

'*Your* story, Wilf. You're the editor, you know.'

'But Tom, haven't you got *anything*? Notes, maybe, or tapes? Can't we get a statement out of this guy? Can we push him? What have you actually *got*?' The receiver gave a short bark of laughter at my naïvety. 'But Tom,' I said again, 'I mean, I thought you were my friend.' Tears were stinging my eyes. I sounded pathetic, and felt it.

'Oh, I'll be back tomorrow afternoon and we can talk about it then. Don't worry. You must simply remember not to get enmeshed in details. Let the lawyers do that if they have to. Bluster. You'll be brilliant. It's your hour, Wilf. Enjoy.'

I was lulled momentarily.

'Got any good tips, then?' I tried to be jocular.

'Put all your property into someone else's name, I would.'

'For the horses, I mean.'

'Fall Guy in the three-thirty. Rank outsider at thirteen to one.'
There was a chuckle, and the phone went dead.

Obscurely, I felt that I had been had.

I fought the phone until early evening, feeling like I'd gone to sleep in the nursery and woken up in Vietnam, then Henry put his head round the door, without knocking as usual. He had a reassuring solidity about him, and a sympathetic look on his face. The helmet had disappeared; he was back in mufti.

'Come on, boss,' he said.

' "Boss"!' I murmured, eyeing him. 'That implies you work here.'

'Oh, I do,' he returned. 'I'm just not responsible in the way you are.'

'Thanks, dearest.'

'Come on out. We've got a couple of bottles here that are giving us irresistibly flirtatious looks.'

'Who's there?' I asked, warily. I wondered if Sibella had come back.

'Just us chickens. Come on, laddie. Stop moping and start coping. Stir your stumps.'

'I am coping. Being in shock is a big help,' I rejoined. 'You know,' I went on to announce to the waiting assembly of Bomber, Henry, Minna, Adam and six bottles of cheap wine, 'it's in moments like these that you learn who your friends are.'

'Who's been ringing you?' asked Minna. She blinked slowly and vacantly at me. You could tell that she'd been at the antidepressants when she appeared to be looking at a point several feet behind your head. She had dark straight hair that ended in a slight, tidy curl under her chin, and she used to wear tight jumpers and long, shapeless skirts; if she hadn't been so bone thin she would have looked like a poorly constructed sack. But she didn't; she was frail and emaciated and a whiz with figures, but we tried to avoid discussing such things. Her interests lay in the darker and more esoteric philosophers – Hegel and

151

Schopenhauer and Nietzsche – and there was always a Penguin Classic of one or other of them poking out from her bag.

'Absolutely no one at all. No one that didn't want to string me up, that is.'

I say we did not discuss figures, but that's not strictly true: I remember a time when we went for a drink together and after the first gin and tonic she launched into a seemingly endless disquisition on the beauty of mathematical form with specific reference to calculus. As my mathematical education had ceased at an early date and I had difficulty recalling the significance of the square on the hypotenuse I listened to her with rapt but uncomprehending admiration. I told her it seemed a bit of a shame for all those brains to be wasted on the feeble figures of the *Arts*. She had nodded mournfully and replied, 'They are, aren't they?'

Bomber was pulling a face. 'So what's going to happen?'

'We fight on,' I said, with what I hoped was a wearily heroic smile.

A small ironic cheer went up.

'I mean, you can prove it, can't you?' asked Minna. 'We, I mean.'

'We can. With Tom's help. He's got the goods.'

'Are you absolutely sure of that?' asked Henry.

'Yes. Oh, yes. And anyway, it's selling the magazine, and that's got to be good.'

We all nodded vigorously. Through the window I watched the unceasing cascade of red and white lights bathed in orange by the streetlights, multiplied over and over by gleaming automobile metal, and listened to the comforting rumble and roar of the traffic, the aimless shouts of the evening's first revellers.

'As long as there's still a magazine to be sold,' observed Bomber, after a little while.

The doorbell rang, a faint tinkle one could barely hear up on the fifth floor. I brightened.

'That must be my car.'

'What for?' asked Minna, helping Henry to another glass of wine.

'He's going to the studios of the *Nine O'Clock News*,' said Bomber, 'may God have mercy on his soul.'

Minna, on the other hand, was obviously impressed, which gratified me absurdly.

'Break a leg, Wellingborough,' yodelled Henry after me as I clattered down the stairs. My pulse began to race; I felt as if I was about to parachute somewhere out over Arnhem when the going was getting rough. I shut the door behind me and was skipping towards the waiting car when I heard a voice. Squinting upwards, I saw Bomber leaning dangerously out of the fifth-floor window.

'Wilf, it's Jimmy. Says it's urgent.'

I hesitated, and was lost. Again. I should have gone on to glory, but instead I dutifully did the other thing.

'You've been having a high old time over there, haven't you?' he remarked, with unpleasantly menacing false *bonhomie*. There was always a sing-song note in his voice, and it was very notice-able now. A sort of verbal swagger, like a boxer going into the ring.

'We're selling like crazy,' I panted, after my rapid ascent of five flights of stairs. 'It's put us on the map sensationally.'

'That's splendid.' His tone was not cordial.

'Aren't you pleased?'

'Why didn't you return my call?'

'I tried to. Couldn't get through.'

'Do you want to know what I've been doing all day?'

No, I didn't really, nothing could have interested me less, but I divined he was going to tell me anyway. He seemed to mistake my lack of response for nerveless expectation.

'I've been having some very illuminating conversations with David Vale's lawyers, and some even more illuminating ones with David himself.'

'David. I see.'

'You'll be pleased to know he has agreed not to sue us for the high six-figure sum his lawyers have assured me they could legitimately expect for that story you ran.'

'But it's true.'

'I'm afraid David is in possession of some letters from the young man concerned which will show that one half of the story is not true, and the personnel department of the Research Bureau has a letter from him which will show that the other half is not true either.'

'And you believe them?' I was incredulous.

'That's not the point, Wilf, as you should know. The question is, will a jury believe them? And the answer – and I have taken expensive advice on this – is emphatically yes.'

I didn't like the way this was going. I felt as if I had taken that parachute jump after all.

'So he's not going to sue? So where's the problem? We're off the hook, aren't we?'

'We are. But – and I'm sorry to have to tell you this, Wilf – you're not. It's not really in his interests to get involved in a legal battle –'

'Because it's all true, presumably.'

'Whatever. But like Salome and John the Baptist, he wants your head on a platter.'

I laughed.

'But you're not going to give it to him, are you?'

'I'm not sure I have a choice.'

For a moment I reflected that he was probably right. Then the enormity of it all hit me. 'But I'm just about to go on the *Nine O'Clock News*.'

'Not any more, you're not.'

I grew mutinous.

'You can't stop me if I want to.'

'Well, let me see. As the editor of *Arts Unlimited* you are entirely to blame for the offending article, and David can sue you. You will need legal help. Costly legal help. Very costly legal help. Unless other counsels prevail.'

'You don't want me to go on the *Nine O'Clock News*?'

'There's a little more to it than that.'

'Not the *Today* programme? What about the *Guardian* profile?'

154

'I do understand your predicament, Wilf. But you're not going to do any of it.'

'*Wogan*? Surely *Wogan*?'

'Any of it.'

'Is that your deal with Vale, then?'

'As I said, there's a bit more to it.'

'And that is?'

'Wilf, you're not making this easy for me.'

Why the hell should I, I wondered.

'Give me a clue. Just one will do.'

'I'd have thought it was obvious.'

'Well, it's not. I was doing what I thought was right. What I thought you wanted. Increasing the circulation.'

'You might have consulted me. Arguably, you should have done so. But I'm not unreasonable. I appreciate what you've been trying to do. It's just that now I'm in a position, through your actions, where I have only one course open to me.'

'And that is?'

'You're fired, Wilf.'

'Fired?'

'Yes.'

'You mean, really fired?'

'Yes.'

'You mean, up-against-a-wall-and-fired fired?'

'As you like. But I suggest we call it a resignation.'

'You're sacrificing me on the altar of pragmatism?'

'On the altar of a considerable six-figure sum. Yes, I am.'

'In spite of the fact that sales have rocketed?'

'I want there to be a magazine to rocket, Wilf,' said Jimmy, eerily echoing Bomber's earlier words.

'You're firing me to placate a grade-one shit who uses his position to ruin the life of some poor underling who had the good taste not to return his revolting advances?'

'You're sounding rather personal, Wilf.'

'Shouldn't we at least talk to Tom?'

He was meaningfully silent. And I thought, oh, what a fool

155

you've been, Wilf Wellingborough. Oh, what a fool you've been. You're the man who printed a Tom Phipps story. A dodgy Tom Phipps story. 'No,' I heard myself murmur. 'I suppose there's no point.'

They say that bereavement comprises four stages: numbness, anger, grief and acquiescence. I did all four at once – even the last, because I knew a *fait accompli* when I heard one. There was more besides: shame, and a dash of self-contempt. Jimmy was right: I wasn't fit to be an editor. But then why did he take me on in the first place? It was his idea. My emotions began running round on little tracks, like squeaking trucks clattering behind an engine on a child's clockwork railway, like a dog chasing its tail. It's my fault, I'm no good, Jimmy is right. Jimmy should support me, I did what I should, Jimmy is wrong. What will my friends think, what will the world think? Trickety-trock, trickety-trock. And why did I trust Tom?

Well, quite.

My anger at myself was eclipsed entirely by my anger at Tom, that spineless, faithless, inept worm. I wanted to flay him mercilessly, tear him limb from limb and pull out his toenails. After that, I'd begin torturing him properly. I hated Tom; I hated Jimmy; I hated myself.

'What it's like,' I said to Milo on the phone not long afterwards, 'is the first minute after the beginning of the universe.'

'Strewth,' said Milo. 'That bad?'

'There's this moment of utter chaos and then shapes begin to emerge. All in the most infinitesimal fraction of a second.'

'Quarks,' he said.

'I beg your pardon?'

'It's all to do with quarks. Those or neutrons. Or protons, or something. If it hadn't been for some chance or other, the whole universe might have been negative.'

Science was very hot in publishing at that time; even so, and despite my own deep ignorance of the subject, I could tell Milo was struggling.

'That's exactly how I felt. I'm not sure the danger's past.'

156

'But part of you is feeling positive?' There was a hint of pleading in his voice.

'From time to time, yes,' I admitted grudgingly. 'But only inasmuch as I know I would get intense satisfaction from kicking the shit out of Tom Phipps's head.'

'But you know what he's like. Everyone does.'

I groaned. Of course I did. Why had I ever allowed myself to forget?

'Anyway, it's not the end of the world, if I may return to our cosmic analogy. You'll get another job. I can't think why you ever wanted to edit the *Arts* in the first place.'

I bridled. 'It's a wonderful magazine. Everything that's worth anything in life is in it.'

'On the other hand, you're not there any more. So you'd better let the scales fall from your eyes.'

'Milo, I have just lost my job, remember.'

'Wilf, this is the eighties, remember. Everyone loses their job.'

This was futile.

'See you later?'

'See you later.'

An hour after my little Pearl Harbor I braved the loyal troops. They were still sitting there glumly. The wine had disappeared, save for one plastic cupful that Bomber held out to me ceremoniously.

'We saved it for you,' she said. Then she burst into tears and flung her arms about me.

'You know, then?' I sounded even more funereal than I felt.

'Door's not that thick,' said Henry.

'Not with your ear pressed against it,' came Bomber's voice, muffled against my stomach.

Impervious, Henry continued. 'Don't worry, old son. The world is full of opportunities for a young man of talent like yourself,' and he dabbed away a tear with a filthy handkerchief.

Minna appeared to be gazing at the wall behind my head. Then, unnervingly, her eyes focused.

157

'Mind you,' she said, 'it was a fucking stupid thing to do.' She got up and walked towards me. A long forefinger tapped me forcefully on the arm. 'But I'm bloody glad you did it. The worst thing about this – apart from you, Wilf, of course – is that that objectionable little prig Vale is going to come up smelling of roses.'

It was the most outspoken remark anyone had ever heard her make. We were silent a moment in appreciation.

'So what are you going to do now?' asked Bomber.

'I think, my children, if I may patronize you all grandiloquently for the first and last time, there is only one thing to do. I'm going to meet my friend Milo and get well and truly smashed.'

The Crepuscule welcomed us with open arms.

The Adverse Quantum Theory of Anticipation

A WORD ABOUT THAT restaurant. It's gone now; I walked past where it used to be the other day and there's an obscenely fashionable hairdresser there instead. 'A haircut?' they sneered as I timidly enquired, just for the hell of it, just for the nostalgia of sitting in the old, now barely recognizable premises. They were booked up for months. I tried to look as if I wasn't blushing from the roots of my tousled curls and to saunter out nonchalantly, and naturally I tripped over the mat. Three hours later, waiting for the tube, I thought of a reply.

I hate it when that happens. I once went into World's End, Vivienne Westwood's shop down the more unprepossessing reaches of the King's Road, with the huge clock outside whose hands circle swiftly anticlockwise; I was in a tearing hurry one late December evening and I needed a Christmas present for Grace. I asked if they had scarves. I suppose, looking back on it, that had to be a strange question to ask, but, you know, I needed a scarf. 'A *scarf*?' The boy behind the counter, who had a lop-sided hat on (remember that 'Buffalo Girls' look?) almost choked. I peered about me and realized that I didn't recognize the function of a single item. I flung myself out the door in a rage. It seems a shame to disturb the privacy of these places.

Anyway, the Crepuscule became something of a haunt of mine. (I mean, more than it had been. I practically lived there, drinking filter coffee and pretending I was Sartre all day.) It was French, and the French restaurants of London are simply the best, whether it's cheap and rough with ties hanging off the ceiling like the Bouillabaisse off St Martin's Lane or whether it's the Jeu d'Esprit itself. The Italians do restaurants wonderfully too, of course, but the French don't try so hard; it's all in the waiter's swagger, the confidence in the wine (even if it's not all that good), the casual arrogance of the menu (even if the cooking isn't absolutely sensational), the manifest assumption that, because it's French, it's right. *Français, ergo sang-froid.*

In the early days Milo and I had met there, then Tom would come along, and others would drop by, and the waiters were all nice to us and called us Mr Glover and Mr Wellingborough in an admirably unctuous manner, and the manager, whose name was Natalie and who had wiry black hair with streaks of grey, and a strong, aquiline face with an intense, disconcerting stare, used to come and sit with us and drink with all the unhurried calm with which the French drink, as if red wine were simply an amiable alternative to tap water and no big deal at all, which is why they don't get drunk the same way we do, getting rat-arsed to celebrate or commiserate. The British don't take drink for granted; it's always there as a means to an end, often oblivion.

After my departure from my beloved *Arts*, as I say, the Crepuscule became a sort of makeshift office, and I began to feel raffish and bohemian. Café society doesn't really exist in London, but if it existed anywhere, I liked to think, it was at my table at the Crepuscule. Tom had dropped out of sight, of course. I heard that he was full of remorse about what had happened, but I didn't believe it for a second; he was simply trying to give the idea some currency in order to soften everyone up, for it can't be denied that his own reputation, shaky as it was beforehand, was now more or less in shreds. Not that this was any great consolation. I missed the *Arts*, though Bomber and occasionally Henry used to join me at the Crepuscule and we would rake over old times forlornly. I treated Bomber to lunch just a few days after my redundancy cheque came through, which was surprisingly quickly; I assumed Jimmy was anxious to avoid further bad blood.

Bomber arrived with her crew-cut bristling healthily, her face

160

as rosy as ever – I loved the delicate mosaic of tiny red veins like the hairline cracks in a pottery glaze that covered the points of her cheeks – and a decidedly shifty air. She chatted amiably enough, until inevitably the subject of my successor came up.

'It'll be someone with ambition,' I mused. 'The *Arts* is traditionally used as a passage to greater things.' I caught her eye. 'Well, usually it is. Look at Kitty Greaves. I wonder who Jimmy will go for.'

'We think he's already decided.'

Something in her voice alerted me.

'Anyone I know?'

'Uh-huh.'

In that moment my natural, irrepressible sunniness was eclipsed by the certain knowledge that I was about to hear something I would not like.

'It's not Tom–bloody–Phipps, is it?'

Bomber looked at me in astonishment.

'Wilf, with intuition like yours it's amazing you ever got near that job. Jimmy Spalding may be unpredictable, but he's not a complete arsehole. Even though he fired you,' she added, patting me on the hand.

'Well, who, then?'

She pulled a face, giving herself two new chins in the process. 'Sibella?'

Two chins became three.

'I see. That explains a lot about her recent behaviour.'

'Yes, but how recent?'

I caught her drift. 'You think this has been going on for some time?'

'We do.'

'Why?'

'Just something to do with the way she turned up the next morning looking incredibly pleased with herself and acting as if she owned the place. It made us wonder a bit.'

If there is anything worse than getting the big 'E' it's knowing that it's been planned. All the while you were happily going about your business, unbeknown to you the shutters were being brought down. You were out in the cold; you didn't know it, but someone else did. My eyes became watery.

'You haven't really come to terms with it, have you?' asked Bomber, kindly.

My voice skated a few notes as I replied. 'Haven't even begun to.'

We were silent awhile.

'And to think I got her into the *Arts* in the first place. She came to my rescue at a *Private Eye* lunch once. She was like a latter-day Boadicea.'

'She still is. She's had everything repainted and the whole office is *totally* minimalist now.' (She said this with relish.) 'Everything's matt black and silver and – I have to say this, Wilf, though I know it hurts –'

'Oh, I know, I can imagine. You're going to say she's much more efficient, aren't you? But presumably not so creative?'

'Wilf, you know she's creative. That's why you hired her in the first place.'

'So, efficient and creative?'

'And dynamic.'

'Oh, good.'

'Wilf, you can't just feel sorry for yourself. You've got to recognize the past for what it is and move on to the next stage.'

I gave her a blank look. One that was intended to convey a measure of disbelief. 'Bomber, has something happened? Are you in love or something?'

'I don't need men in my life,' she snapped. 'That's offensive.'

'I didn't say it was a man.'

'That's still offensive. You're saying I need to be in love to be – whatever you're saying I am. That's *really* offensive. What *are* you saying I am?' Her eyes had narrowed and she looked cross. I relented.

'All right,' I went on. 'I'm being frivolous. But you're sounding like an agony aunt.' The truth dawned. 'How nice is Sibella being to you?'

162

She looked shifty again.

'Deputy editor?'

She blushed.

'I'm good, aren't I?' I tried to sound caustic, but really I was too fond of Bomber to be bothered. 'Well, that's brilliant.' I leaned over the table and hugged her, burying my nose in the gap between the collar of her leather jacket and her neck, and finding it an enticing temperature. I was surprised by the warmth with which she responded. When we unclinched there was an amused grin on her face and her eyes were glistening.

'I do miss you, you know that, don't you? Even though we're much more organized now. Women do things better.'

'What about Henry?'

'Not so good. She's gone off him.'

'Too old school.'

'Too drunk, too smelly, really.'

'Same thing. So what's he doing with himself?'

'Don't know, I'm afraid.'

'Poor old sod.'

'He'll be fine. He's a survivor. Anyway, Sibella wants to have a leaving party for you.'

'Don't be silly.'

'Yes, she does.'

'No, I mean it's a crazy idea.'

'Why? It's no good being petulant, as I've told you often enough.'

'I'm not being – well, if I am it's because – she can't possibly – it would be absurd – I mean, surely nobody would –'

'Forget it. You're not going to finish that sentence. Let's talk about Milo.'

'No, wait. Did she mean it?'

'Of course.'

'I'll think about it.'

'Big of you.'

Sibella, it turned out, did mean it. She took me out to a new Thai place in Frith Street and flirted outrageously with me,

163

something she'd never even hinted at doing before. It was as if I was a sort of phantom that needed to be laid to rest. Or maybe just laid. Or maybe she'd done that already, as it were.

'And you know, Wilf, I do want to give you this party. I want you still to feel part of the magazine. I mean, I'm changing it, of course. Less traditional, less male, less exclusive. More about women, more appealing to women, more *for* women. Wider. More welcoming. But, you know, still intellectually rigorous.'

'You could get Kitty Greaves to write a column, maybe, if she's got the time – I'm sure she could find it. An expansive column about worldwide women's affairs. Call it "Broad Issues".'

She halted for a split second, and frowned.

'Not a bad idea.'

Then she brightened.

'And not a good one, either. You're ghettoizing as usual. I want everything to mesh. The regulars, the features, all of them. The trouble with the *Arts* is that everything has always been in pockets. Docketed in pockets. Very male, clubbable, passé.'

Crushed? You bet I was.

'But, you know, it would be great if you did a little writing for us. The occasional review, perhaps something longer.'

'I'll do you two thousand words on the adverse quantum theory of anticipation. AQUA, to give it its loose acronym.'

'Come again?'

'It's something I've been working on with Milo Glover. It goes like this. You know how a quantum particle can be a wave or a particle, but you never know what it is until it's observed?'

'Schrödinger's cat.'

'I was about to say. Well, my theory of predicting the future is that whenever you know with absolute certainty that something is going to happen, whether it is good or bad, that certainty turns what's going to happen into the reverse of what you're expecting. It's the only way to describe, scientifically, the strange waywardness of life.'

'Wilf, are you feeling sorry for yourself?'

'Probably.'

164

'I thought so. Never mind this codswallop, what about something on the redundancy of men?'

'You could have phrased that better.'

She had the grace to chew her lip and look disconcerted, but she recovered quickly. 'Well, the unnecessariness of men in the late eighties. Make it upbeat, though. Funny, even.'

'Why don't you get Henry to do it? The perfect candidate. He's a good man, you know.'

'Good for what?'

She had me there.

'Quiz pages, I seem to recall. You were his discoverer.'

'Too *ancien régime*, dear. What *else* is he good for?'

'Oh . . . company.' I waved my hand vaguely. It was no use. 'How long do you want this thing, then?' I asked, with dread in my heart. It seemed so humiliating, but what is pride to the defunct editor? 'And where's this party?'

She smiled beatifically.

'Your choice. Within reason.'

It had to be the Crepuscule.

'I think of you as my friends,' I explained expansively to Natalie.

'Thank you, Weelf,' she replied. 'And is this *Arts Unlimited* of yours solvent?'

'Oh yes, it's owned by someone very rich.'

'That,' she remarked philosophically, 'is not the same zing.'

'Not the same zing at all, Natalie. Couldn't have put it better myself. But you'll be OK.'

Her eyes narrowed, and she pressed her lips together in an expression of beady contempt. But she relented in the end. We had the party on a Monday night and she closed the restaurant.

Leaving parties became serious business in the eighties. I remember Milo saying they were having one a week at Pegasus and something called leaving-party fatigue was setting in; every time the same tired sausage rolls appeared, accompanied by bizarre little fishy things with sesame seeds on top, mini pizzas, salt and vinegar crisps and chicken drumsticks, all of it looking as if it had been left over from the last one. The same clichés were trotted out in the speeches, where everyone was terribly polite and pretended that Jim the head designer's departure was a natural progression for his already distinguished career, and not that he had been shafted good and proper.

It was the extraordinary hypocrisy of it all that made me feel listless as the evening drew nigh. Jimmy had apparently insisted on coming, and my soul squirmed at the thought. Added to which I knew that it would be a wrench to see everyone again. But at least I felt on home territory at the Crepuscule, and I begged Natalie to be there. I also made sure Henry knew he was wanted.

On the evening itself my stomach felt as if it were in my shoes and if anything it sank lower as time went on. Nobody turned up for the first half-hour and I felt like death; then they all came at once and I felt deliriously relieved. Milo and Flora and Paul and Henry and Adam and all our contributors came; then I caught sight of Helen, which was an electrifying moment, but the thought of Jimmy made me feel sick with apprehension.

'Where is he?'

'He couldn't make it.'

The room was getting noisy.

'I'm sorry?'

'I bet you're not.'

'You mean he's not coming?'

'He got stuck in some piece of business. He sends his best wishes. Don't look so pleased, Wilf, it's rude.'

'So are you staying?'

'Why not? There's a babysitter. I don't often get out. I mean, I get out to witness incidents of extreme violence, but I'd like to have a good time, for a change.'

At the end of the party, after Sibella had made a fantastically cloying speech about following in my august footsteps, which she then spoiled by extolling to the skies the virtues of Jimmy Spalding, presumably for the benefit of Helen's ears (and Helen did indeed look irritatingly pleased), Natalie took me aside.

'Weelf, she is married to someone else, no?'

I was baffled. 'Who?'

'Hélène.'

'Helen? Yes, she is, the guy who fired me, as it happens. Why?'

'You have been following her around with your mouse open all the time.'

'My mouse? What mouse? Oh, I see.' I wasn't sure whether to be worried by the fact that she'd noticed or the fact that she was telling me. What was she, my mother? 'What, fully open?'

She laughed. 'It's up to you, Weelf. It's your life. And yes. Like a fish.'

'So why is the party ending?'

'You have run out of wine.'

'Can't we get some more?'

She shrugged and pulled a face. 'Your Sibella says no more money.'

Things were definitely changing at the *Arts*.

I saw Sibella giving me a curious look as the crowd drained away into Beak Street and Golden Square while I remained, like a rock deserted by the fleeing tide, surrounded by the debris of the evening, with only Helen for company. I supposed it must have seemed peculiar that I was chatting animatedly to the wife of the man who had put me out to grass.

'So Sibella is flavour of the month?' asked Helen, *sotto voce*, but not so *sotto* that I didn't catch a slight edge in it. Sibella caught her look and beetled over.

'Happy, Wilf?' she asked.

'You could say that,' I replied guardedly. 'Actually, I'm mildly disappointed not to be asked to dinner. Everyone seems to be going home to bed.

'Well, it *is* eleven o'clock,' she observed.

'That late? So it is. I hadn't noticed.'

'I'll take you out, Wilf,' interjected Helen.

Sibella grinned broadly at her. 'You won't get into trouble with James, will you?' she asked, with a slight, self-mocking shake of her head.

167

'We're old friends,' returned Helen, equally sweetly.

'I must confess I was dreading Jimmy putting in an appearance,' I said. 'I was so glad it was just you. You see?' I looked at Sibella. 'Splendid example of AQUA. Positive as well as negative. You really should let me do that piece.'

They looked at each other in consternation.

'Don't ask,' said Sibella. 'Remember,' she went on, turning back to me. 'The meaninglessness of men. With wit, panache and brio.'

'What if I like being meaningless?'

'As if,' she smiled, and went to settle the evening's business with Natalie, who had gone to sleep with her head on the counter.

'Where are we going?'

Walking down a pavement in Soho even on a Monday night is a precarious business. You can't simply saunter along like you can in Mayfair or Covent Garden; people keep coming straight at you. I don't suppose there is an electronic game which simulates walking a Soho pavement, but there should be. You have to concentrate very hard not to be bounced into the road and the path of a passing taxi, or alternatively bounced the other way into some den featuring X-rated mags, videos and poppers (what *are* they? I'm sure I should know). Conversation tends to be perfunctory, as you weave in and out, dodging the youths, the drunks and the interested businessmen.

So it was some time before I could focus on Helen's question, at which point I realized that I didn't have an answer. What I did know, and what had been nagging me for some minutes, was that I did very much want to sit and talk to her. I felt like a dam holding back a great reservoir of mashed feelings, a sloppy, messy, glutinous mass of things I wanted to talk about, and hadn't been able to for ages, since before Flora, since the time when Grace and I had been happy. It was as if an immense vat of pullulating emotion sensed a small crack in the wall and was bearing down on it. Poor Helen. She was about to be submerged in an outpouring of fetid, antique neuroses.

'How about here?'

The thing about London restaurants is that when you have spent enough years in them you get blasé, and going out to eat is about as glamorous as visiting the dentist. And Helen, of course, was a bumpkin who knew nothing, poor soul, about the fast-changing world of Soho eateries, so we ended up in the restaurant without either of us thinking twice about it.

It was only when I sat down that I noticed it was the same one in which Flora and I had begun to go our separate ways. The waiters had changed, but the menu hadn't. A great mournful mood of loss came over me, not just for Flora, because I was never enough in love with her – I had some little instinct for self-preservation after all – but for. . . Well, for what? For things I hadn't done, for relationships I hadn't had, for things that I'd lost, for what I hadn't been able to do. One does, I think, have the right to be maudlin after one's own leaving party: *especially* when one's been asked to write a vivacious article about the meaninglessness of men for the magazine from which one has been so unceremoniously booted.

Helen didn't say much. She didn't have much opportunity for a while. I prattled unceasingly but diplomatically, tiptoeing round the subject of Jimmy while remembering the uncertainty of her feelings towards him, pouring out my heartbreak over the loss of the *Arts* for no greater reason than that here was a new and sympathetic ear as yet unassailed by my litany of complaint, reassessing the enigmatic Grace, and mildly mocking Flora, which I suspected she would like.

I was aware that I was at a fulcrum; that my life was changing and that I had to change with it. I was trying to give the past a recognizable shape so as to divine the future it implied; put another way, I was trying to wipe away the grime so as to catch a reflection of what was to come. Relationships have their own lifespan; their ending need not be anyone's fault, as Helen and Flora had both, in their own, patient ways, explained to me. I had thought of my life with Grace as a wave running up a beach and disappearing pointlessly into the sand. Now I could see that it had simply run its course.

Other people's perceptions are liberating like that. They reshape your ideas of yourself, the ones that tied you down like the myriad tiny ropes of the Lilliputians binding Gulliver. It's not hard to fall in love with the people who do this for you.

I've done a lot of falling in love. I was in love with the *Arts*. I was in love with the idea of it and the influence it had, far beyond its stature. I loved the spontaneity of the people writing for it, responding to all the wonderful things happening in the city (it was a very London magazine; we never had the resources for much else). And I felt betrayed by that love, because I had not used the *Arts* like everyone else had; I had come to a full stop, fulfilled by it, not wanting anything else. I should have been bigger than the magazine, should have gobbled it up in my triumphant progress. Instead, I hung up my hat on the old art deco hatstand that was the only thing Kitty had left behind.

The flood slowed at last. At some moment Helen had laid her hand on top of mine, which was infinitely calming, and it stayed there; then, as natural as anything, my hand turned palm up, and her hand stayed still, and I found myself gently running my fingertips the length of her small pretty fingers, the motion not so much sensual as a kind of nervous release, like counting worry beads. Touch is such a fine sense, and hands so much express personality, that holding hands sometimes feels like reading someone's nature, a perfect act of intimacy. Of course I did not think for a moment about where it might all lead. It was about tenderness, that was all. At the time. It was one creature comforting another. Though I remember the pleasurable shock of it, too.

I found that I had been looking into her eyes for some time.

I might have died a little death, but I felt a little life stirring.

And I decided to tell her about Jimmy and Grace at the Coliseum.

Maybe not now, but sometime soon.

Pastoral

I FOUND WORK, EVENTUALLY. It was just a matter of trying, of ceasing to mope in bars and cafés feeling my stubble. Beginning to fall in love helped, I'm convinced: I started to glow a little. Given that the object of my love lived on the other side of the country it was a lukewarm sort of a glow, but people began to be more responsive. I started going to parties again. One day I had a call from the *Sunday Times* Colour Magazine, who wanted to have someone writing on gardens on a regular basis: not a column, but then after the *Arts* the very mention of the word used to bring on aversion-therapy-strength horror. And though, to be honest, I didn't know a whole lot about gardens even after all the writing I had done on the subject for the *Arts*, it's amazing what you can pick up, and what canyon-sized cracks can be papered over by sleight of word. The Colour Mag seemed to think that gardening was the coming thing, which, with a great deal of hindsight, was extraordinarily prescient of them. But it meant that, joy of joys, I was able to mount expeditions to Inverness and Cornwall – at the penniless *Arts*, after I had covered Chelsea Physic Garden and Kew I had spent the features budget for the month – in search of happening horticulturalists, and I could happily have gone on doing nothing else for ever.

Once I had decided to tell Helen about Jimmy and Grace I couldn't let go of the idea, indeed I became obsessed by it. It began to loom larger and larger in my life. I thought of it, slightly crazily, as a doorway to happiness. Which shows, I suppose, that I was not really as recovered as I thought I was. I told the Colour Mag that the most exciting garden in the country was on the Welsh borders, beside an old mill where the river had worn a long gully, in which many species of shade- and moisture-loving plants were being nurtured by some enterprising professionals from Birmingham: their mail-order business was growing exponentially. I went there with my own camera and spent a deliriously happy day splashing about in the stream photographing marsh marigolds and exotic ferns, then stopped off for a night at the Lion Hotel in Shrewsbury, where Helen met me for dinner. I had gone off the Prince Rupert as a venue.

It was not easy. Since our conversations at Monkridge and in the presence of the bear-like Jethro, and since my own débâcle, we had neither of us discussed Jimmy much, and of course I had done the subject of Grace to death that night in Soho. So when I asked abruptly, 'How's Jimmy treating you, then?' by way of conversational gambit, it felt and was about as subtle as if I had been holding a placard inscribed, 'Introducing an Important New Topic for Discussion. Listen Up.'

Her eyes narrowed, but she only went on looking thoughtful.

'I mean – is he – does he still. . . ?' I went on, making it worse, shaking my head from side to side, trying to make the point without actually specifying what it was.

'I don't think he has a much higher regard for me than before,' she replied slowly, resting her forehead on her hands.

'Is that what you want?'

'Respect? Yes, it's one of the things I want.'

'How do you get on with Ranulph?'

'He's like James, really.'

'Meaning?'

'Both long on charisma and short on human kindness.'

'He's still hard on you, then, Jimmy?'

'You know he is.'

I plunged in.

'Does it ever become more than words?'

'I don't want to talk about it, thanks.'

'Are you sure? Because –'

She put her hand on mine, not lovingly, but with the firm pressure of dismissal. I could not stop.

'You know, I saw him a while ago at the Coliseum.'

'Nice for you.'

I felt my voice rise in pitch slightly.

'Does he know Grace fantastically well? I mean, does he see her a lot?'

She looked at me directly.

'What are you trying to say?'

I drew a deep breath.

'Well, they looked pretty close to me.'

She did not reply. I was irked. Having committed myself, I wanted a reaction. I wanted the reaction I wanted.

'I mean, they *were* kissing.' I accented the word absurdly, flailing a little. 'I mean, you know, not . . . but. . .'

'Wilf, you must learn to finish your sentences.'

I was stung.

'Doesn't it bother you if they're having an affair?'

Astonishingly, she laughed. She laughed unhappily, and not altogether convincingly, but she laughed all the same.

'You could say I'm not surprised.'

'Why not?'

'They've always been close.'

'Not that close.'

Into the silence, like a mouse sidling over a kitchen floor, crept a doubt.

'Do you mean you knew?'

'As I said, I'm not surprised.'

'But that's terrible. I mean, how can you live with that?'

Her hand rested on mine again, this time more softly.

'Wilf, you know, I hate to say this to you, but I think most people would not be surprised. You, yes.'

'So, all the time −'

She nodded.

'God, that makes me feel bad.'

'I don't mean they used to leap into the sack at every available opportunity, but it's an old friendship. A close one.'

'You sound like you don't mind.'

She reflected.

'Oh, I don't know. It was always there, I suppose.'

'I don't understand how you can accept this.'

'It's not a problem.'

'Of course it's a problem. It must be tearing you apart.'

Her voice hardened.

'I said it's not a problem.'

I was aware that we were the last in the dining room.

'I have plenty of other problems with Jimmy.'

I thought, let's leave it at that for now.

As we left, I slipped my fingers through hers and felt liquid with happiness as hers curled warmly through mine in return. But as I bent to kiss her she placed her fingertips against my chest.

'I have to go,' she said.

'Can I see you tomorrow?'

'Don't you have to get back to London?'

'I'll manage.'

Our eyes met. There was something distant about her expression; appraising, too. I felt like a specimen under a microscope.

'Come at twelve,' she said. 'You haven't been round the gardens in summer, have you?'

That night, restlessly turning, I analysed my motives meticulously. Jealousy, desire, despair, anger, revenge: yes, they were all there. Then at around four o'clock, that time in the morning when, either waking or sleeping, the mind seems most able to discern a sense and an order in things, a little door opened, and something else, something a lot better, which was small but promised much, stepped into the arena. I had not quite realized it was there, waiting in the wings to be recognized: feeling, strongly, very strongly, for someone else. Welcome back, I thought.

I'll never forget the sight of Helen as she stood outside the front door at Monkridge that next day. She was dressed in white, a linen dress that left her arms bare, and she seemed to shine in the early summer sun. I was no longer conscious of all those cantankerous feelings, only one of passionate, celebratory longing;

something had changed in her, too, as if a screen had been rolled aside, an inhibition discarded, or a problem solved.

She took a cold bottle out of the fridge, and we bore it into the garden with some ice and two glasses, just as we had, eccentrically, taken out coffee in the winter. The garden was reaching fullness of leaf, the beds punctuated by the very last of the tulips, dark maroon and crisp white and green, before the contented sufficiency of the great poppies whose green pods hung expectantly on long stalks. Here and there deep pink cistuses and geraniums flared in the sunshine. Every movement of Helen's sent waves of pleasure through me; I studied the small hairs on the back of her neck, and worried that she was too thin, and revelled in the way she would turn away from my gaze and then turn back and return it coolly but steadily. As she poured the wine over a lump of ice in each glass her loose dress fell forward to reveal her body descending into it and for a moment I almost felt vertigo. We wandered into the rose beds, the distance between us palpable: the closer she was, the more I thrilled with improper anticipation. The roses were beginning to bloom, their names as evocative as their intricate, eddying flowers and their giddy-making scents: Tuscany, Cuisse de Nymphe, Fantin Latour, Boule de Neige, Charles de Mills, Souvenir du Docteur Jamain, Rosa Mundi, Nathalie Nypels, Ballerina, Roseraie de l'Haÿ, Ispahan. As we named them, the sensuousness of the words and their meanings was as heady as the cold wine at midday. We found a bank in the middle of the rose garden and sat at either end, with the glasses between us. Helen's attention seemed absorbed by the roses; unable to restrain myself, I stroked her shoulder, and her head turned abruptly, catching my hand between cheek and shoulder.

'I'd quite like to eat you,' I said.

She ducked her head quickly and kissed the back of my hand and smiled.

'Why don't you?'

As we kissed I was aware of her fully: her light body beneath the dress, the warmth and the extraordinary softness of her

175

lips – as if they were hardly physical at all – the slight perspiration on her brow. After a while we lay on the grass. She coiled a leg around me and her dress slipped over her thighs. I traced their smooth skin – a small sigh escaped her, then a low cry as my fingers worked their way inside her. We were on fire for each other: every touch seemed to liberate new, unprecedented feelings; as the dress floated over her head and her breasts tumbled on to my chest, the mere shape of her almost winded me. I felt the tiny stroking of the grass against my back and then the warm, wet rush as I entered her. I thought I might faint.

Her pale body crouched over me intently; I teased apart her legs and ran my tongue up into her deep, mauve saltiness, then over her clitoris, which stood out like a small pebble. I licked until she came in a shuddering silence. Then I rolled from under her and entered her from behind as she rested her head contentedly on her arm. I was slow, as slow as I could be; her whole body was dozily relaxed.

Afterwards, we lay together in the sun, drifting in and out of sleep. When I was with Grace I always started to worry after sex: about my job, about my friends, about my clothes. With Flora, for some unaccountable reason, I simply thought about food, and how hungry I was, and what different things I could be putting in a vast sandwich or how good it would be to make one's own bread. With Helen, I thought:

'Someone's coming.'

In blind panic we grabbed our clothes and hurtled, crawling, among the rose beds. There seemed nowhere to go. If we stood we would be seen; all around the beds were lawns. If we ran for the woods we would be unmissable. We lay on the grass underneath a vigorous Blanc Double de Coubert and frantically pulled on our things. I was too terrified to find it absurd, but Helen kept bursting into fits of giggles.

'Who is it? Who was it? What did you see?'

We lay like a couple of children, side by side, peering among the rose stems.

'Ranulph,' she panted. 'I think it was.'

176

Slowly, I peered over the bushes. Sure enough, some distance away, moving purposefully, Ranulph's patrician head and shoulders seemed to float over a turbulent sea of roses.

'Did he see?'

'No. He's almost blind, anyway, poor thing.'

'Are you sure?'

'He wouldn't care. He doesn't get involved.' It was an odd choice of phrase.

Her dress was covered with grass stains. 'Come on,' she said. She took my hand. 'Let's see if we can dodge the nanny.'

For some time after that my thoughts were all confusion, and I found it difficult to concentrate on work. What was I but a lovelorn freelance gardening correspondent, a latter-day swain? I thought about Helen constantly, awaiting her calls, which were, to say the least of it, erratic. She had a difficult time getting to the phone, she said, but I was never certain she was trying hard enough. To distract myself I started wandering into Soho in a way I had not done for months. Milo had become a denizen of some new club in Frith Street: he shouted joyfully when I put my head round the door one evening.

'Wilf! Where have you been? Why don't you call me back? I've been worried about you.'

It was a small club, sparsely furnished in contemporary beech-wood benches and cushions, with a tiny bar. Its membership was very exclusive and very literary; essentially, you had to know its president personally, and even then there was a five-year waiting list. I sat down and looked around: a huddle of middle-aged men, many of whom wore corduroy somewhere about their person, and most of whom seemed to be a mass of wrinkles from their foreheads to their trouser-seats, sat glowering into a club sandwich or a copy of the *Spectator*. There was only one woman, who outwrinkled them all.

'Aren't you a bit young for this place, Milo?' I enquired.

'Yes, of course. But you know it doesn't do to be too youth-obsessed. I mean, the young, among whom let me charitably include ourselves, don't buy books the way the oldies do. You want to do well in publishing? Oldies are where it's at.'

'One bestseller and you age forty years, Milo.'

'Wilf, you're writing about gardens. It's not exactly the Wag Club.'

'Does that still exist?'

'I'm not sure.'

'More clubbed against than clubbing, you and I.'

'Almost witty, Wilf.'

'Thanks. I've been out of circulation again.'

'So how are you? We missed you.'

'Really? Who?'

'You did take it hard, that *Arts* business, didn't you?'

'I did. How's Sibella doing?'

'Have you seen it lately?'

'Can't bear to look at it.'

'I thought you were supposed to write for it?'

'I was.'

'Well, it's different.'

He leaned over to a nearby table and plucked something from it. A beautiful woman in wraparound shades stared moodily from the cover. I didn't say anything.

'I mean, to be fair,' Milo went on, 'this is that new thing at the Donmar. But it's more like *The Face* than the old *Arts*, isn't it?'

'And the circulation figures?'

'Up.'

'I may go and live in Shropshire permanently.'

Milo shook his red locks at me.

'Don't be ridiculous. Move out. Move on. Move up. But don't give out or give up.'

'How's Tom?' I changed the subject.

'I'm supposed to be meeting him here, actually.' He grinned. 'Can you face it?'

'I think it's probably time I did.'

'You mean it? Oh, here he is.'

A theatrical look of delight struggled visibly with an authentic expression of horror upon the face of Tom Phipps as he saw me, but with his customary chutzpah he swaggered to our table – he was more roly-poly than ever – and clasped me in a bear-hug. He stepped back, held me by the shoulders, squinted thoughtfully at me as if I were a rather lovely old painting in an auction room, then sat down and remarked inconsequentially, 'You've lost weight.' He grinned beatifically. 'I mean, you look lovely, darling. Didn't expect to see you here. Now, let me see.' He studied his nails, chewed his lip and looked quizzical. 'Have you been away? Don't seem to have seen you in a while.'

I considered laying hold of a nearby fire-extinguisher and driving it into the back of his head, but recovered myself.

'All friends here, then, are we?' twittered Milo.

'I seem to have been bamboozled into a situation that requires forgiveness,' I complained. 'I don't think these things ought to be presumed lightly.'

'Champagne?' suggested Tom.

'If you insist.' I nodded stiffly, like a frosty old dame in a costume drama.

Milo asserted himself.

'If you're not going to kiss and make up,' he said, 'I'm leaving.'

We both looked at him.

'As good a reason for hostilities as any.'

'Not funny, Wilf.'

'Well, I need the practice.'

'And you haven't said what I want to hear, either, Tom.'

Tom extended a flabby hand towards me.

'I'm sorry,' he said. 'I was right,' he could not resist adding, 'but I'm sorry.'

'Now there's graciousness,' said Milo.

I took Tom's hand without great enthusiasm, and astonishingly experienced a surreptitious spasm of relief.

'Let us assume the past is now behind us,' said Milo, with endearing inanity.

'What do you mean, you were right?' I asked Tom.

'Wilf –'

179

'No, Milo, I want to know.'

Tom's eyes rolled.

'David Vale had that boy fired because he didn't return his favours,' he said. 'Everyone knows that – knew that. It was scandalous, outrageously so. He hounded him for months; accused him of dealing coke, being an alcoholic, you name it.'

'Can you fire someone for that?'

'Can we talk about something else?' asked Milo. 'I mean, can – we – talk – about – something – else?' With every word he made an emphatic, lunging, exasperated movement of his hands and head as if he were a clockwork toy.

'How about Jimmy? We haven't had a Jimmy conversation in ages. Not all that surprising, I admit,' Tom said, clocking me out of the corner of his eye, 'but I miss them. How is the old bastard?'

'Tom, I'm a peripatetic garden feature writer, and I've been spending a lot of time at my parents'. I'm out of touch.'

'Your parents live extremely close to where he does,' Milo pointed out.

'Yes, well, I suppose they do.'

'So, what's the gossip?'

'He's not there all that often, so far as I can make out. How's his flotation coming along?'

'Don't you go and see Helen? She must be bored – or is she immersed in Shropshire life? Can't imagine it somehow.'

'I do, now and then. But this flotation?'

'It's imminent,' said Tom.

'And will he be *very* rich?'

'I rather suspect he will. So long as nothing goes wrong.'

'Such as?'

'Fraudulent accounting. Gross sexual practices. Who knows? He's capable of either.'

'Good businessman, though.'

'I'm not saying those things will happen. It's just that, a man like Jimmy, you never know.'

'Personal or business?'

'The City doesn't usually care if a man horsewhips his

180

wife – or vice versa – and sells his children into slavery so long as
the profits and prospects are good. Which they are, in Jimmy's
case. But, you know, there's a recession looming and everyone's
a bit jittery. If you're trying to float a company and you're
heading for a messy divorce, with a touch of GBH thrown in,
who knows where it's all going to end up? If I know Jimmy, and
I like to think I do, he'll be very, very careful to make sure every
nut and bolt and nook and cranny of the business has little pink
and blue bows on it. He'll be fine, though. He's always fine.'

My reconciliation with Tom took me by surprise, but I
quickly got used to it. He had recently bought a flat in Camden
with the daughter of a film producer – an American one, and
therefore egregiously rich, as opposed to the home-grown
variety (he was no fool, Tom; a liability, perhaps, but no fool) –
and he had done so, it was assumed, with her money, since he
was famously penniless. I thought I had discerned an air of added
sleekness about him, but he seemed to have changed a little, too,
in himself: less fractious, more grounded.

'Love, eh?' I remarked morosely to Milo, after Tom had left
for Annabel's. Annabel's! What were we all coming to?

'Hard to believe?'

'I can't quite help being disappointed by the smoother, lovelier
Tom. I know I sound jealous –'

'No, no –'

'But that's not what he's about. That's not what he's *for*.'

Milo had changed, too. He was now a sought-after publisher,
far less prone to satirical denunciations of that appallingly
philistine company of his. Even Flora seemed to be going to bed
earlier.

'What do you mean, you need to sleep? Why can't you come
over and console your old friend?' I demanded of her, on one of
her visits to London. My flat in Stockwell was about the size of
a garden shed, and that is in itself sufficient reason at ten o'clock
at night for the dogs of depression to set about one.

'Dearest, I need my sleep. I always did. It's just that you kept
me up.'

'You did enjoy being kept up, didn't you? I mean, what we had was wonderful.'

'It was and I did. But New York's a hard-working place. It's for alphas, not betas. So I don't go out so much at the moment. Not on a whim.'

'All the more reason to come over here.'

'You want me to leave the Dorchester for a corridor in Stockwell? Tell me, Wilf, is that your idea of fun? Because it certainly isn't mine. I don't want to be rude or anything —'

'You're doing well, then, considering —'

'But — you know what I'm saying?'

I did.

'You could come here for breakfast,' she added, encouragingly. 'But it would have to be early. Do you do early?'

After I put the phone down it rang immediately with a sort of explosive urgency, as if the person on the other end had been ringing constantly, waiting for me to finish.

'Wilf, it's Helen.'

'Helen! What have you —'

'Listen. Do you know what? Do you know what Jimmy's doing? I need your advice. I need your help. Damn it, I need you.'

This sounded promising.

'We're having a dinner here next weekend. Do you know who's coming?'

'Let me —'

'Grace.'

'— guess.'

We spoke at the same time, and I was confused. Had we both said the same thing?

'Come again?'

'What do you mean, come again? I told you.'

'Say it again. I missed it.'

'What do you mean, you missed it? He's invited Grace. Grace. You know, tall blonde girl with a dopey expression. You went out with her long enough.'

182

'Not long enough, actually. Not as far as I was concerned.'

'Never mind that. It's a bloody disgrace.'

'Well, tell him you don't want her to come.'

'How can I? He'd want to know why, and I'd have to tell him. I'm not ready for that. Are you sure you saw them together? I mean, *really* together?'

'You bet I'm sure. He was —' But she wasn't listening. She knew. 'Anyway, I thought you didn't mind. You didn't seem to.'

'It's a bit fucking much to have her under the same roof. There are limits.'

'Yes, well, I can see that.'

'Will you come too?'

'That's a monstrous idea.'

'Isn't it? I mean, is it? We would be seeing each other again. . .'

Weak, weak, weak. But I rallied.

'No.'

'You have to be friends with Grace some day, you know. You did it with Tom Phipps.'

'That was different. Considerably different, if you think about it.'

'How?'

'I had no choice. It was sprung on me. And I never went out with Tom.'

'Don't be facetious. Will you come?'

'Oh, all right.'

'I love you.'

'You do?'

'Of course.' She sounded defensive.

'Hmm.'

'So you really will come?'

'This weekend?'

'This weekend.'

'I'll be there. What's cooking?'

'Anything you want, baby. Anything you want.'

I enjoyed the way she said that.

Thinking it over afterwards, I could hardly believe what Jimmy was doing. It was brazen cheek, and as such very much in character. And yet it was too bizarre. Perhaps he was in love. Not ordinary love; it would have to be obsessive love for him to do this. In his own mind he must be insulting Helen; so must Grace, and that was not in character at all. The realization ran through me like acid that the pair of them couldn't leave each other alone; both out of character, then, for Jimmy was never one to yield to his emotions. That trickle of acid again. And Helen wanted me there, so she must hate them both. As we sat at dinner she and I would know about each other, and we would know about Jimmy and Grace, and Jimmy and Grace would know about each other, but they would not know about us. Which would give us a very strange and exciting and reprehensible advantage. It didn't bode well for Jimmy, nor Helen, but in recent memory he had fired me and so had Grace, so I didn't feel I owed anything to anybody.

And I loved Helen. I was pretty sure about that. I'm very cautious about deciding whether I love someone. Given that I'm keen on love as a rule, it is true that it often takes me some time to admit it's there. Seriously there; when it comes to being meaningful about people and what you feel about them, love is at first a small bright flame that surprises you when you're not looking for it; suddenly there it is, a little unforeseen leap of faith, an ambush, a watershed. Suddenly the maps are changed; suddenly the landscape is irrevocably other. Suddenly we are learning something new about the world.

It was hard to discern the presence of love at that dinner. It was never going to be an evening of unrehearsed gentility, but even I had little preconception of what was to come.

Jimmy was in a filthy temper. He was preoccupied, and his usual sang-froid seemed to have snagged on something that was at him like a piranha. One is not always aware of people's moods immediately; and I was too distracted by meeting Grace for the first time since she had finished with me. Much had happened in between, but no matter how long one has been separated, the

184

pain is still fresh. There is that piquant relish to be had from the notion that one has moved on and grown since parting, but it didn't quite work for me; the reason being that I had not moved on and grown. I had had a marvellous and mind-expanding time with Flora in New York, so my life had not been entirely sterile, but the role of roving gardening correspondent would have to be presented as the result of wild romantic enthusiasm to have any impact, and I was uncomfortably aware that many there that night would be unimpressed.

Apart from the four of us, Helen had invited Jethro, who was a welcome if slightly obnoxious sight, since he was in fully velveted wizardly attire, with a long black gown over a satin purple polo-neck shirt. Hideous Shropshire chic, but I could see that it fascinated Martha and Timothy, Jimmy's neighbours, who ran a nearby organic farm. Between their bemused interest, Jethro's outright and sinister oddity and the rest of us, the party had a quite opulent potential for going disastrously wrong.

Grace was full of the brooding intensity that I adored, yet found too distracting, too aggravating, to feel comfortable with; her indifference still had the capacity to reduce me to ribbons. She leapt to her feet when she saw me, arms swinging a little awkwardly at her sides; even Jimmy paused and smiled and strode towards me in beaming camaraderie. They wanted to be friends. That was what this was all about. It was time to make up. We were awash with conciliatoriness.

And there was Helen, reminding me that my life had moved on somewhere new, somewhere neither Jimmy nor Grace — damn their kindly hospitable condescending eyes — knew anything about. I was with Helen; we were in love. Love was our weapon, our protection, our exclusivity, our pride. Love was our revenge.

'Wilf, I'm glad you could come.' Jimmy at his most unctuous, determined that benevolence would overcome resentment, knowing I would not have come had I not been willing to allow it to do so.

And Grace, throwing her arms around me with an excess of

enthusiasm, earnestly warm and good. And someone else's. Possession is ten-tenths of the law of love.

'You look different, Wilf,' pronounced Grace.

'Really?'

'Yes – you look happier.'

I ask you.

I caught Helen's glance quickly and held it a fraction of a second longer than was wise. Co-conspirators.

I gave Jethro a cheery wave. He bowed portentously.

Jimmy put a glass of champagne in my hand. The frosted glass and surging bubbles restored my spirits. I sat on the arm of the chair in which Helen was coiled with her customary elegance, and began making animated conversation with the farming couple about milk yields and the problems of growing wheat without chemical weedkillers; simply put, it appears one gets a lot of weeds. In compensation, one can raise one's prices considerably for being organic. This gratifying state of equilibrium did not prevent them holding forth for about half an hour on the subject, after which I sustained another half-hour on the merits of vegetarianism and the wickedness of meat, but from time to time I felt Helen's hand brush my thigh or the small of my back, and as she did so I was incandescent with the intimacy of it. The intimacy and the secrecy. What was more, she was looking devastating. Her deep grey dress clung to her body, and she wore a black velvet jacket cut short to the waist. By contrast, Grace was clad in bright woollens from Edina & Lena; fabulous deep crimsons and yellows. It seemed to me that it was she who looked happier, more at ease with herself, more vibrant than I had ever seen her. Let's face it, I was still dotty about her somewhere deep down inside, and the feelings were threaded with nostalgia, which is about as bad as you can get.

It was all, however, about to get a whole lot worse.

Explosive Devices

DESPITE HIS EFFORTS at *bonhomie*, Jimmy remained distracted. His body twitched slightly, as if he found his clothes constraining. From time to time Helen glanced at him, appraising, cool, but not entirely unconcerned. Grace hardly stopped looking at him, which was typical of her artlessness, and foolish, too. Helen was all too acutely aware of what was happening, and I could see it pained her, though to what extent I found it hard to tell.

I grew adventurous over dinner.

'How is the *Arts*, Jimmy? Thriving?' Helen gave me a surreptitious look of mock horror and I drove my fork into the lasagne with satisfaction. It was vegetarian, thus pleasing our agricultural companions.

'Doing well,' he returned crisply, then scowled at his plate. 'But not well enough.' He looked at me and put on a huge false grin. 'Still, better than under you.'

It was a typical Spaldingism – laconic, slightly flat – but the message was clear. I wasn't stupid enough to think he was joking. Entirely.

'Jimmy,' scolded Grace. I managed to raise my eyebrows at Helen, though I had to find my moment to do it. So they were on scolding terms, were they?

'I should think so,' I rejoined. 'Jimmy fired me,' I explained pleasantly to the farmers. 'But, you know, I'm OK with it.' Jimmy's attention seemed to be focused with extraordinary intensity on the corner of a silver candlestick, and I thought we had lost him for good. Suddenly he roused himself.

'She's doing a good job. A very good job. There's a lot more to be done, though.' I fancied he was addressing himself rather than us.

'You're never going to turn it into *Vogue*, darling,' put in Helen.

'He's thinking of something along those lines, though,' said Grace. So he confided in her. More than Helen. The tension between the two women was like static. It had been there in the background, a soft crackle resembling gravel under a car wheel, but now they sat opposite each other like rearing snakes.

Sublimely indifferent, Jimmy said suddenly, 'This is lovely, darling, but why is there no meat in it? Lasagne has to have meat. Otherwise it's a pasta sandwich.'

'Jimmy is unreconstructed meat and potatoes,' said Helen, shortly, glancing at her guests.

'Meat and lasagne would be fine,' he retorted.

'Jimmy!' came from Grace again.

'Grace, dear, you know he's never going to change.' There was the whiff of brinkmanship about this from Helen, as if she were about to go all the way and reveal what she knew. Something about her tone subdued Grace.

'Don't you ever miss meat, Martha?' he asked.

'Never,' smiled Martha.

'It's not about morals, it's about economics,' explained her husband. He was tall and gangling, a saturnine Art Garfunkel. I had met both of them from time to time over the years; she had been at the High School and he had been sent away to Radley, returning with a thin veneer of sophistication which had easily been removed by the lonely vigils of farming life. She was blonde – that is, I remember the time when she wasn't, but you wouldn't know it now. And perfectly made-up – immaculate lipstick, dangly diamond earrings, the works. Shropshire is like the old Soviet Union: the women dress to kill in an old-fashioned sort of way, quite the farmer fatales. There was a heavy air about her, a faint aroma of the burdensomeness of life, yet her eyes moved like globes of mercury on a china plate: instantly, fully focused, not missing the merest morsel of a sentence.

I was trying not to drink too much; there was instability all around me, a sensation of underlying toxicity. I was holding back because, watching Jimmy recharging his own glass and everyone else's with a powerful Cabernet Sauvignon, listening to his opinions becoming ever more forceful and unbuttoned, and catching Helen's contemptuous but wary looks towards him, I found myself increasingly desirous of being elsewhere.

'How's Byron?' I asked. Helen was taking a sip of coffee from a tiny bone-china cup, the kind I hate – I prefer my coffee in vast invigorating vats. The candles' flames were reflected in the polished wood of the old dining-room table; Jethro and the others were engaged in some long-running saga to do with a discothèque in Church Stretton; and Jimmy sat, chin in hand, immobile, giving the impression of some brooding energy at rest, his mind, like Yeats's long-legged fly, fixed upon silence.

'Do you want to go up and have a look at him?' asked Helen. The honest answer was no, not in the slightest, but the opportunity to escape was too tempting. Helen almost ran down the corridors and hallways, as if pursued by devils, her arms folded, hugging herself, her head inclined slightly, brooding. When I caught up with her I put my arm round her waist. She did not respond, but stood on the threshold of Byron's room for a few seconds without speaking. I took my arm away.

'Go in,' she said. 'Go on, go in.'

It was only a child's bedroom, but it felt like a foreign land. The air had an indefinable sweetness, and the rubble of infant-hood spread over the floor and seemingly up the walls like coastal wreckage. There was a bed in the corner, where I could dimly discern a huddled form. All around, as if from another element, another dimension, were long-forgotten images of Mickey Mouse, Mrs Tiggywinkle, Alice, Winnie the Pooh. I felt as if the past were coming to reclaim me, threatening to pluck me back into something I had lost and did not want to find again. Nervously, I tapped my foot against an Action Man. Lego spilled out of a large plastic box. There was a TV and video. Aeroplanes hung from the ceiling. One door of a wall cupboard

189

was open to reveal tier upon tier of toy heaven. The kid wanted for nothing.

I found Helen was standing by my side, and I clasped her out of desperation as much as affection.

'Hold me,' I gasped, panic-stricken. 'Hold me.'

I felt her hands grip my arms tightly. In my madness I thought it was passion. Steadied somewhat, I went on, confidently.

'What's going *on* down there? I think I'm going to die from the tension. Jimmy's gone off the rails, Grace is fawning all over him, and all I want is to be making love to you. That time we had in the garden was so astonishing, I wanted you more than anything I've ever known —'

I looked round. Even I wasn't going to suggest sex in a four-year-old's bedroom, when he was asleep in it.

Maybe I was more drunk that I'd realized, though.

A strange expression seized Helen's features. She was staring at something on the wall by the bed. For some reason I assumed it was a mouse, and searched in vain for it. Then I noticed a small red light glowing comfortably. I had never seen anything like it. It looked like some sort of kitchen appliance: a small white box, attached to a socket, with a red light.

Agitatedly Helen pulled at me. I was as keen as she was to find a bedroom, though I wondered whether we really had time, given that we were supposed to be taking a quick peak at a slumbering infant.

When we were outside in the corridor she took hold of my hand and pulled me forcibly some distance. Let's go. Now. On this rich blue deep warm carpet. Inviting like the Mediterranean.

'Shut the fuck up,' she hissed.

'I didn't say anything.'

'The fucking baby alarm's on.'

'Baby alarm.'

She turned a small circle, dancing in agitation.

I had no idea what she was talking about.

'Baby alarm. Baby alarm. Intercom. In case he wakes up. It's a long way from the dining room. We leave it on so we know if he's awake. He might wander around and get lost. What the hell did you say that for?'

Danger and embarrassment is a lethal combination. The adrenalin works likes a snake in the bloodstream.

'Do you think they heard?'

It sounds dumb, but one had to ask.

Helen could hardly stand still.

'Of course they did. They must have done. Maybe they didn't. What can we do? Wilf, I'm going to kill you for this.'

An overwhelming sensation of weightlessness overcame me. Walls and floors seemed to recede.

'What are we going to say? What are we going to do?'

She didn't reply.

It wasn't fear, exactly, but a biting nervousness that gave everything a hard clarity, like learning you have an incurable disease, or hearing that one of your parents has died. The world assumes a metallic freshness, a charged immediacy, like it's coming for you.

I remember the light as we entered the dining room: from the candles, from the wall-lamps. I remember its harshness, how it set off the edges of everything: the bookcases, the Conran side-tables, the gilt frames of oils commissioned from friends, the silhouettes of people standing awkwardly around the table, napkins clutched nervously to their midriffs. And like some avenging angel, the horrible fulfilment of the guilt one had hoped absurdly to avoid, Jimmy, standing four-square in the middle of the room, hands in pockets, a thunderous expression on his face.

We had had it.

'I think you and I have some talking to do,' he said to Helen. The words were thick and slurred. I'd never heard him talk like that; he seemed unmanned, not himself. Something in his tone was borrowed from elsewhere – films, maybe. For once, maybe for the first time, he was uncertain of what he was about. It was a Jimmy I did not know.

Then he looked at me, and it was a Jimmy I did know. I had seen this Jimmy often when we were rural gangs in the shrubbery

191

at ten years old: domineering, snide, his features luminous, mobile, intent.

I have a very, very practical response to such situations. I run. When I am attacked by strangers in the street, I put up no resistance. When I'm fired, I have no comeback. When my girlfriend throws me over, I accept it. I'm not one of life's great confrontationalists. So as I stood there, sensitive to every slightest movement, I thought carefully about the distance that lurked between myself and the wide open road. And, it should be said, I thought about whether Helen could make it with me. Could she run as fast as I could? Would that long, pencil-like dress impede her? For an infinitesimal second I pictured her throwing off her garments as she ran; then soberingly I noticed that Jimmy had disappeared, that the others were sidling away from the dining table, and that Helen was tugging at my sleeve. The tugging became increasingly frantic.

'Get out,' she was saying.

I remembered what happened to poetry Jimmy didn't like. I needed no second warning.

Reaching the door I turned slightly to catch a glimpse of Helen, and saw as if in a dream the noisy, thunderous bulk of Jimmy cascading back into the room. His right arm rose swiftly and a picture behind my head exploded in a shower of glass. Animal fear possessed me and I ran like a dog, aware of my living self as if it were a pulse in my throat, the rest of me pure motion, a madman close behind.

I made it out into the open, going well, my blood crashing in my ears. After a while I realized I needed to know where my pursuer was. With a wrenching effort of will I made myself slow and turn; in the floodlight in front of the old house nothing was moving. Either he was somewhere in the darkness between, or he was still in there. What was he doing? Something must have slowed him down. Was he going berserk and massacring them all? Had he done away with himself in a final gesture of despair?

I had heard no further shots. Should I call the police? Helen was still there, still facing the music, vulnerable, exposed, guilty. Should I go back? How could I? How could I not?

It was raining heavily. Water dripped from my nose. I was hot, drenched, in turmoil and in trouble.

The organic farmers left quickly, their movements assuming the clockwork rapidity of those who do not wish to give the impression that they're leaving as fast as they possibly can. Moments later their Land Rover came to life and raced up the hill, passing not far away from me. As they shot under one of the occasional lights that illuminated the drive I could see the shock on their faces.

I sat and waited. My skin must have wrinkled like a pink prune under the deluge, but I was hardly aware of it. Hour after hour began to pass. It was warm even for July. Eventually, however, as I mentally thawed, I became conscious of my bedraggled state and an encroaching physical chill, so I decamped to the protection of a nearby oak. As I did so I saw Jethro scamper out of the house, and within a minute his bike was roaring up the hill. I staggered towards him. He saw me and slowed, took off his helmet and eyed me as I approached. He said nothing. Neither did I, for a minute or two. He grinned suddenly.

'You look a mess.'

'What do I do now?'

He sighed. 'What do you do? God knows.'

He looked pensively into the distance. Jethro being a responsible adult was a new one on me.

'Go and have a hot bath by the look of it.' A sardonic look overcame his features. 'You're worried about your arse, aren't you? Well, don't be. Jimmy will kill you if he ever gets the opportunity, but they've got enough problems.'

'Is Helen safe?'

'Yes, just. I thought he was going to go for her, Wilf, I really did. I think he would have done, but there was a sort of seismic shift in him when he looked at the other guys standing around, and me, and then Helen again, and he just raged at her. *Molto* recriminations, man. Verbal abuse big-time. Not funny. The gun was still hanging in his hand, and he wouldn't put it down however much she asked him to. You didn't want to have been there, Wilf. I know Jimmy, and I know what he can do, and I was pretty fucking terrified. I mean, what a fucking mess, Wilf.' He eyed me meaningfully.

'Let me get this straight. Recriminations with Grace there?'

'Why not? She still is. Staying over. We needed her there, let me tell you.'

'Grace and Jimmy are sleeping with each other.'

Extenuating circumstances. Jethro flinched.

'They're not the only ones, by the sound of it. And anyway, how do you know that?'

How did I? I suppose I didn't. When one examined the evidence in the cold light of day, there was a considerable body of reasonable doubt. And the cold light of day was just beginning to make its presence felt. It had missed a long, wet, rotten night.

'Give me a lift home?'

Jethro looked at me, sodden and pathetic as I was.

'Get on.'

I lied to my parents. That is, I didn't tell them the whole truth. I said that Helen and I had got close, that Jimmy had heard me say something unguarded, that Jimmy had taken a shot at me. They listened intently – no one gets into the state I was in without something serious having happened – and at the end my ma smiled sweetly at me.

'That's fine, Wilf, darling. And when you want to tell us the real story we'll still be here.'

I thought of the expressions on the farmers' faces in the lamplight.

'Well, I think there might be some fairly vicious rumours about.'

'I imagine that's quite possible,' said my father.

We all knew what was being said.

194

When I got back to London I intended to lie low: very, very low. I didn't want calls, or newspapers, or anything. I wanted to insulate myself completely, to batten down hatches and tuck myself up into my own little hermit shell. I sat in my flat and read Tolstoy, Dante, Aristotle and an abundance of Richmal Crompton. I felt shocked and estranged, but in a good, still-in-one-piece sort of way, as well as a useful sorting-out-where-I-go-from-here sort of way. I missed Helen like crazy.

The summer was turning out blazing hot, and the tubes were perpetually on strike, so when I needed to I walked into town up the South Lambeth Road and over Vauxhall Bridge, past Victoria Station then round Buck House and up the Mall, from the squalid south London landscape of battered tower blocks first thrown up in the ruined acres left by the Blitz to the airiness of St James's Park; the heat and light made it radiant, cleansing the city of its appetite for the abyss. On those days London seemed all mine, and I flung myself along its pavements in a flapping whirl of old and battered linen.

Every so often I would stop on Vauxhall Bridge to gaze upon the water, sometimes low and muddy and disreputable, sometimes high and silver and self-confident, always with something distracting going on. One evening, with the world turning a brick red in the sunset, I found the face of someone nearby swimming into recognition. She, like me, was leaning against the parapet; unlike me, she was dressed smartly. Lots of people used to stop to admire the view, and I always felt a comradely sense of community with them. We were a diverse crew, we river-watchers, and the bridge was in a different dimension from the rest of London. It was a point of transition, a solid highway crossing a liquid one, a physical embodiment of an equals sign, where vistas opened and perspectives could be gained and yet where nothing could be effected, only equated. The bridge was a place of purpose, but on it, momentarily, for us watchers, purpose was suspended.

She was not dressed for disengagement, though: she wore a smart black suit, and her hair was short and bobbed and glossy

195

and black, like a billiard ball. She dressed as if she had life sorted, but she leaned on the parapet with the rest of us as if she were pondering the greater questions, like whether having life sorted was all it was cracked up to be.

When I looked at her again her posture had changed: one perfectly shod foot had found its way behind the other, her shoulders had slumped slightly, and her features were assuming a disturbing familiarity. They gave the impression that they were coming together at me out of a fog, out of the past; indeed they were coming at me out of the past, my own past, and my mind made little forays and feints to try and catch half-seen intimations of people I once knew. And as these elusive old images coalesced from the deep hinterland of recollection, the face before me assembled itself to match the rapidly approaching impression of memory, and the two were as one.

Of course, some people may not have the same problems with recall that I do.

I sidled along the parapet.

'Hermione?' I ventured.

She turned, and her face assumed an expression first of suspicion, then alarm, then scathing bewilderment – all of which were irritating, because it's humiliating to recognize someone who doesn't return the favour – and then, at last, 'Milo?'

'Wilf,' I corrected. But we were in the right arena.

'Wilf. Of course,' she echoed, enthusiastically. She looked away, slightly nonplussed, then laughed self-deprecatingly. 'Do you come here often?'

'As a matter of fact I do, what with the tube strikes and the sunshine and everything. What about you?'

'I live just over the bridge, so sometimes, yes.'

'Whereabouts over the bridge?'

'Just over there.' She waved a hand.

'What, in that squat? You can't do.' There was very little residential housing on the south side of Vauxhall Bridge, apart from a dilapidated square which had been well colonized; technically it was a squat, but all the buildings had been done up to match the last word in Bohemian chic, and I had known a few old friends pass through it.

'Why not?' She gave me a look of one who perceived unjustified assumptions, possibly leading to prejudice. I remembered that she had watched me shower Iris Murdoch with champagne, that she had been a brilliant PPE student – politically radioactive – and that she had been one of the few people I had ever met capable of taking a serious interest in the prayer-life of the Bishop of Oxford.

'Well, you don't look as if you do, I suppose,' I said lamely. She gave me a pitying look, then seemed to think better of it, and smiled. She had a big, brassy smile: strong teeth and full lips; the lower one having a small thrusting will of its own.

'Have you been there?' she asked.

'Not for a while,' I returned, guardedly. Several years, in truth. To me it was just a folk-memory, a place I had been to once or twice; not wildly different from other London squats: just crumbling and chaotic, hoping to become a housing trust. But we were walking the same way home, and as we came to the small, unobtrusive turning off the cacophonous main roads that hug the Thames south of the bridge, she invited me to take a look. It had changed utterly: once a heap of fetid dereliction, Angley Square was now a much-loved haven of exuberant good taste. Pavements had been dug up and planted with palms, gigantic phormiums and yuccas; sword-like leaves sheared through the unyielding urban landscape, somehow challenging the memory of falling bombs and, in their scything vigour, cleansing their surroundings of decay. In place of ripped-up pavements were euphorbias and hellebores and silver birches, a tulip tree and real plantains, the pale greens, whites and creams shaping the streets with their silky definitions. Variegated ivies and passion-flowers embraced the old walls, and Moroccan brooms, pampas grass and scintillating verbena were outspoken neighbours. Hollyhocks crowded round a children's play area. There was an intelligent harmony; it was a good place to be.

Hermione's flat was almost bare of furniture, the walls were whitewashed and hung with kilims; the bare floorboards were covered with them, too. Just like old times.

'I brought lots back from Morocco,' she said, as I admired them.

'And when you're not in Morocco, you're in the City?' I hazarded.

She frowned. 'God, no. I'm at Saatchi's.' She did not elaborate. Whatever it was she did there, I could not imagine she didn't do it well. She kicked off her smart shoes with subtly reckless abandon. Plucking a chilled bottle from an old fridge covered with children's magnetic letters – v. chic – she uncorked it with relish and offered me an enormous blue balloon of a glass.

'So where have you been since we last met, whenever and wherever that was?'

I told her. The words, or at least the events they described, seemed to take form as I spoke, like breath misting on cold air.

There was a knock at the door before I finished; without waiting for a response, a tousled figure in a dressing gown appeared.

'Hermione,' he said, as if making sure, 'I was wondering if you had any camomile tea?' He had a rather beaky expression, and he eyed the room questioningly, like a bird. 'I seem to have run out.' His glance alighted on me.

'This is an old friend – well,' she laughed, looking in my direction sheepishly, 'someone I once knew – and this is Sebastian. Sebastian lives upstairs.' For some reason this last remark seemed important to her, for she repeated it, with emphasis. She rummaged in a brown pot by the stove and flung him two small packages.

Sebastian stood gazing at me absently, then suddenly woke up enough to murmur his thanks, and disappeared.

'He's an architect,' she said flatly, as if this explained something.

'So what kind of people live here?'

'Oh, drop-outs, people like me, people like Sebastian. Families.'

'You've got some good gardeners somewhere.'

'We sure have. This place is unique. Of course, it's a housing trust now, but it wasn't always. There's the toil and trouble of years all around us, you know. Just stopping it falling down was an achievement.'

'Have you been here long?'

'Seven years. I'm practically the oldest living inhabitant. It's changed a lot. I've changed a lot.'

'We all have.'

'Have we?'

Her expression was full of sardonic appraisal, and I sensed an implied truth. Around me the furniture was beautiful, the glasses lumpy and distorted and expensive, the paintings equally so, and it was not so very far from my life in Notting Hill with Grace. In fact, it was practically identical. Though free, of course.

'Yes.' I like to be emphatic when I can. 'Not always for the better.'

Her look softened. 'Tell me about it,' she invited quietly. So I did, some more.

As I walked back I felt discernibly lighter. It wasn't as if bemoaning my fate was new to me; it was simply that she was virgin territory. I had landed on *terra incognita* and I was colonizing it with my miserable autobiography like Cortez did the Aztecs with guns and syphilis (or was it smallpox? Or both?). Like Jethro, she thought the whole thing was a mess, but because I hardly knew her it felt like a stamp of approval. A *new* kind of mess. Being licensed to feel sorry for oneself is small comfort, but it felt unaccountably like a big one as I slipped along the Stockwell pavements home.

On entering my street, which was wide and spacious and lined with vast late-Victorian houses all converted into flats, I saw a figure sitting on the low wall that boundaried my front garden: a drunk, a beggar, some vagrant. It was hunched in a big overcoat, head in hands, and it wasn't moving. The light was beginning to fade, and there were several large sycamores to embolden the gloom. I felt timid about approaching it, so I passed by on the

199

other side and walked round the block. When I returned it had not gone away, so I did the same again, this time stopping to read the paper over a cup of coffee in a nearby café; but the figure was still there when I got back, and I realized I was being absurd. I'm not one for premonitions, by and large, but as I walked towards it the figure rose and turned to face me. In the darkness beneath the tree above us I could not make out its features, and I hesitated, then stopped. What did it want with me? It came towards me, its head shaking from side to side like the red dwarf in *Don't Look Now*; I swear I was about to turn and run, when it spoke.

'Wilf, where the fuck have you been? I've been waiting fucking hours.'

'Helen? What are you doing here?'

'Come to see you, of course. Do you think I sit alone in strange bits of London for the good of my health?'

She had taken hold of my lapels. I could not make out whether she was genuinely angry or not. Her smile was of the fixed kind that does a passable imitation of a bare-toothed snarl.

'How long are you staying for?'

'I'm not going back.'

'You're *what*?'

'I'm staying. With you. I've come to stay. How many different ways do I need to put this?'

'But what about Jimmy?'

'I've left him.'

'What about Byron?'

'I've left him too.'

'But you can't.'

'Just watch me.'

'No, really, you can't.'

'Let's go inside.'

'No, wait.'

Madly, we struggled.

I felt rising panic.

'Wilf, what *is* this? Aren't you pleased I'm here?'

200

'You can't leave Byron.'

'Wilf, look. Listen.' She put her hands, fingers outstretched, flat against my chest in her characteristic way as if she were holding down an unruly sheet of paper. 'Byron will be fine. Jimmy can look after him. Jimmy can handle it. It'll be good for him. And I am going to live my life. This will be good for me. So it's all worked out. Don't argue with this, Wilf.'

She looked up at me under glowering eyebrows and I was dumb.

'It hasn't been that easy, you know.' Her voice wavered and thinned.

My head span like a roulette wheel.

'Why did you leave?' I asked, as we walked to the door.

The overcoat she had on must have been an old one of Jimmy's. She was lost in it; she looked worn out, waif-like, drained.

'Because I didn't want to be with him any more. Because I did want to be with you.'

She leaned against the wall as I took out my keys.

We climbed the stairs to my flat.

'We can't stay here,' she said, running her hands through her hair distractedly.

'Why not?'

'Jimmy will find it. He knows where you live.'

'Well?' I said it to sound like 'So?'.

'Well, you know what he's like.'

'You want a safe house? I don't know a safe house. I don't know what a safe house is.'

'Somewhere quiet. Somewhere off the map. Somewhere with a lot of people going through.'

I thought for a while.

'Let me get you a drink.' I said. 'I've got an idea. That is, if they've got a phone.'

Random Episodes of Senseless Violence

'IF YOU HAVEN'T got camomile, raspberry will do. Or lemon verbena; I'm happy to consider lemon verbena.'

We had been denizens of Vauxhall for two months. It was a new world, a new-found-land. Being a bit of a flop at life wasn't a stigma, far from it. If anything, it was actively encouraged. It was not as if Sebastian ever found any work as an architect, and apart from his insatiable desire for herbal teas he was the most affable of companions. The rooms they found for us were basic – someone had once removed the plaster from the walls and no one seemed to have yet found the appropriate moment to put it back – and we had two mattresses on the floor. We put all our food in Sebastian's fridge. Hermione gave us a kettle and a corkscrew, and we picnicked on cheese and wine, side by side on the mattresses, until the evening began, when people would gather to sit around and do copious drugs in an accommodating neighbour's flat. Most often it was at Sebastian's – though he had no visible means of support, he managed to bestow narcotics among us with uncommon philanthropy. He held some sway among the shifting community of travellers and wanderers and Saatchi executives; it was something to do with his slow, slightly lugubrious gravity and the spark of wisdom in his eye (both of which he cultivated assiduously, I suspected).

It was both heaven and hell being with Helen. I was numb at the thought of Byron – but I quickly told myself that it was not my business. Told myself, but as so often when I gave myself advice, I didn't listen to it. And why shouldn't a woman take control over her destiny? Men walk out on their families all the time. No one approves of it, but they accept it happens. I'd never heard of a woman doing it – or was I having an atavistic prejudice about the nurturing instinct brutally but rightly shattered? What did I know about the nurturing instinct, anyway? Zip, that's what.

And I could not make Helen out on this. I could make her out on most things, but she blanked me on Byron. She had achieved a terrifying composure. I could only guess helplessly at the feelings coursing behind each poised gesture and word, but I knew they were there, for everything she did and said was fractionally too fast, too light, too tense, like violin strings wound a semitone too high for their correct pitch. Inside she was wearing herself out, exhausting her emotional reserves little by little, and as she did so those strings were being wound tighter. But she held it together.

It wasn't that she wasn't in touch with home – she went out to the phone box frequently (calling the nanny, I supposed), always returning white as a sheet. After a while, though, it transpired that her pallor was due to something I don't think she can have reckoned on: Grace had moved into Monkridge, leaving the job, leaving everything. This drove her crazy. I thought she would snap, but then I could see the mulishness rising in her. She still had this stubborn ability to make herself mistress of her condition at extraordinary speed, and keep things that way.

'The point is,' she would say, and as she did so she bowed her head and splayed the fingers of her left hand, thrusting them out before her in a peculiar gesture of priestess-like concentration and affirmation, 'the point is that he is better off without me there. Two parents who behave like Jimmy and I did are no good for a child. I did this for his sake.'

The unhappy thought occurred to me that Jimmy and Grace were not necessarily the ideal replacement relationship, but I said nothing. What, again, did I know?

'This is the choice I have made,' she went on, as she always did; this part was a mantra for her. 'I'm very happy with it. This

203

is what I want. I've got you,' here she would relax, 'and I've got a life. I like it here.'

She did like it. More than I thought she would; someone who marries into the Spalding family could justifiably be thought to have an eye for the luxuries of life. Maybe she was over-compensating, but she threw herself wholeheartedly into Vauxhall ways, often remarking that this was an experience she had missed out on and that she was going to hug it to herself for good.

I wasn't so sure. It was nice to play at being students again, especially ones that were doing things in a boho way that was never easily attainable the first time round. We began picking up odds and ends of furniture from junkshops on foraging trips to Brixton and beyond, and I brought some stuff from my flat, including my computer. But something in me wanted to get back to the fray: to taste monkfish rather than lentils, to drive something more powerful than the communal Deux Chevaux which we took turns in trundling along to Sainsbury's at Nine Elms to fill up with groceries for the week (it was a minor miracle that it ever made it back). I still wanted somehow to count a bit in the great world that, like the relentless gale of traffic along Wandsworth Road, whirled unceasingly past us beyond the sedate confines of our new alternative village.

It was not long before I had the idea of approaching the Colour Mag about this place. It hadn't been covered by anyone, so far as I knew, and with my horticultural hat on I could wax enthusiastically about redeeming urban decay and so on, while branching out by writing up its human side.

The editor was keen.

'So that's where you've got to,' she said, over the phone. 'We were wondering.' There was something strange in her voice, but she left it at that.

I got straight into it, clearing a table and setting out the objects that I loved to have around me when I wrote: an old stone picked up at a church fair in Oxford, made smooth and shiny by some sort of lacquer, sky-blue heath milkwort painted against the light grey; an ancient cactus that had stayed loyal and alive through the years, obscenely healthy and sprouting priapically out of a pot that was too small for it. I felt good about this piece. It was going to be the making of me.

That evening we gathered in Sebastian's flat, one floor below ours. It was in exquisite taste: whitewashed walls, one huge and violent painting where the enamel was so thick it threatened to climb out into the room and walk, and the reds so powerful and hot they made you break out in unseemly perspiration. Almost everything else was culled from junkshops: ancient chandeliers, their rust glowing in the light thrown by lava lamps, so popular in suburban seventies sitting rooms, whose little blobs of molten wax rose and sank in glass shaped like old Corona bottles. In the corner stood the torso of a mannequin, with a badge inscribed 'Who's Your Friend?' pinned to its left nipple.

Halfway through the meal Hermione, who had painted her face white for the evening and, with her black hair and spangled clothes, looked like something out of the *commedia dell'arte*, began complaining piteously about the latest tube strike.

'I thought we were supposed to have entered a strike-free era,' I reflected, deliberately politically provocative. Someone had just put a large ladleful of bean stew on my plate and I felt seized by a bout of Thatcherite aggression.

'Well, someone should tell the drivers. They've been out again for the last week,' observed Sebastian. 'Anyone for a soupçon more?'

'I don't think I've seen a newspaper in months. Amazing and wonderful how isolated we are here.'

'You *must* read the papers, surely?' Hermione sounded sceptical.

'No. Don't know why. Just don't.'

'Do you, Helen?'

She assumed a hunted look. 'Not really.'

'Not never?'

'No, I suppose not.'

Sebastian was looking at his plate. Then, as if addressing

himself to the assembled beans, he said slowly: 'You must have seen some, though, I would have thought.'

'No.'

'Come on, Sebastian. Are you an avid devourer of newsprint? I wouldn't have thought so.'

'Devoted to the *Six O'Clock News*. But I read the newspapers sometimes. Enough.' His voice trailed off. His meaning, for he evidently had one, eluded me.

'What are you driving at? *Are* you driving at something?'

'I think he is wondering,' interrupted Hermione, 'whether you know about Jimmy Spalding.'

'Of course I know about him,' I replied. 'More than most. Apart from Helen, of course. I've known him for ever.'

'Well, quite.'

'Well, quite what?' An atmosphere was gathering about us, a huge great prickly one with spines like a monstrous porcupine. Helen's hunted expression had become almost abject. A horrifying thought struck me.

'It's not about Byron, is it?' I blurted out. With a low, disturbing moan Helen swung out of her seat and her heels were heard clattering on the stairs.

'It was at first,' said Hermione. '*Guardian* front page. I mean, only once,' she added, seeing me recoil. 'It's the business pages now. I can't believe you didn't know all this.' Privately, neither could I. Where had I been when I needed me most?

Hermione was exasperated. 'He's trying to float the company, but he's under a deep black cloud because Helen's left him and there are all these rumours, and people are wondering if she's going to press charges. I mean, is it true?'

'Probably. What are they?'

'Well, did he beat her up?'

'Is that what they say?'

'Not specifically. But that's the kind of thing they're hinting at.'

From somewhere in my mental hinterland an old defensiveness arose.

'I hope they're not dragging Grace into this.'

'Grace who?'

I was relieved. 'Just someone.'

'Is she the one he's living with now? With the boy?' asked Sebastian.

We were quiet. The other guests looked on apprehensively. In the silence I could hear a train crossing the bridges over at Nine Elms. Somewhere upstairs a lavatory flushed.

'Helen's still up then,' I remarked, hoping desperately to lead the conversation, as if by a ring through its nose, into the realms of facetious asides – anywhere away from where we were.

Then someone – it wasn't Hermione or Sebastian – said: 'She went downstairs, though.'

It took me a few seconds to register this.

'Well, she can't have done.'

'Yes, she did.'

'There's no one upstairs. We're all here.'

Doggedly: 'She went out, though. I heard the door slam.'

'Who's up there, then?' Another voice.

'Better go and look, Wilf.' This was Hermione. She seemed quite serious. 'Lavatories don't flush themselves.'

'Oh, come on, this is stupid. I mean, you don't expect – you don't think we've got a toilet-flushing pan-rinsing ghost, do you? How many joints have you had?'

'None, as it happens. So don't be offensive.'

There was an inescapable logic emerging here. Someone should go and see what was going on. That someone was going to have to be me.

I climbed the bare wooden staircase in trepidation. I felt the whole thing was absurd: of course it was Helen. Who else could it be? A burglar would not pause in his or her burgling to pee, although I had heard that the excitement of theft sometimes led to the urge to drop a turd, often in the middle of the room, like a territorial marking.

I undid the latch and went in. With a whir and a thump someone in black shouldered me in the chest and knocked me

207

winded against the wall. At such moments those things nearest to oneself rapidly thrust themselves upon one's attention. Family jewellery, engagement rings, photographs, treasured etchings.

'My wallet. Please don't take my wallet,' I gasped.

He stopped as he descended the stairs and rummaged in a holdall, fishing something out and throwing it up at me.

'There. That's just to show I'm a nice burglar. Nothing in it anyway,' he muttered, then vanished from sight.

When I got back to the others they were on their feet, but they had otherwise utterly failed to apprehend the fleeing suspect.

'Did you manage to intercept him?' I asked, with all the dry irony I could muster.

'Did they get anything?' Sebastian asked irritatingly.

'Well, funnily enough they didn't get my wallet. No, they missed that.'

'They?' asked Hermione. 'Outnumbered, were you?'

'All right, he, then. Anyway, we'd better get the police.'

There was a rich and stagnant silence.

'Surely even you need to get the police in sometimes.'

'Only if it's really necessary,' sighed Sebastian wearily, as if my experience was wildly inflated.

'Well, it *is* really necessary.'

'Did he get anything of significance?'

I realized I had no idea what he had taken. There had obviously been a great deal of digging into things and strewing them about, but our room always looked like a garbage spillage and it was hard to see where home-grown squalor ended and looting began.

'Oddly enough, the one thing I noticed missing was a piece I was writing about this place for the *Sunday Times*. Why would he take that, do you think? It can't have been for reading on the bus.'

In an evening which was becoming conversationally challenged with pregnant pauses, the mother of them all now occurred. We reassembled at table. I was extremely shaken, and not really concentrating. I felt abused and humiliated. And no recourse to the hopeless but reassuring Metropolitan Police. And Helen had disappeared, and it was about Byron, and why shouldn't it be? I massaged the back of my head where it had struck the wall.

'Wilf, I don't believe you just said that. I *can't* believe you just said that.' It was Hermione.

'What?' I blinked.

'That you're writing about us.'

'I'm not. It's more about the vegetation. At least' − I felt compelled to be honest − 'it'll start that way. I think I've got a copy on disk, though, so I foxed him there. He seems to have been looking for documents,' I mused on. 'All the drawers with letters and papers in have been emptied.'

'There are codes of behaviour,' said Sebastian. 'Even here. Dammit,' he thumped the table theatrically, '*especially* here.'

'Yes, well, obviously he hadn't been made intimate with them.'

'And obviously neither have you.'

'Me? Please, Hermione, I've just been burgled and attacked. You can sympathize if you like.'

'You don't come here and then make a fast buck out of doing press features. If we ever find you doing that we'll help him finish off the job.'

They were looking very cross. I realized I was getting in over my head but I couldn't help it. I was outraged.

'Come on, Hermione, now it's you who's being offensive.'

'*Offensive*?' she screamed. '*Offensive*? You freely come and live here and *write* about it? Who the fucking hell do you think you are?'

Someone with their right foot firmly embedded in a hornet's nest.

Foolishly, I retaliated.

'Well, you know, surely it would be a good thing. You've done so much here; it's a miracle of urban renewal, or regeneration. People should know about it. It's inspiring: a happy commune of, what, five hundred people, who have created this wonderful synthesis of brick and plant; it's a whole new way of living. It's the future, or the future of a lot of derelict, defunct and decrepit housing around the country, maybe around the world. You should be proud of what you've done.'

'The point is, we did it for ourselves. It's ours, and we don't want publicity. And it's not your right to do this. Especially since you're getting paid for it. It's exploitative.'

'Do you want a cut of my fee?' I couldn't believe that she did, and God knows I didn't want them to have one, but I couldn't think of any other response.

'For Christ's sake.' There was a – what would it be called? An astringency? – an astringency of pursed lips around the table. I felt like someone in an old Bateman cartoon: the man who mentioned cash in a commune. Yes, I should have known better.

There was a sudden blur and Helen was with us again, plainly trying to look as if she had been there all the time. No one had the courage to ask her where she had been, or perhaps everyone had the tact not to. Besides, my concerns for her feelings were momentarily superseded by my concerns for my own. My nerves seemed to jangle louder the more time elapsed. The figure of the intruder turned into a silhouette in my memory, then back to flesh. I realized with a slight shock that he had been wearing a balaclava, like a terrorist.

Helen, when we told her, was cool.

'What did he take, exactly?'

'I haven't checked, exactly. I mean, I did look, but I haven't checked in detail.' I was beginning to feel slightly dizzy. 'I'm not sure I could tell.'

'Apparently, he purloined a piece Wilf was penning about us,' intoned Sebastian, looking even more like an idling bird of prey than ever. 'About which we're extremely pleased, as you can imagine.'

'I can.' She said this to herself, abstractedly. She stood up. 'If you don't mind, I'm going to bed.'

I followed, glad of the excuse and the company.

'Where did you go?' I hissed. 'I thought it was you upstairs.'

She did not answer, but blew through the flat like a whirl-wind. When she came to a halt she stood arms akimbo and remarked decisively, 'You know what this is about, don't you?'

'Not a clue.'

'It's Jimmy.'

'What, the man in the balaclava?'

She seemed to reflect, and a wry, appreciative smile broke upon her lips. 'Well, you know, it's the sort of thing he might try.' She sounded, unbelievably, admiring. Then she shook her head. 'Pull yourself together, girl.'

'All right, what do you mean?'

'This is Jimmy's style.'

'I know he's capable of lots of things.'

'You don't know him like I do.' Defiant, almost proud.

I thought I did.

'So what is a half-written article of mine going to tell Jimmy?'

'It's going to tell him quite a lot about what I'm doing here, isn't it? God knows how he found me.'

She peered out of an open window. 'Very agile,' she remarked.

'Really, I don't think Jimmy would –'

She held up a hand.

'Really, he would. Believe.'

'How on earth do you go about hiring burglars?' I wondered out loud. 'Especially intelligent ones, ones that read bits of paper and make judgements about their usefulness.' I intended to be mildly sarcastic, but it seemed pointless. Helen didn't answer.

'Unsettling,' I murmured.

But Helen seemed to find it all far from unsettling. Over the ensuing days and weeks a certain confidence appeared to buoy her up; she became more inclined to affectionate confrontation with Sebastian about the relative merits, and more especially demerits, of Richard Rogers and Norman Foster; I once came in to find her lying on her back with her legs in the air, twirling a

211

tea-tray around on the soles of her feet. By contrast, I assumed some of her old moodiness like a protective cape, knowing that I must be buried deep in the ordure of public scorn, at best by association, and still nagged by the burglary, its suddenness and violation and inanity. It was an occurrence whose poison leeched out but slowly, and after a while the longings for my old life increased, and I sneaked out to a phone box on the Wandsworth Road and phoned Milo.

'Wilf! Where have you *been*? I've been terribly worried about you.'

'I'll tell you. But can we meet? What are you doing tonight?'

'Not much. Tom's around. Thought we might go and see a film. You want the Crepuscule?'

'Very much I do.'

'With or without Phipps? Are you friends or foes?'

'Actually, very much friends. I've got some things I want to ask him.'

'How's Helen?'

'How do you know about Helen?'

'Come on, Wilf. I'm not completely deaf or blind, you know.'

I foresaw there was some catching up to do. The pips went.

'Crepuscule, seven o'clock,' I bellowed down the phone, and hung up.

It was good to be back. I felt as if I had been in hibernation, wrapped in the violent and exotic world of Helen and Jimmy and Monkridge. I still was. But seeing Milo's dear manic features and wildly enthusiastic grin, and Tom's fat, voluptuous, reliably untrustworthy face, lit a little long-dead flame in me. A single-male-in-the-metropolis-at-night-with-old-pals flame. The much-polished patina of the chairs, the broad and unhurried red-and-white check of the table cloths, the racks of bottles on the wall, the spidery handwriting of the menus, the great voyeuristic windows on to Beak Street, the set of Tour de France posters, the good French food and the air of a restaurant that feels at ease with itself – all filled me with fortifying vigour.

'I've invited someone,' said Tom through a mouthful of onion

212

soup and baguette. 'Someone you might like to see.' He eyed me roguishly.

'Is this wise, Tom?' murmured Milo, rolling his eyes anxiously.

'Oh, yes?' I parried.

'He'll be along later.'

'Can't wait. What I want to know is, what all this is about Jimmy?'

'Grammar,' said Milo.

'What-all-this-is-about-Jimmy,' said Tom, slowly. 'No, I think it makes a sort of louche, devil-may-care sense. It even has a kind of rhythm. But that could be improved upon. If you lay the stress on the "what" and the "is" and the "Jim" it's a sort of bunched-up, boozy, drum roll; if on the "all" and the "is" it's a quiet ballad in a musical between two more rumbustious numbers.'

'Get on with it,' I said.

'What don't you know?'

'Everything. I haven't read a paper in two months.'

'Impossible.'

'You don't know where I've been.'

'That's often said about you.'

'Thanks.'

'Where *have* you been, then? We all know who with.'

'*How* do you know? Tell me about that first.' It was time to find out the full extent of the damage.

'My dear Wilf, it was everywhere. You don't elope with the wife of a press baron without someone noticing.'

'Press baron's a bit rich. And we didn't elope. Oh, God.'

'As is Jimmy Spalding. And whatever. And quite.'

'Front page, I hear.'

'Worse. Page three of the *Daily Telegraph*. Along with the axe-murderers and the Soviet tanks massed against the East German borders able to reach Paris in twenty-four hours.'

'So the effect was?'

'Haven't you spoken to anyone? Didn't you phone home or something?'

213

'Tom, I'm not a child. I thought no one knew. And I was lying low. I thought everyone would disapprove,' I ended pathetically.

'They do, but not of you.'

'Who, then?'

'Whom. Jimmy.'

'*Jimmy*? Why?'

'Because it was clear why she had left him. All the sympathy is with her. He's obviously a beast. I'm afraid,' said Tom, regarding me pityingly, 'you're only a bit-player in this.'

'So now Jimmy is seriously in the poo,' proffered Milo, elegantly.

'Because of Helen?'

'Because,' said Tom, 'if you want to sell your lovely company serenely on the stock market in pursuit of Byzantine wealth, you don't want to have a filthy court case hanging over your head.'

'The papers said that about him? About the abuse and stuff?'

'And stuff. And stuffed him. Except that I don't think it's proven, is it? I imagine he's petrified about where she is and what she is going to do.'

'We had a very interesting burglary the other day.'

'What did they take?'

'Something I was writing about where we're living. They couldn't have said this in print, though, could they? Libellous, surely?' Screwing my eyes up at Tom.

'There are ways and ways of putting these things, Wilf.'

'Bygones, you two,' called Milo.

'Bugger bygones,' I returned, but my heart wasn't in it. I turned back to Tom. 'So the police aren't going to take action but everyone thinks it's just possible they might, and even if there's no truth in it whatsoever it's damaging his reputation, and he doesn't think the City will support his flotation?'

'Wilf, how many times have I told you, the City doesn't give a damn about reputation. But even they might balk at a criminal record for domestic violence. Not to mention the disposal of assets in the divorce; what happens if the disaffected ex-wife takes possession of a large bundle of shares?'

'So, let's count the scalps. He screwed me, I've screwed his wife and his business? Looks like two–one?'

Milo looked shocked, and a slow grin spread wide across Tom's face.

'That's a nasty vengeful streak you've got on you there,' Milo commented.

'Here's our friend,' said Tom, rising unexpectedly.

Out of the Beak Street darkness, to my utter astonishment, emerged, blinking into the light, Jethro, more outrageously blackly bearded than ever. He was clad in full leather biker togs, the kind that make you look as if you have walked off the set of a particularly dilapidated episode of *Star Trek*. He entered with a swagger quite unlike the moronic slouch he affected in Shrewsbury. As a result, not only was I unwilling to believe it was him, but for some time I didn't even recognize him at all. He had a casual *savoir-faire* that was entirely in keeping with his sur-roundings but was not remotely in keeping with the Jethro I knew.

'Jethro!' I shot out eventually. Tom's head swivelled inquisitively.

'Jethro? Why do you call him that?'

'Stephen *is* my name, Wilf,' said Jethro.

I suppose it was, originally. I could see why he might want to drop the Jethro. I couldn't remember why we had thought it so funny. And here he was, a creature transformed, casting off his crusted old carapace to emerge pink and blinking into the metropolitan brave new world.

'Stephen. Yes, of course. How on earth do you know these two?'

'I don't think I've had the honour,' said Milo, utterly bewildered.

'In my role as monitor of all things Spalding, which I took to be a public service of the greatest moment, Stephen and I have been having a number of clandestine meetings which are proving extremely useful,' intoned Tom.

'You're not shopping Jimmy, are you?' I asked in amazement. 'After all he's done for you?'

Jethro looked offended.

'What's he done for me? And what do you know about it, anyway?'

'Can someone tell me what's going on?' interjected Milo with some heat.

'Last time I saw Stephen here I was soaked to the skin having been shot at by Jimmy Spalding.'

'Yes, I heard about that,' murmured Tom.

'What, literally shot at?'

'Literally. Live ammunition, glass exploding everywhere.'

'I didn't know that.'

'Surprising how quiet it was kept.'

'We wonder how he managed it,' said Tom. 'Anyway, Wilf, Stephen's not shopping anybody. He's just a good source of off-the-record information. Have a drink, Stephen.' He poured him a generous measure of Semillon Chardonnay. 'Relax, Wilf,' he went on. 'On his occasional visits to London, Steve and I just trade gossip. He likes to know what I know about Spalding and I like to know what he knows. Together it happens to add up to quite a bit.'

I could see who was being useful to whom. I wondered what Jethro was getting out of it.

'So what *is* going on?' I asked.

'He means, how's Grace?' observed Tom, sweetly, and with disconcerting accuracy.

'Not coping all that well,' grinned Jethro.

My treacherous heart leapt a little.

'With Jimmy? Who can? How's he treating her?'

'Oh, no, Jimmy's fine. He's so taken up with business he gives her no grief at all. Don't think he knows she's there, half the time. And he's not there the other half. When they're together, though, they're pretty soft on each other. Sorry, Wilf.' He looked at me sympathetically. It didn't help. 'No, it's Byron who's the problem.'

216

'Byron?'

'Who's Byron? Someone help?' pleaded Milo.

'Helen's and Jimmy's son.'

'Have you met him?'

'I did once. And sort of caught sight of him another time.'

'Grace thinks he's the kid from hell.'

'Well, if his mother's left him with a strange woman I'm not surprised he's pissed off about it.'

'He doesn't seem all that bothered about that. He told me the other day that mummy had gone to town to do some shopping and would be back soon.'

'Will she, Wilf?' queried Milo, *sotto voce*. I didn't answer.

'He won't, however, do a single thing Grace tells him to do. Asks him, I suppose, would be fairer; she's sensitive about that. Doesn't want to impose herself – you know what she's like. She'd bend over backwards for that kid; for Jimmy's sake, that's one reason, but she's really aware of what's happening to him, more than he is in some ways. The thing is, you see, she can't understand why Helen left, just can't understand it.'

'I'm with her on that,' said Milo.

'Oh, Milo,' I said.

'Wilf, I'm sure you're Romeo and Casanova and a titan in the sack, but I can't see why she would leave her son.'

'She's a very intelligent, self-determining woman.'

'Self-determining is right.'

'And the man beats her up.'

'Wilf, we don't know that, so far as I can see. I mean, do we?' Tom pouted slightly. 'The rumours are strong.'

'That doesn't mean you know the truth of it.'

'She's even left her child because of what he was doing to her.'

'She has left him. That's true. Though she may not have done so for the reasons you think.'

Tom and I looked at each other. I don't think either of us had any clear idea why Helen was no longer with Jimmy and Byron. I had a fond idea it was because she loved me. And she did. I know she did. She told me so. Often.

'Go on, Stephen,' insisted Tom.

'Byron's a nightmare to her. She buys him teddies and he secretly puts them in the washing-machine so they come out all shrivelled. She gives him food and he feeds it to the cat or throws it at her when her back's turned. Once he ran away from her in the middle of Shrewsbury and she experienced ten minutes of terror before she found him holding a policeman's hand about ten feet away from where she had last seen him. He's developed perverse eating habits: one day it's jam and peanut butter and nothing else, the next it's Marmite and marmalade.'

'Sounds quite normal to me.'

'She doesn't know what normal is in a four-year-old, though. She puts him to bed and he howls the place down, or sits sulkily sucking his thumb while she tries to read him Postman Pat.'

'I'd do the same, I think.'

'He refuses to put his clothes on and wanders around without anything on at all, like one of those blanket protesters, only without the blanket.'

'That *is* impressive.'

'She can't control him.'

'What does Jimmy do?'

'He's just too distracted to notice. And Byron worships the ground he walks on.'

'Nothing new there.'

'I think she's at the end of her tether, you know.'

'Why?'

'Well, she told me so, for one thing.' Jethro looked at me meaningfully. 'You know, he's desperate to get Helen back.'

This struck me as illogical.

'He's living with Grace, and he wants Helen back?'

'What a mess,' said Milo.

'Who told you that, Jethro . . . sorry, Stephen?' I asked.

'He did.'

'Were you supposed to tell me that?'

'Of course not.'

'Were you supposed to tell Helen that?'

218

'Maybe.'

'And have you?'

'Well, Wilf, old son, we don't know where you are, do we? Although I sometimes wonder whether Jimmy hasn't found out, from one or two things I've heard him say.'

'I shouldn't be surprised, either.' And I told Jethro about the break-in. He was, happily, suitably struck.

'Tell you one thing, though,' he said.

'What's that?'

'Jimmy doesn't give up easily. Are you planning on staying there much longer?'

As I walked over Vauxhall Bridge I seemed to see men in black wraparound shades all about me, but the paranoia didn't last too long. I felt sorry for Grace, a little, and shameful *schadenfreude* a little more. Towards Jimmy I had a similarly crowing heart.

I should have known better, as Jethro had tried to point out.

As I approached the railings that ran along the pavement in front of our terrace – incongruously, for there was no traffic – I saw a white bag hanging from the spikes. I wondered vaguely whether someone had lost it, and whether some other, charitable, soul had hung it there to be found later. Then I wondered why Lambeth Council had not removed it, since today was the day the binmen came round; it was always late in the morning when they arrived in our street. I thought I must have missed it when I'd gone out. Then I noticed that it was misshapen, elongated and heavy looking. And as I drew nearer I saw that it was, ineluctable and deathly white, the putrid carcass of a dead cat. Its eyes were open but discoloured in the lamplight, as if by cataracts. I was instantly, violently sick, overwhelmed by the rancid odour of decay. I pulled myself upright, inhaled a headful of rottenness and bent double again. Then I staggered past the monstrosity, upstairs to our rooms, and lay prone on our mattress bed, empty as Helen was away visiting her sister, who was about to give birth. Nausea invaded me in every part and I could hardly move.

On the outer rim of my shivering consciousness came a

219

tearing sound and a sharp bang, followed by the thump of boots moving quickly along the hall. It took the merest fraction of a second before I realized what was happening. He wasn't giving up easily.

I threw myself across the room and tried to heave an old Victorian wardrobe towards the door. A moment before I was incapable of stirring, but it's amazing what fear can do to help in these situations. The wardrobe refused to give. I began to sweat. It was not meant to be handled by one person alone: it was mahogany-heavy. It required, almost as a matter of dignity, a small army to shift it. Muscles screaming in agonizing protest, I began walking it inch by inch towards the door. The boots were nearly at the top of the stairs. In desperation I flung myself against it and found it start to slide over the polished floorboards. I could hear my heart like a drum, and I became incongruously aware of the aromas of the bathroom, the soaps and shampoos, the damp towels left to hang too long.

The boots were at the door.

I hurled myself against the back of the wardrobe and it toppled. It fell square against the door, which rattled furiously under an onslaught from the other side. Almost immediately, so it seemed, something was being driven into the wood of the doorjamb, and it began to splinter. I sensed, rather than saw, the skylight in the kitchen. Underneath it was a chair covered with junk, all of which I swept off with one gesture, save an old Olympus Trip which, for sentimental reasons, I held on to: I'd bought it when going on holiday once, and it was a rather unusual puce colour. I switched it to flash. This could be my final moment. I wanted a record of the occasion.

Standing on the chair, I shouldered the skylight.

It refused to budge. The bolt was rusted by steam and seemingly impregnable.

A fusillade of blows was tearing at the door. I brought a can of baked beans up against the bolt.

The top panelling of the door ripped open. An arm snaked through, met the back of the fallen wardrobe, and withdrew.

220

Instantaneously a renewed onslaught opened up on the door's lower panelling.

I braced myself against the skylight again and heaved.

Nothing.

The panelling gave.

One more try.

The skylight burst open in a shower of rotten woodwork.

Leaping upwards, I heard a bellow of fury as someone tunnelled unwillingly through the back of the wardrobe. I swivelled in the ruined skylight and a face appeared through the opening wardrobe door, wraparound shades hanging rakishly from one ear. It was a pudgy, open face with a surprised look on it. I raised my arm.

Click. Flash.

'Smile, please,' I said brilliantly. 'You're on camera.'

Beneath my feet the tiles of the roof were slippery in the late-summer drizzle. The ground was a terribly long way away. I looked across the line of the housetops to the gable end. If there was an easy way out of this, I couldn't see it.

There was movement in the kitchen below. As I shifted to try to gain height, and the angle of the roof, my right foot shot out from under me and my chin struck slate with a numbing, humiliating crack. Immediately I found myself tumbling over and over, my hands tearing desperately at the slimy, moss-covered roof.

I came to a halt, spread-eagled, a few feet away from the gutter, my cheek hard against cold slate. I was immobilized; the slightest move would put me over the edge. I was acutely aware of every nerve, every muscle, of the whereabouts of every limb. It felt like I was there for hours, but my fingers gradually found the upper edge of tiles above my head and I began to will myself upwards, urging myself to be weightless, light like feathers, pitching myself against gravity, aware of the drop squatting infatuated behind me. I crawled with lumbering caution, a great antediluvian lizard, then with the speed of returning hysteria. There was a fierce pain in my hands and jaw as I sidled

221

spider-like on all fours, getting more confident; I was all animal, every sense attuned to the roof, the whole of my being concentrated on what I could feel beneath my fingertips and toes. When I reached the summit I felt like it was Canary Wharf.

I turned to meet the foe, but there was no one there. He must have missed me in the darkness, must have given me up for dead. Either that, or homicide was not, after all, on the agenda. I began to shake. Gradually, I made my way back down to the skylight. It had been shut from inside. The wardrobe had been pushed under it. I, the river and the rest of south London were alone together. I felt cold and shaken, but adrenalin made me intensely alive to the night, to the sibilance of the traffic on Wandsworth Road and the churning of propellers in the river. I felt victorious, strong enough to stay there till dawn.

Which was just as well, really. It was several hours before anyone could be bothered to come and help.

Return of the Pink Elephants

I HAD NOT SEEN Kitty since New York. It was not a meeting I sought – meeting Kitty is never something you look forward to, not if you're simply mortal and of merely average looks, minimal social cachet and zero glamour – but I had been invited to a party by Tom Phipps, who obviously felt that we had buried the past and were the firmest of friends, which I suppose was fair enough. It was the launch of a men's magazine, still a fairly unusual concept in those days, even after the success of *Arena*, and Tom told me there might be opportunities for idle gardening correspondents. Tom's was a generous spirit, quick to soften and quick to lend, though of course he rarely had anything to give, despite his partner, who seemed well able to hang on to her wealth. This made his geniality the more moving; we all knew he would have, if he could have. Not that he was a good man in any conventional sense, but he dealt open-handedly with the world, and if he danced on the tables, as he often did, he did it to entertain and uplift the company rather than to draw attention to himself (though this was a welcome secondary effect).

And that, if I may say so, is what you might call forgiveness.

'I'm not an idle gardening correspondent,' I said to him with heat. 'I'm not idle. And I'm not just a gardening correspondent. I'm branching out.' I thought I heard him raising an eyebrow down the phone. 'Seriously.'

'Wilf,' he said. 'You're on the threshold of infamy. This is just the right time to go public.'

I brooded. Helen and I had decamped to a room in Milo's flat the size of a filing cabinet.

'When they said second bedroom in the estate agent's details,' Helen had remarked uncharacteristically tactlessly, 'they did mean for human beings? Not rabbits?'

The gossip columns were full of us, or seemed to be. Jimmy Spalding brought to his knees by the desertion of his wife, reputation in ruins, company prospects nose-diving, that was the line of attack. Another was desertion of child by heartless wife. And a third, which I struggled to promote through Tom Phipps, was Jimmy the gangster finally lets rip and victimizes boyfriend of runaway wife. Nobody was greatly interested in this one, explained Tom, because it was unprovable and therefore libellous.

'And I hardly need remind *you*,' he admonished me portentously, 'how dangerous *that* can be.'

We had had to leave Vauxhall.

'Of *course* they have to go,' Sebastian had declaimed, rising to his full height like a pantomime dame. '*He* wants to write articles about us, and they're attracting some very unpleasant attention. *Violent* attention.'

'Sebastian,' scolded Hermione in exasperation, 'this is not the Iranian Embassy siege. This is a squat in Vauxhall. A very nice squat' – his face had become even more beaky and disapproving than ever – 'but a squat none the less. We should be defending them.'

We were out in twenty-four hours. Alternative society is so ruthless.

Unreality crept furtively in like smoke under the door as we discovered how public our story was. Our story: it sounded like Romeo and Juliet, but we had indeed become a sort of media artefact. We were an idea in the minds of others, others who were looking for a narrative, something that could run. Jimmy featured in the business pages; we were in the diaries. We were becoming celebrities, a peaceable Bonnie and Clyde; everything we did felt as if it could be used; we began to wonder whether we were the story, or whether we were being created by the diarists, or whether we were creating the story *for* the diaries.

At Tom's party (as usual with Tom, it was clear he was there simply for his entertainment value and the confident expectation that he would commit some outrageous and eminently reportable *faux pas*) we sank bucketfuls of champagne. (Not that I can remember a party when we didn't.)

'I love you,' I murmured to Helen.

Without warning, indeed I didn't even see her move to do it, she suddenly emptied the entire contents of her glass into my face.

I was utterly disorientated for a few seconds.

'What the hell did you do that for?'

'Act horrified,' she hissed in my ear. It was not difficult. The whole room had turned to stare. She swung on her heel and sped from the crowded room; they had hired the Travellers' Club, apparently the most manly place in London.

'Darling,' a gravelly voice exploded in my ear. 'Was that entirely appropriate behaviour?'

I felt too angry to be intimidated by Kitty. And I knew her New York venture had been a disaster, which could not fail but to diminish her éclat a touch. The champagne was cold, very cold, and I hated the way it dripped down the inside of my collar.

'Your prerogative, do you think?'

She looked frozen daggers.

'What *do* you mean?'

'Like you did to Jimmy Spalding. At the Coliseum. *Madam Butterfly*,' I added helpfully.

She ignored the remark. As ever, her gaze made me feel as if I were invisible.

'And is there any reason why that young woman' – she referred to all women, apart from the chosen few friends of the moment, as if they were pathetic creatures who had just had the folly to emerge from under a rock – 'poured liquid all down your chest? Come on, Wellingborough' – as I sought a way of expressing my outraged incomprehension – 'there's got to be a reason. There's got to be something behind it. So you were watching, were you?' she went on, testily, without pausing. It took me a moment to realize we had returned to the Coliseum.

'You could have chosen somewhere less public. And anyway, he was with my ex. Couldn't help noticing.'

'*Was* he?' Her eyes softened. '*Such* a shit, that man.'

'Ferdy's daughter, Grace.'

That basilisk stare, again. I could see clouds rolling away in her mind; like all self-obsessed people, Kitty had an extraordinarily selective memory. She was looking through me, but I knew that what I had said was engaging her attention. And engaging the attention of Kitty Greaves gave me a surge of pleasure, like a schoolboy when his work is praised in class.

'Yes. I suppose you thought that was an odd thing to do,' she barked.

'Throwing champagne over someone in a public place? Well, perhaps I shouldn't. It seems to be something people do more often than I thought. Fling it or spill it. But he did fire you – I assumed it was because of that?'

'And he gave the job to a vacuous innocent who fucked it up and then got fired himself.' She bared her teeth in a sudden ferocious grin.

So she did mind.

'I didn't think you were all that bothered.'

'You're right. I wasn't. And it wasn't about that. Not entirely. I'd forgotten about you and Grace. How is she?'

'Living with Jimmy.'

Realization dawned, and her eyes widened in mock astonishment.

'So you're with –'

'We do love each other, actually.'

'I can imagine you do.'

'I think it's time I found a towel.'

'Wait, Wilfred.' How her moods could change. 'There's something I want to talk to you about.' She put her hand momentarily on my forearm. Suddenly, it seemed we were intimate.

226

'Here?'

She checked herself.

'No, let's meet and talk. Come round to my house. What are you doing early evening tomorrow? Before dinner.'

I pretended to consider. 'I think I'm free.'

'I hadn't realized we had all that in common,' she pronounced, as she plunged into the crowd.

When I got home I found Milo reading a bulky typescript.

'You're back early,' he yawned.

'Why didn't you come?'

'Had to read this.'

'Any good?'

'Derivative tosh. We paid six figures for it.'

'Is Helen here?'

He raised his eyebrows. 'I thought – I assumed – she was with you. Are you wet? I mean, literally?'

'Thanks.'

'I'm not trying to be funny.'

'Yes, you are.'

'Well, all right. But you are, aren't you?'

'Helen threw a glass of champagne over me.'

'Why, what had you done?'

'Kitty Greaves was there.'

'I'm thinking of commissioning a biography of her.'

'She'd like that.'

'Not the one I've got in mind. But tell me about Helen.'

'I don't know. I don't know why she did it and I don't know where she is.'

'Is everything all right?'

'Oh, yes. Well. I don't know. I mean, she seems to going away a lot.'

'To her sister's. To help with the new baby.'

'Yes.'

'Does she need a lot of help?'

'I wouldn't have thought so, no.'

227

We looked at each other.

'She's a deep one.'

'You think so?'

'Can't read her. Never could.'

'Typical publisher. As if she were a manuscript.'

'Even so,' he persisted. 'Can you?'

Could I? Can anyone read anyone? Sometimes I spend months trying to understand someone, but others can get their number in seconds. I'm too cerebral about it. I wait for cause to effect. She said that so she means this. I like everything to unfold step by step, a succession of consequential conclusions. I'm structured and practical and Newtonian; in quantum physics, you can twiddle a particle on one side of the universe and an answering particle responds on the other. I need to be more quantum in life. Or just a bit quicker off the mark.

The next day I rolled out of bed thinking she wasn't there, but she was. I tried to wake her but she wouldn't be woken; just turned over defiantly. I got myself a bagel out of the bread bin, started making coffee, then saw that the bagel had mould on it. I went out for some fresh, buying *The Times* on the way back. Helen and I were in the diary. Lead item. 'Crying over spilt champagne?' the piece began, then more about the 'runaway lovers'.

As I say, was I living this story, or was it living me?

She had been eating Neal's Yard muesli for a quarter of an hour before I felt calm enough to put the question.

'So? Are you going to tell me why you did that last night?' Hostile, yes. But to the point.

'High spirits.' Her teeth crunched on a nut. She grimaced. 'God, I hate this stuff.'

'High *spirits*?'

'Come on, lighten up. It was just a bit of fun.'

'Where did you go?'

'Can't remember.'

'It's in *The Times*.'

She moved like lightning, tearing open the paper until she

228

reached the right page, reading it to herself, motionless, almost hungry for it.

'Do you like being in there?'

She looked up slowly, thoughtfully.

'That depends.'

'Depends on what?'

'On who sees it, and what they think about it.'

I know what she meant now, but I didn't then. And she didn't answer. I hate it when people go opaque on me. Especially when I love them.

'I mean, do you like being written about? Do you like being the centre of attention? You practically put that story in the paper.'

'We're celebrities, Wilf. We're making news. Enjoy it.' She smiled beatifically at me.

'Did you do that deliberately just to get in the paper? You can't have done. I mean, you *can't* have done.'

'Of course I didn't.'

Well, I know now, but I didn't see anything to worry about at the time. I was more preoccupied with Kitty's enigmatic behaviour, and I remained in a stew of curiosity all day, so much so that I arrived at her Notting Hill house fifteen minutes early, and found myself wandering down the Portobello Road as it closed for the night to kill the time.

'Oh, hello,' she said, when she opened the door. She didn't sound as if she was crazy to see me. But she left the door open, and after a moment's hesitation I went in. It was a long time since I had been there, and she had changed it all with a triumphant blaze of mildly oppressive but peculiarly tasteful kitsch. The wallpaper was of mutedly flaring pink lilies, the lamps the glazed pink Ganesha elephants from Rajasthan that used to recline repugnantly in her office at the *Arts*, and there were lava lamps on the mantelpiece, just like in Sebastian's flat. I noticed that the leather-topped desk, the armchairs and the sofa were the ones she had reclaimed from her old office, though it was to be some time

229

before I found the signed Craig Raine poem and the sixties covers of the *Arts'* first editions, the former in the first-floor lavatory and the latter huddled together in the top bathroom. The poem was hung next to a *Private Eye* diary spoof of Kitty and signed by Craig Brown, thus demonstrating a gentle wit on Kitty's part that I had not hitherto suspected. It also echoed Tom's long-standing assertion that Craigs Raine and Brown were in fact the same person. She had the Patrick Heron seascape illuminating one wall of the living room, and other paintings full of greys and disturbing perspectives dotted throughout the house, but above all, soothingly and satisfyingly, there were books in racks, books in stacks, books in piles and books in floor-to-ceiling bookcases. It was book heaven.

She saw me gazing in admiration.

'If I had my time again,' she said, 'I'd be a book publisher.'

I thought of Milo.

'I'm not sure you would, you know.'

'You'd like a drink?' Without waiting for a reply she fetched a chilled bottle of Sauvignon. 'Tell me about Grace,' she went on.

'Determined. Passionate. Selfless. A great believer in lost causes. I used to think she was a big softie, but I learned better.'

She wasn't interested in small talk. That is to say, she never was, but it was clear her mind was on other things.

'How did she feel about her father's death?'

For a moment I wondered if I could be hearing aright.

'How did she *feel*?'

Kitty was obviously troubled, in a way I had never been. She sat in a large chintzy armchair with the bridge of her nose clamped between thumb and middle finger.

'Wilf, this is not easy.'

She wiped her eyes with her thumb, in a graceless moment of pure human emotional ineptitude that was fantastically unlike her. I began to wonder if I had walked into the wrong house. But no, only Kitty would have had those elephant lamp bases.

When she took her hand away from her face she looked

230

utterly dejected, her brow puckered in unhappiness, her lower lip jutting in petulant misery.

'You see, it was my doing.'

'What was?'

'His death.' She leaned forward, and her great dark eyes narrowed as they looked at me. 'We fought.'

'How do you mean?'

'What do you mean, how do I mean?' she snapped. 'We always fought. Seriously. Like cats.'

'I don't remember.'

She didn't answer.

'Why are you telling me this?'

Still she was silent.

'You were – what?'

I was once more terrified of her. How could I talk of her most intimate secrets?

'Lovers, yes.' Sullenly, as if she had been given a parking ticket. 'Like you and Grace.'

'It didn't really work, you know. After Ferdy's death – you did ask – it wasn't that she went to pieces, though I suppose she did. It's more to do with me. I don't think I was much help to her.'

'Why should you have been a help to her?'

The harshness took me back.

'Well, I wasn't.'

'Did she expect help?'

'I'm not sure. I think so. I know I wasn't giving her any.'

'Why not?'

'I didn't know how to. And over time, I just know, I was failing. I wasn't doing what I should have done. For her. And Jimmy obviously was.' My eyes stung, and I thought, not in front of Kitty Greaves.

'Obviously.'

'I don't know what I *was* supposed to do.'

'It was her problem, not yours?'

'It was hers. She wouldn't talk to me. But it was my problem because I didn't know how to talk to her.'

231

'How to comfort her.'

'That, too.'

'How to speak to someone who has just lost the most important person in their life.'

'Yes.'

'I had no one either.'

'She was his daughter, though.'

'That's why I asked you here. I saw him before he died.'

I nodded. 'I'm glad.'

She looked scornful. 'I mean, I saw him just before he died. I was the last person to see him. He came to find me at the hotel I was staying in, some poxy little place I'd gone to escape all the shit about Spalding's buying the *Arts*. He came to my room, drunk, and I wouldn't let him in, and he just stood there, leaned there, I should say, against the wall. He said he was sorry, that he had to sell, that he was desperate for the money, and only Jimmy was interested. So that's what he had done. He was sorry.'

'He wanted your forgiveness?'

'That and a whole lot more.'

'He'd done that to you and he wanted forgiveness?'

'I should have forgiven him. It's not ours not to forgive.'

'I suppose not.'

'I refused to see him. I told him about Simon.'

'Simon?'

'You know.'

'Spicer?'

'But it wasn't true.'

'It wasn't?'

'Not then.'

'But it was afterwards?'

'Don't you get this, Wilf? It wasn't then.'

'You made it up?'

She sank further into the chintz.

'To spite him? And it wasn't true?'

'Not then.'

'Did he come into your room?'

232

'Not your business. But no.'

'You froze him out?' I didn't want to be harsh, but sometimes nothing else will do. 'So, drunk, damaged and despairing, he got in his car and drove himself to perdition?'

'I think so.'

'And you told no one?'

'No.'

'Were you surprised by what happened?'

She crackled into life.

'Of course I was fucking surprised. Surprised? You think I wanted that to happen? I loved that bloody man. What do you think I'm saying?' She rose and walked, shaking, her hands stretched like claws, seeking comprehension, to the darkened French windows. 'Why am I telling you this? Not because I'm interested in your *opinion*. I want to talk to Grace, but she's with James. Can't do anything about that. But I want to talk to that child.'

'Are you sure she would want to talk to you?'

'No.' She kept her back to me. 'No. But, Wilf, this is the first time I have talked about this to anyone. It's confidential on threat of death.'

She never could resist melodrama.

'How was he, that night?'

'Smashed. I don't know. Not that smashed. But soggy, perspiring, smelling of booze. I'd seen him pretty wild before, but he seemed helpless, lost.'

'Why was he so desperate?'

'I don't know. I thought –'

'Yes?'

'Grace might know.'

So that was it. So very Kitty. Shielded by the pretence of wanting to help, she was looking for illumination, for an understanding that would exonerate her, for, ultimately, forgiveness.

'I don't think she knew much about her father's business affairs.'

She collapsed back into her chair, looking tired.

233

'She might know something. Anything would do,' she murmured.

'What if there's nothing to find out?'

'Do you know there isn't?'

'No. But I don't see Grace any more.'

'Are you and what's-her-face inseparable?'

'I think so.'

'You think so. Can't you do better than that?'

'No. I can't.'

'That good, is it?'

I'd had enough of this. I got to my feet.

'Kitty, if I see Grace I'll tell her what you said.'

She bared her famous snarl at me.

'And what was that?'

'Well, that you want to see her, to tell her, you know, about Ferdy. . .'

Her expression grew contemptuous again.

'Darling, *I'll* tell her all that. You just tell her I want to see her.'

I wasn't going to do any such thing; I wasn't going to call her, talk to her, or even – indeed especially – think about her.

Oh, but wasn't I? Hadn't I been thinking about her all the time, in some vague, echoing, indeterminate way? Well, I was determined not to call, even if, in the circumstances, I would have had the perfect excuse. *Because* I had the perfect excuse.

And as I made my way unhurriedly towards Holland Park Avenue, the light fading with the warm violet hue you sometimes get in London in early autumn, the restaurants opening and the stores shutting and the pavements alive with people, I admitted to myself that I did mind about Grace leaving me and that I did mind about Jimmy. It was an emptying sort of thought, even amid a busy night in Notting Hill, when the world seems so very available – providing you are of a certain youthfulness and in sufficient funds. I headed back to Milo's place, where he met me at the door. He wore an expression of studied concern, the kind where the lower lip slides across the teeth and the face becomes lopsided.

234

'I think you and I,' he said, 'need to get out.' His cramped quarters were now at the Shepherd's Bush end of Uxbridge Road, and it was a walk to find anywhere half decent, but we got most of the way down Shepherd's Bush Road before he would reveal what was bothering him.

'Over to you,' he said, fishing an envelope out of an inner pocket.

I read it under the passing lamplights. The handwriting was Helen's.

'Darlingest Wilf,' it started. 'Sometimes we have to come to difficult decisions, and it is never easy, and we must be forgiving.' That word again. 'Jimmy called me today. He is desperate.' That one, too. 'So am I – not for him, but for Byron. He and Grace – I hope this does not hurt you too much – are not happy. I will not say I am myself happy to return to him. I will not say it. Yet he was more passionately determined than I have ever known him, and although I feel that Byron is in perfectly good hands, and I have never felt anything other than a real and true love for you, James has persuaded me. He tells me Grace is leaving. I am returning tonight. Wilf, I love you, but I need to go home.'

I went numb. That's what shock does; helps you not to feel for a while. It seems hard to believe, I know, but it was just the same after Jimmy fired me, and after I found out about Grace and Jimmy from her diary. Now, as then, I was conscious that there was an acid bath of pain just heating up nicely somewhere in the green-room of life. I knew I was going to feel betrayed, humiliated, lost, distracted; that the not-having Helen, and the mystery of her sudden departure, were going to wring my insides out like you do a sopping wet towel; that it was going to go on and on – but just for now I was somehow under anaesthetic, dimly aware of my emotional immune system going down, fighting valiantly.

We found a restaurant, and I threw the letter over the table at Milo. His left eyebrow rose as he read.

He pursed his lips. 'Practically Jane Austen.'

Which was not quite how I felt. Later, as things began to fit together more, I realized why Helen had adopted such a curious tone, and what she'd been hiding, but for now I was overtaken by a brief flurry of feelings, outriders of grief; I ran the gamut of the deadly sins and back again over and over (even sloth, for what could I do?). Gluttony was the exception. I made up for this, however, by ordering the most expensive item on the menu.

'The love of your life has just walked out on you and you order *foie gras*?' asked Milo.

'Not the love of my life, actually' – too defensively – 'and what do you expect me to order?' I retaliated. The restaurant was famous for the creativity of its menu. Next I had scampi and chips, to redress the balance. Milo attempted, as ever, to flirt with the waitress, with the usual lack of success.

'Milo,' I asked, still stung by the heartlessness of his previous question, 'it may seem strange, given the present state of my life, but how is yours going? I mean,' I added, to press the point home, 'is there anyone in it?'

'Well, Wilf, I wanted to talk to you about that. There is, as it happens, and it's someone you know. You did ask, Wilf,' he continued, as I shot him an apprehensive look.

'Who?'

He closed his eyes in the manner of one deliberately exploding a bomb. I can almost see his hands descending on the plunger.

'Flora, as it happens.'

'Oh, great.'

There was a long pause. 'So, how long's that been going on?'

'About four months, actually,' said Milo, looking rather ashamed.

It could have been worse. I mean, it *could* have been worse, I realized. I genuinely did. Had he said 'Grace' I think I would have had a real problem.

'Good,' I enthused. Warmly. And meaning it. 'Good. I mean, really good. She is good, too, isn't she? I mean, if you like that sort of thing, and to be honest with you, Milo, I always did.'

He looked at me coldly.

'Spiritually, I find her extraordinarily illuminating,' he said.

'Flora? In your dreams, baby.'

'I have obviously located an aspect that you signally failed to encounter.'

'Practically Jane Austen yourself,' I scowled at my friend.

'More D. H. Lawrence, actually.' And a corner of his mouth twitched.

'I'm glad to know it. But can I point out to you that tonight I have lost both my girlfriend and her predecessor to others? You may haggle over the niceties concerning the latter,' I added, seeing that he was about to, 'but the thing is Milo, what about *me*? Why is this happening? Why do they all walk out on me? Am I a pathetic worm?'

'No, no.'

'I am a pathetic worm. I feel like a pathetic worm. A pathetic worm that's just been dumped. A pathetic worm without a female pathetic worm to entwine with.'

I couldn't sleep all night, but, once again, at three or four o'clock I calmed down a little. When I was small I remember lying awake one night, quite certain that there was a monstrous beast in my bedroom; a dragon, I think it was. I knew precisely which corner it was in; and how big it was (it was very big), and how terrifying, though how it got there I can't recall. As the night wore on, and my fear ran rampant, I evolved a strategy. I would befriend the horror. We threw a few jeering exchanges at each other, which became badinage and chiding, and after an hour or two of this we were real pals. Then I fell asleep.

For several days and more after Helen's desertion I just thought about how miserable I was, because that's the way I am, and I couldn't think of any good reason why I shouldn't. The gossip columns, of course, lost interest instantaneously, and I was left to wonder why Helen had gone back. I obsessed about it, and talked to Milo deep into the night. My bewilderment was an anaesthetic; I simply didn't get it. But somehow I knew she wouldn't be changing her mind. I certainly couldn't bear to ring her. Which made me think of Grace, who would have been on that number before, and was now presumably cast out. I experienced a little grim satisfaction, but then I began to think about how she must be feeling, and it occurred to me that it would not be too different from me; maybe quite a lot worse. After all, I was getting a lot of practice at this.

'She's staying with her mother,' said Milo.

'She must be in a bad way. How do you know?'

'She called. Wanted to know how you were.'

'That's thoughtful.'

'Well, she is.'

'I wonder whether –'

'I think you should.'

'Kitty wanted me to call her.'

'That will do if you need a reason.'

Weekend Feature

THERE ARE RELATIONSHIPOHOLICS, which is mundane, and there are badrelationshipoholics. These are the ones who like their relationships to erupt dangerously and erratically like some foul-tempered boil. They relish the emotional fix; it's how they know they're alive. Appalling rows, merciless needling, stormy sulks and worse; they hunger for catastrophe, braving the abyss while confined claustrophobically within their own needfulness. It's what soaps are made of.

Well, I wasn't one of those. Not me. I think I was once a bit of a relationshipoholic, but after Helen – I don't know, maybe it was lack of opportunity or something – I was single, just myself and me, for a long time. I didn't go home much any more; I think I simply wanted Helen and Jimmy and whatever it was they had been about out of my life. I didn't want to go near them. I didn't see Grace, either; when she answered the phone, I outlined what Kitty was after; there was a pause and then she asked for her number. Poor lamb; she must have been feeling wretchedly unhappy and humiliated, and now she'd have to put herself through her father's death all over again. I felt for her.

'Is there anything I can do?' I asked. 'Vodka and sympathy?'

'I'll let you know.'

She didn't call back.

I found myself a job – a proper job – as features editor on a new broadsheet that was starting up. It was something I fell into, but there was a sudden vortex greedy for hacks and editors and dreamers of all shapes and sizes as long as they could string some decent words together in the right order, and I could just about stretch to that. To top it all, I was, as I was discovering

239

surprisingly slowly, tinged with mild celebrity after my fleeting visit to gossipland. The country didn't really need a new broadsheet, and it folded after about three years, but one way or another I had entered calmer waters.

I never heard from Helen, or Jimmy, again. Well, that's not quite true – life being what it is you inevitably bump into people here and there, however frostily – but it's true enough. I had a lot of opportunity for reflection, and in the end I worked out what had happened, though I found it hard to believe. Helen must have wanted Jimmy to hear about our spat and to think we weren't happy any more. All along, it had been she who had been writing the plot, for all of us, even the diarists. I realized unwillingly that the best people, the kindest, most generous and sweetest people, will go to extraordinary lengths to get what they need; deep needs lie deep, and there is nothing stronger than the will to survive.

The September of the year after Helen left seemed like my new state of mind; it was fresh, crisp, but not cold, a refreshing hangover-cure for the fetid summer that had only recently passed away. The sunlight was clear and subtly golden, and there was a resonance to it that seemed to last for years afterwards, during which I felt clearer and fresher and better about myself and didn't worry about that elusive someone else. But I didn't run away from people, either. You can't, if you're the features editor of a brand-new broadsheet, however rickety it is.

Another important element of my life at this time was, believe it or not, Milo and Flora. I privately greeted this stellar conjunction with profound scepticism, but time went by and they were still, in their weird way, together. It shouldn't have worked, but it did, just. It was like watching Punch and Judy.

One day Milo rang me in a state of great excitement.

'Hot tip,' he said, almost yodelling into the phone. 'We're renting a barge.'

'Really? I've always wanted a holiday on the canals. Sitting out of an evening, as the glass-like water serenely reflects the last fleeting clouds of the day and the china blue of the sky turns to vivid orange. One might take up smoking a pipe, in order to puff contentedly. Do they still sell meerschaum pipes?'

'We're not going on a barging *holiday*, we're renting one to live on. By Chelsea Embankment. You know, where Edith Grove turns left to avoid running into the river.'

'What, live on together?' This was news. Flora had moved back to London so they could be in the same city, but thus far they had yet to make it into the same domicile. It was part of their mystique, their magnificent mutual egotism, that they could not yield to each other's lifestyles.

'Yes. At weekends.'

'If they can afford it, most people rent somewhere in the country.'

'Yes, most people do,' he said, witheringly.

'So let me get this straight. You'll actually both live on this barge only at weekends but actually together?'

'Anything wrong with that?'

'No, no. Whose idea was it?'

'Mine, of course,' he replied in a tone that made me suspect it had been Flora's.

'I think it's brilliant. I love the idea. When's the house-warming? The barge-warming? The barge-*chauffage*?'

'Soon. But Flora thought you could do something on it for the paper. The barge, I mean. Houseboat, I should say, really. And us. I mean, it *is* a variation on the weekend country cottage, isn't it?'

'If it was Flora's idea, why didn't *she* ask me?'

'Wilf, are you being obstreperous?'

'No, just curious. I like to observe the quaint convolutions of human behaviour.'

'Well, you do know a certain amount about them.'

'Milo, only you two could think the fact you are renting a houseboat to be the only place in which you cohabit, and that only at weekends, and one moored next to Battersea Bridge, was anything other than completely bizarre.'

'So you won't do anything?'

241

'Oh, I might. You're both unremitting self-publicists, but I suppose it's one way of making sure I get an invite.'

'You'd better believe it. It's a dog-eat-dog world, Sunny Jim.'

'It's a palm-grease-palm world.'

'Oh, stop being prim. We're going to let you do this piece for free, you know. Generous, or what?'

'What, I think.'

So that was it. People may use each other, perhaps we all use each other to one end or another, and Flora and Milo were past masters at it. Their union was a mighty one; friends constantly remarked on their titanic rows and their almost equally noisy peaces. They were content, I think, in all this: squalls blew through them, and kept them trim and ebullient. They were waltzing tempests rather than mooning lagoons, and they made it seem very happy rather than wildly unstable, and I couldn't help but be impressed, and a little envious. But as I loved them both, I succeeded in being magnanimous. I think.

The paper was reasonably intrigued by their houseboating, but as ever it was because of Flora rather than anything else. I kindly kept this from Milo. The salient point was that Flora was the more interesting of the two, since she was big in New York as well as London, and thus had an ineffable charisma. Milo was adrift on the heaving seas of corporate publishing and therefore too focused on survival to cut the sort of dash that could possibly rival the buccaneering exploits of Flora, whose every predatory outrage in the shameless business of stealing other people's clients caused significant ripples on the sensitive pudding-skins of literary London dinner parties.

I put the idea to the editor.

'I don't know much about him,' he said. 'But I do know about her.' The first sentence was pure ignorance – poor old Milo – but the second contained a mildly lascivious lilt.

'She's very hot,' I observed.

He smirked. At that moment I hated him.

Of course, I knew Grace would be at the party. I thought, very seriously, and for a long time, about not going simply for that

242

reason, but I had a living to make and I told myself I was being sentimental, which in retrospect I don't think was quite true. I was, simply, beginning to value my new-found independence. There is a languid, easy-going happiness to being alone, but it's a happiness that has to be waited for, lain in wait for even, because it's a long time coming and, like the beauty of the desert, you only appreciate it when you find yourself surrounded by it. Then it suffices. And so even was my temperament becoming at that time that I didn't want it disturbed by the past. If I was going to be at ease with myself and life in general, I had to avoid falling from the tranquil little plateau I had surprisingly attained.

The editor was frank. 'I don't need scandal. That's not what you're for.'

'Houseboat chic,' I murmured, 'is what I had in mind.'

I felt proud to have recovered from the débâcle of *Arts Unlimited*. There are two ways to experience London, and I imagine it's the same for other cities, too, not to mention the entirety of existence. You're either struggling, or you've cracked it. What's interesting is that you're not really aware of where you are on this elusive sliding scale until you have moved on. You won't know that you have secured a place on the great teeming metropolitan termite-mound until, looking back with the benefit of hindsight and perspective, you spy yourself finally sinking a toe into the rearing edifice.

I was back. And I was single. Wilf Wellingborough 1; Life 1. But I was OK about being single, so I won on penalties. I had been transfixed by that teenage sense of the overpowering social, moral, intellectual, biological, philosophical and (incidentally) sexual need for a partner and I was beyond that, now.

But, you know, chocolate is good, too.

Anyway, I had to go to Milo's and Flora's barge-, houseboat- or whatever-warming for another reason. As life draws on apace and you hit thirty, which amazingly turns out not to be the end of everything, some gatherings are like milestones, or, even better, checklists, where you mark off the progress of everyone you know.

243

For instance: emaciated actor turned travel-writer, now living in the country with neurotic wife and three children, still travelling. Mohican haircut, masochistic punk, brilliant dancer, now with a child and clowning on the fringe-theatre circuit. Middle European scientist, invented new kind of contraceptive pill before reaching Oxford, now immensely important – and immense – banker. Early cross-dresser charms lovestruck gallery-owner and thereafter attains significant position at the ICA. Ebullient egghead becomes frighteningly rich barrister and succeeds in looking exactly the same as he did ten years ago, unlike the rest of us. The finest mind of your generation is teaching deprived children in an East End comprehensive and spends much of her time trying to prevent her pupils being deported.

They were all there.

I found myself thinking about this as I walked down the King's Road from Sloane Square tube station. It's a long walk and maybe I should have taken a taxi and maybe Fulham Broadway would have been a little closer, but the weather was changing and I felt invigorated by the wetness and the wind, the drifting yellow leaves and the magnificence of the turning year. And I have always loved the King's Road; every time you walk down it, a new set of shops has gone under and an equally sharp set has replaced it. As I trudged past warm, glowing, endlessly enticing windows in a street that had leapt to prominence in the sixties but was still there twenty-five years later (in a way that, for instance, Carnaby Street was not), I thought of how it had changed from cheekiness to sloppiness to aggressiveness to unashamed sleekness.

Everything turned round in the sixties. It all turned round in the eighties. It's generational; twenty years per cycle. A decade of change followed by a decade of stasis. I sometimes wonder if the history of the century is like this: after the great cull of the First World War, for instance, the newborn reached maturity in 1939, ready to fight the next one; after the Second World War, it was 1965 that saw the boomers roaring through to change the world.

Nineteen eighty-five was the middle of Thatcher's decade, when her ideological children were at university, infatuatedly mopping up her views.

Looking for patterns as usual.

Milo's barge was not the sort of highly ornate gypsy-caravan-*sur-mer* that I had hoped for, but a clinical-looking glass and aluminium floating gin-palace of no recognizable charm whatsoever, save that it was on the river. Conrad thought the Thames was a gateway to darkness, which of course it was, but now it is a river to love: rising and falling patiently to the rhythm of the tides, just the right size and not a little over, reliably reflecting the lights of the city that pulses along its banks, polluted but beginning to get better, the Thames is not a charismatic or fabulous river, but it is one that it is easy to become sentimental about, now that Empire's gone. Its moods are few, and when it is still the city looks glamorous in its depths.

The interior was predominantly white and beige, with subdued lighting. There were fitted carpets throughout. Horsefall was there, and Spicer, and Tom and his girlfriend whose name I could never remember, and Sibella and Bomber, and Paul and Charlotte. Among the celebrities were long-forgotten faces, faces last seen at Paul's wedding or before, beginning to look a little the worse for wear, some more bruised than others. If I looked as old as they looked, I thought to myself, I would be dead already.

'Are you all right?' asked Milo solicitously. 'You look as if you've seen a ghost.'

'Several,' I replied. 'And there's another one.'

Grace had arrived. I watched her surreptitiously as she slid unnoticed through the guests until she found Flora. They embraced, wreathed in smiles. I turned to make dull conversation with a young, rather spiderish-looking Labour politician of some sort who also worked in television. He was engaged in an ecstasy of gossip with several young men, one of whom was, to my delight, at first, laying into my nemesis, David Vale.

'Such a complete shit, I mean he was to *me*. I did like him, sort

245

of, but he wouldn't leave me alone. Whenever I turned round there he was, theatre tickets, flights to Mauritius, he *was* passionate and, you know, it was flattering and lovely but' – here his lip curled – 'he's such a pig. I mean physically. Beautiful inside *no doubt*. Then there was all that business with that stupid magazine and he forced me to write letters to support him, but, you know, he'd made my life hell and do you know what they did me for in the end? Using the wrong parking space. I mean they were right, the press, but even after all he'd done and the beast he'd been I couldn't really let him down. You'll think I'm insane but I sort of felt he was my friend, I did sort of fall for him for a while. . .'

I turned away and circled warily, from a junior cabinet minister to a suave poet with a voice like a dainty Whispering Bob Harris. I succeeded in staying on the other side of the cabin from Grace, until after an hour or so I found myself cornered. Grace was once more deep in conversation with Flora, when the latter caught my eye.

'Wilf, we're wondering whether you're avoiding Grace for any particular reason.'

It was the sort of question where both yes and no are admissions of guilt, so I brazened it out.

'I've just been meeting all your fascinating friends, Flora. I'm only here,' I added, turning to Grace and addressing her as if we had never met before, 'because they have persuaded me to do a piece about their urban retreat.'

'You're getting paid for it, aren't you?' asked Flora pointedly. 'And I'm not even taking a commission.'

'Love the boat, though, Flora.' I changed the subject.

She looked about her with some irritation. 'Do you? It's all right.'

'You can't be getting tired of it.'

'I suppose not.'

'What I should have said,' I explained to Grace afterwards, 'was, "You can't be getting tired of Milo."'

'I don't know about "should".'

'"Could", then.'

'Do you think that's it?'

'You know what Flora's like.'

'Poor Milo.'

'You were always soft on him, weren't you?'

'Was I? I thought you said you didn't remember much about our time together.'

I blushed. After Flora had moved on I had found myself affecting an outrageously immature carelessness with Grace, which gradually evaporated as I discovered that we seemed to have been abandoned, quarantined in our own corner.

'I think they want us to talk,' she said, rolling her eyes back and forth like windscreen wipers.

'Well, we are, aren't we?' But I knew what she meant. I caught a glimpse of Tom Phipps flashing me a huge and encouraging grin.

'I feel like I'm a goldfish in a bowl. An irritated goldfish in a bowl.'

'Me too.'

'I'm thinking I might just make it an early night.'

'Me too.'

So now we were leaning against the parapet of Battersea Bridge on a still-early October evening, watching the river. Before us the Albert Bridge shone gaudily like a fairground attraction.

I said: 'I didn't remember it for a while, but it's coming back. I was surprised how the memories just vanished. Self-protection, I suppose.'

'If they're coming back, does that mean you don't need protection?'

'Well, you know, time heals, and stuff.'

As if in answer she plucked a packet of Silk Cut from her pocket.

'Want one?'

'No, I don't think I do. Thanks.'

She lit up and inhaled fast through pursed lips, to get the hot nicotine hit as sharp as possible.

'You didn't use to smoke.'

She laughed in a tired, smothered, restless way that didn't seem like her either. She ran her hand over the bangles on her wrist and rubbed her forehead with her long thin fingers.

I tried to think of something to say that wasn't utterly crass, and watched the clouds of mud swirling lazily in the water, picked out by the bridge's lamps. Every lamp created its own circle of intimacy; beyond the warm, soft brown of the water beneath, the river ran like liquid jet.

'Was it awful when Helen came back?'

'Was it awful when she left?'

'I asked first.'

She picked at the tiny lichen on top of the parapet.

'It was.'

'Did you understand why? I mean, I didn't. I've got an idea, but –'

'Well, it's in *Gatsby*, isn't it? They're careless people, Jimmy and Helen. They smash people up. Then they retreat into their carelessness and leave everyone else to clean up the mess.'

'Haven't read it. Saw the film, though.'

She sighed.

'But I think I know what you're saying. She wanted him to come crawling. She wanted to humiliate him. Then it would be on her terms.'

She took another drag.

'That's kind of what I'm saying.'

'And we're smashed up? Are we?'

She didn't respond.

'You've been through it, though, haven't you? Poor baby.'

'I have. I fucking well have.' She laughed again, explosively, as if she were close to tears.

'Did he want her back for her own sake? Or was it the humiliation and the gossip and the business?'

'All that. All of it. She doesn't take prisoners, Helen.'

248

I felt fantastically angry for a moment. And then I thought, oh, what the hell.

'Probably better out of it.'

She looked at me fleetingly.

'You've changed.'

'So've you.'

'You've done it better.'

'You've had it worse.'

'You want to know what it was like when Helen came back?'

Something in her voice worried me.

'Yes. But not now. Later. Let's go and eat. You want to eat? Then you can tell me. My ears are yours alone. Anyway, was it OK with Kitty?'

Piling on the agony, I suppose, but I couldn't resist asking.

'Kitty was good. Kitty was really good.'

'Really?'

'Yes, really.'

'No, I mean, really, was she?'

'Yes. We talked lots. Lots and lots. She knew Dad, knew him well, had him down just like that.'

'Seems to me it wasn't just Ferdy died in that crash. There was quite a bit of you in there, too.'

'Yes.'

'And a bit of us.'

'Yes.'

'So you forgave her?'

She took a long while over this.

'I've almost got there,' she said eventually. 'He had sold her down the river. That wasn't her fault.'

'And the story about her and Spicer?'

'What story?'

Kitty Greaves, crafty to the last.

'It can wait. Where are you staying?'

'With Kitty.'

'Good, that's good.'

'She's helped me a lot. She's a good friend.'

249

'She's a great woman.'

A cold breeze suddenly rose up at us off the river.

'Shall we go?' I asked. 'Do you want to wear my jacket? I think that was a bit of autumn, just then.'

'Yes, let's. I'd like that. Where shall we go? There's San Frediano in the Fulham Road.'

'I don't know it, but whatever. I wish you'd wear this jacket.'

'It's not far,' she said. 'And I'm not cold.'